"You saved my life. Of course I trust you, Max," Erin said, pushing aside her uneasiness.

"Now, why do I get the feeling that statement lacks conviction?" he mused, watching her. His fingers slid beneath her chin and tilted it up. "Never mind. I suppose after what you just went through, you're entitled to a few doubts. What you need now is a stiff shot of brandy and bed." He cocked one eyebrow. "I suppose you'd object to spending the night at my place?"

Erin shot him a dry look. "You suppose right."

"Ah, I see. You trust me with your life but not with your delectable body. Is that it?"

"How perceptive of you."

D0311076

Dear Reader,

Sophisticated but sensitive, savvy yet unabashedly sentimental—that's today's woman, today's romance reader—you! And Silhouette Special Editions are written expressly to reward your quest for substantial, emotionally involving love stories.

So take a leisurely stroll under the cover's lavender arch into a garden of romantic delights. Pick and choose among titles if you must—we hope you'll soon equate all six Special Editions each month with consistently gratifying romantic reading.

Watch for sparkling new stories from your Silhouette favorites—Nora Roberts, Tracy Sinclair, Ginna Gray, Lindsay McKenna, Curtiss Ann Matlock, among others—along with some exciting newcomers to Silhouette, such as Karen Keast and Patricia Coughlin. Be on the lookout, too, for the new Silhouette Classics, a distinctive collection of bestselling Special Editions and Silhouette Intimate Moments now brought back to the stands—two each month—by popular demand.

On behalf of all the authors and editors of Special Editions,
Warmest wishes,

Leslie Kazanjian
Senior Editor

GINNA GRAY
Fools Rush In

Silhouette Special Edition

Published by Silhouette Books New York

America's Publisher of Contemporary Romance

SILHOUETTE BOOKS
300 East 42nd St., New York, N.Y. 10017

Copyright © 1987 by Virginia Gray

All rights reserved, including the right to reproduce
this book or portions thereof in any form whatsoever.
For information address Silhouette Books,
300 East 42nd St., New York, N.Y. 10017

ISBN: 0-373-09416-7

First Silhouette Books printing November 1987

All the characters in this book are fictitious. Any
resemblance to actual persons, living or dead, is
purely coincidental.

SILHOUETTE, SILHOUETTE SPECIAL EDITION and colophon
are registered trademarks of the publisher.

America's Publisher of Contemporary Romance

Printed in the U.S.A.

Books by Ginna Gray

Silhouette Romance

The Gentling #285
The Perfect Match #311
Heart of the Hurricane #338
Images #352
First Love, Last Love #374
The Courtship of Dani #417

Silhouette Special Edition

Golden Illusion #171
The Heart's Yearning #265
Sweet Promise #320
Cristen's Choice #373
Fools Rush In #416

GINNA GRAY

A native Houstonian, Ginna Gray admits that, since childhood, she has been a compulsive reader as well as a head-in-the-clouds dreamer. Long accustomed to expressing her creativity in tangible ways (Ginna also enjoys painting and needlework), she finally decided to try putting her fantasies and wild imaginings down on paper. The result? The mother of two now spends eight hours a day as a full-time writer.

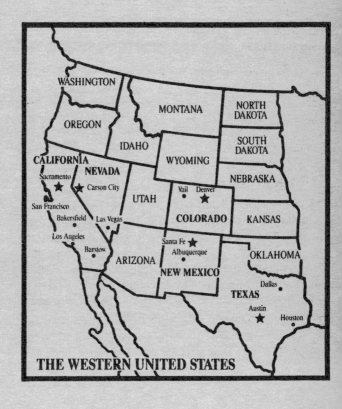

THE WESTERN UNITED STATES

Chapter One

In the space of a heartbeat, Erin Blaine was jerked out of a sound sleep and plunged into terror.

With a strangled cry, she jackknifed up in the bed. Her heart was pounding against her ribs like a wild thing trying to escape. Shivering, she clutched the sheet to her breasts, her panicked gaze darting around the darkened room.

Then, as though drawn by a magnet, she turned and looked at the phone, which was barely discernible in the glow from the digital clock on the bedside table. A second later, when the shrill ring pierced the silence, she was already reaching for the receiver.

Erin didn't need to hear a voice to know who was on the other end of the line.

"Elise, what is it? What's wrong?"

"Oh, Erin! I ... I ..."

A harsh sob choked off her twin sister's words, and Erin gripped the receiver more tightly. "Elise? Elise, what is it?

Tell me!'' Swinging her legs to the floor, Erin groped for the lamp and switched it on. She listened intently, but the only sounds coming through the phone were choppy, incoherent gasps. Raking her free hand through her tousled red hair, she pleaded, ''Elise, get a grip on yourself. If you don't tell me what's wrong, I can't help you.''

''No!'' Elise burst out. ''I don't want you to help me! You can't! If you try, they'll kill you, too!''

The fine hair on Erin's arms stood on end. Her twin's fear was palpable. Even across the distance separating them she could feel it coming at her in waves. ''My God, Elise, someone's trying to kill you? Who? Why?''

''I saw them. I . . . I wasn't sure I had locked the vault, so I went back to the office, and I saw them!'' Her voice broke, and she gave a terrified whimper. ''Oh, Erin, they're going to kill me!''

''Who? What did you see?''

''I tried to sneak out, but I bumped into something in the dark,'' she continued in a breathless rush, as though Erin hadn't even spoken. ''I ran, but they saw me.'' She whimpered again. Her breathing grew more erratic, and then she blurted out, ''I can't stay here. I have to get away before they find me!''

''For the love of God, Elise, if someone is trying to kill you, go to the police.''

''I can't! Don't you understand? I can't! He's one of them! He'll kill me, Erin! Oh, God! Please promise you won't contact the police. Please! You've got to promise!'' Her normally soft voice was high-pitched and raw with panic, and Erin knew her sister was teetering on the edge of hysteria.

''Who is 'he'? And who are 'they'? Darling, you're not making any sense.'' Erin drew a deep breath, striving to get a grip on her own fear and keep her voice even. ''Look, instead of my coming for a visit next week as we'd planned, why don't I take the next plane and—"

"No! You mustn't!" Elise said shrilly. "I only called to tell you to stay away from Santa Fe. You've got to promise me you will, Erin. And that you won't contact the police. Promise me!"

"All right, all right. I promise. But, Elise—"

"I've got to go. Someone's coming." Her sister's voice had dropped to a low, urgent murmur that frightened Erin even more than the hysterical babbling.

"No! No, don't hang up! Tell me—"

There was a click at the other end of the line, and then the dial tone droned in her ear.

"Damn!"

Erin immediately called her sister back, but when the connection was completed the phone rang incessantly to no avail.

Frowning, she replaced the receiver slowly. For several seconds she sat motionless, gnawing on the tip of her index finger, going over and over the chilling conversation in her mind. Finally she snatched up the phone again.

David would know what to do, she told herself, punching out her brother's number. Whatever trouble their sister had stumbled into, he would handle it. When David had been with the FBI, Erin and the rest of the family worried endlessly about him, but for once she was grateful for those ten harrowing years. He had left the Bureau a year ago to practice law, but he still had contacts, and he still possessed the sharply honed skills of a hunter. Erin had the uneasy feeling that she and her sister would have need for both.

"Please be home. Please, *please*, be home," she pleaded, listening to the rings at the other end of the line. Her heart leaped when her brother said hello, only to plummet again when she realized she was hearing a recorded message on his answering machine.

She drummed her fingers on the bedside table and waited for the canned spiel to end. At the beep, she jumped right in.

"David, this is Erin. I just got a frantic call from Elise. She's in trouble. From what I can gather, she stumbled onto some sort of crime and she's terrified that the people who committed it are going to kill her. I'm heading out there on the next available flight. Try to meet me at her apartment in Santa Fe as soon as you can."

From the back seat of the taxi Erin stared out at the sun-baked landscape. Deep arroyos and steep, dry hills dotted with clumps of stunted vegetation bordered the road on either side. Many of the houses along the way were made of thick adobe, some a faded sienna, others cream or tan, all blending with the parched earth so that they seemed to grow right up out of the ground. In the distance, purple mountains thrust up into a sky so blue and so vast it hurt her eyes to look at it.

It was a rugged land, beautiful in a harsh, majestic sort of way, awe-inspiring in its grandeur. Still, Erin had difficulty imagining her sister adapting to such stark surroundings.

Elise was a sweet, gentle soul, the kind who evoked images of summer breezes and lemonade on the veranda, of shimmering pastel dresses and fireflies on a warm velvet night. She seemed somehow out of place in this land of sharp edges and vibrant colors.

As for herself, Erin found it vastly appealing. But, then, she wasn't Elise. Physically, she and her twin were identical. In personality and nature, however, they were opposites, Erin thought with a touch of wistfulness.

Once, for the sake of her marriage, she had tried to model herself after her sister, but the attempt had been doomed from the start, she had come to realize. Erin loved her sister, but there was something in her own makeup that craved,

even thrived on, adventure and challenge. Her restless spirit
and insatiable curiosity constantly sought new horizons,
new experiences. To her, life was something to be embraced with open arms. If that meant being alone, and at
times taking risks, well, that was just part of the price one
paid.

Elise never took risks. Her natural tendency was to opt for
the secure, the safe, the familiar. Ever since childhood all
Erin's sister had wanted out of life was to someday marry
the boy next door, settle down in their sleepy east Texas
hometown of Crockett and raise a brood of children.

Well, she'd married her Tommy, Erin thought sadly, only
to lose him to leukemia after three short years.

To Erin, Tommy Holman's death had merely emphasized how fleeting life was and how imperative it was to live
it to the fullest. However, the tragedy had had the opposite
effect on Elise. She had become more cautious, more reserved and more firmly entrenched in the tranquil, safe
routine of her life. Until six months ago, when she had up-
rooted herself and moved, not just out of town, but to another state.

Erin had been working as a translator for a construction
firm in the Middle East when her sister wrote with the news
that she had taken a job with an import firm in Santa Fe. At
the time Erin had been stunned by her twin's decision. But,
she reminded herself, that was before she had known about
Max Delany.

A wry smile tilted Erin's mouth as she recalled the glowing references to the man that had filled her sister's letters
over the past months. "Max this" and "Max that" had
peppered every page. According to Elise, her boss was a
cross between Pierce Brosnan, Sylvester Stallone and Al-
bert Schweitzer, with a little Robert Redford thrown in.

Erin shook her head. It was amazing the things a woman would do when she was in love. And there was no doubt about it: her sister was definitely in love.

According to Elise's recent letters, it appeared as though Max Delany shared her feelings. Erin hoped so. After two years of widowhood, it was time her sister found happiness again. Unlike Erin, Elise was the kind of woman who needed love and the security of marriage to be truly happy.

"Well, this is it, lady," the cabbie said as he brought the car to a halt in front of a new apartment complex.

As she handed the driver his fare, Erin glanced at her watch and grimaced. Almost twelve hours had passed since her sister's frantic call. To her annoyance, she hadn't been able to get a flight until that morning. Then, since no major commercial airline flew into New Mexico's capital city, she'd had to fly to Albuquerque and take a bus to Santa Fe.

For a moment after the cab pulled away Erin remained on the sidewalk, gazing at the jumble of buildings. They were a soft vermilion, multileveled and boxy, with thick walls, exposed ridgepoles and the rounded edges typical of adobe structures. Artfully juxtaposed over the hillside, the complex resembled a child's carelessly scattered building blocks.

Knowing her sister's penchant for rambling old Victorian houses with shaded porches and picket fences, Erin wondered if Elise really felt at home in this curious blend of ancient and modern architecture. Nothing about it bore the slightest resemblance to the homey old place on the edge of Crockett that she and Tommy had so lovingly restored.

Hefting her bag, Erin pushed open the ornate iron gate set in the adobe wall fronting the complex and stepped into a charming courtyard.

Water splashed in a three-tiered fountain, and hummingbirds flitted among the colorful bougainvillea that draped the outer wall and trailed up the face of the apartments ringing the courtyard. In one corner, a large cottonwood tree provided a spot of dappled shade, its dangling leaves clattering in the breeze. Sparrows hopped over the sun-drenched flagstones, pecking at seeds and other tasty morsels. In the somnolence of midday nothing else stirred.

Erin's low-heeled yellow pumps tapped against the uneven stones as she walked from door to door, looking for number 114. She found it at the rear of the courtyard, a ground-floor apartment in the corner behind the cottonwood tree.

She raised her hand to ring the bell, then noticed that the door was ajar. Pushing it open a bit farther, she poked her head inside.

"Elise? Are you home?" she called. When there was no answer she gave the door another push and stepped inside. "Elise?"

She set her suitcase down and looked around. An icy tingle trickled down her spine, making her shiver as she crossed the tiny living room and peered over the bar into the kitchen. Then she told herself she was being foolish. Elise had probably just overreacted. No doubt by this morning she had calmed down and seen things more clearly and decided to go to work.

It was a good effort, but not for a minute did Erin believe her own pep talk. Though Elise was soft and exquisitely feminine, she wasn't the hysterical type, nor was she a quaking little mouse who saw a threat around every corner. And she was too cautious to leave her door unlocked, much less open.

Erin's uneasiness grew. Something was wrong; she could feel it. An ominous, pervading sense of danger, an almost tangible feeling of fear, permeated the air.

A faint buzzing noise reached her when she stepped into the hall. It grew louder as she drew near what she assumed was the bedroom.

"Elise?" She paused outside the door. "Elise, are you in there?"

The buzzing continued.

Every nerve in Erin's body began to hum like a high-voltage wire. Her breathing grew shallow, her chest suddenly tight. Shivering, she rubbed her chilled forearms and fought down an uncharacteristic urge to run. Drawing a determined breath, she squared her shoulders and walked into the room.

After only three steps she came to an abrupt halt, her eyes widening.

Everywhere was vivid evidence of a hasty departure. A dresser drawer lay on the floor, its contents scattered over the tan carpet. The rest of the drawers were open and empty, except for a beige slip hanging forlornly over the edge of one. The closet was also open, and more clothes were strewn from there to the bed, which bore a rectangular imprint that looked suspiciously like that of a suitcase. The little writing desk beside the window had obviously been riffled through, yet Elise's car keys lay in plain sight on top. As Erin took it all in she felt her scalp crawl.

Elise was so compulsively neat that she couldn't tolerate so much as a magazine out of place or a towel hanging crooked. Nothing short of a dire emergency would cause her to leave her apartment in such a state.

The incessant buzzing was coming from the alarm clock on the bedside table, and finally Erin roused herself enough to cross the room and shut it off.

In the pulsing silence she once again surveyed the untidy room, her hand convulsively gripping the shoulder strap of her purse. She should have known that Elise would run away if something had frightened her. Open confrontation wasn't her sister's style. Even under normal circumstances she avoided unpleasantness and strife whenever she could.

Erin sighed, torn between anger at her sister for taking to her heels without leaving word, and pity, knowing how terrified she must be, all alone and fearing for her life.

She had to find her, do whatever she could to help until David arrived to take over and clear up the whole mess. The question was, where had Elise gone?

Nibbling on the tip of her index finger, Erin frowned. Maybe, since she was so crazy about the man, she had turned to Max Delany for help. Then again, Erin thought, maybe he was tied up in whatever it was that Elise had stumbled onto.

She considered the possibilities for a moment, then turned and headed for the living room. In any case, Global Imports seemed a logical place to start.

She picked up her suitcase and started toward the door. Just as she reached it she hesitated, then retraced her steps to the bedroom, scooped up Elise's car keys and went out the back way.

As she had suspected, her sister's blue Chevy was parked in the covered carport behind the apartment. Erin tossed her bag into the back seat and climbed in.

Global Imports had stores all over New Mexico and the Southwest, with the biggest in Santa Fe, across the Plaza from the Palace of the Governors. The offices and warehouse were located several miles northwest of town in a somewhat isolated spot partway up a mountain.

As Erin drove through the gate and pulled into a parking space, a burly blond man on one of the loading docks stopped what he was doing to watch her. When she climbed from the car he was standing at the edge of the dock, his feet braced apart, his beefy fists propped on his hips, staring at her. The intense scrutiny sent a flutter of uneasiness through Erin, but she ignored him and walked into the office as though she had every right to be there.

There was no one at the reception desk in the lobby. She waited, drumming her fingers, but after a few minutes she gave up and wandered down the hallway until she found a door that bore Max Delany's name.

She knocked, but when no one answered she knocked again and at the same time opened the door and stepped inside.

Looking around, Erin smiled, knowing from the immaculate desk, the abundance of carefully tended plants and the precise arrangement of the magazines on the table beside the small sofa that she had found Elise's office.

Behind and to the right of the desk was another door, which Erin assumed led to Max Delany's office. She had barely taken a step in that direction when the door flew open and a tall, angry man came barreling out.

"Where the hell have you been?"

Taken aback, Erin glanced over her shoulder before she realized that he was talking to her. "Me? Why, I—"

"I return a day early from a trip and find that the damned phones are ringing off the wall, my secretary hasn't shown up and no one knows where she is."

As if on cue, the phone rang. Max snatched it up, bellowed "Call back later" and slammed it down again.

He glared at Erin as though it were her fault. "I've been here almost an hour, and all I've been able to get done is one lousy letter."

Well, well, well, Erin thought as her gaze slid over the irate man. If this was Max Delany, no wonder Elise was smitten.

Not even the intimidating scowl lessened the impact of the man's appeal. Sable-brown curly hair framed an angular face with an intriguing cleft chin, a stubborn jaw and high-boned cheeks. His mouth was chiseled perfection—not too full and not too thin. And to top it all off, he possessed the most incredibly sexy blue eyes. It was, Erin decided, a handsome face that was barely saved from being beautiful by a crooked, off-center nose, which appeared to have been broken at some point and left to mend as it might.

Not only had Mother Nature been generous in the looks department, but the man had a body that wouldn't quit— tall, broad-shouldered and muscular with lean hips and a flat middle. Standing there glowering at her, he radiated that supremely arrogant masculinity that made a woman tingle right down to her toes.

Poor Elise, Erin thought with a touch of amusement. She must have been bowled over when she met him at that party in Dallas. No wonder she'd kicked over the traces and snapped up the job when he offered it.

While Erin had been inspecting Max, he had been doing the same to her, and his angry expression held a faint touch of surprise as he took in her casual white cotton slacks and matching unconstructed jacket, worn over a bright yellow-and-white-striped tank top.

"If you had some problem or needed a few hours off, the least you could have done was call in and tell Sam or Wilma that you were going to be late," he continued in an aggrieved tone. "You're usually such a conscientious little soul. I was beginning to think you'd had an accident."

Understanding dawned. He thought she was Elise!

No wonder he'd looked so puzzled over her outfit, she thought, fighting back a grin. He'd probably never seen Elise in anything other than a very proper dress. "But you don't understand. I'm not—"

He held up his hand, cutting her off. "Knowing you, I'm sure you have a good reason; but I don't want to hear it right now. I've already wasted enough time this morning, and we both have work to do."

Erin opened her mouth, her explanation poised on the tip of her tongue, but suddenly it occurred to her that she'd be a fool to trust Max Delany. Just because he was Elise's boss didn't mean he was a safe bet. True, he hadn't threatened her or acted particularly menacing—grouchy and a bit harassed, which was understandable, given the circumstances, but not menacing. Still, that didn't mean that he wasn't somehow tied in with whatever had caused Elise to take flight. He could very well be one of the "they" she had babbled about over the phone. Erin eyed him, one brow arching. Her sister obviously hadn't turned to him for help. Then again, how could she when he's been out of town? her conscience reminded her.

"There's some correspondence on your desk that needs to go out today." Max gave her a sour look that spoke volumes. "Since no one was here to take dictation, I wrote it out in longhand. When you've finished with that letter, come in and I'll go over the new contract I worked out with Gerlings while I was in Germany."

When Erin didn't move he snapped, "Well, are you going to just stand there gaping all day? Or do you think we could get a little work done around here before it's time to go home?"

"I . . ." Erin hesitated. Her uncertain gaze went from the fuming man to the computer sitting on the desk. She used a word processor sometimes when transcribing written material from one language to another, but her portable machine bore little resemblance to that monster. And she was no great shakes as a typist. For that matter, on a scale of one to ten, her secretarial skills rated about a minus two. "I, uh . . ." Meeting his glower once again, she drew a deep breath, held it a second, then let it out slowly. Oh, what the hell, she decided.

"Of course, Max. I'll get right on it," she said with aplomb. Just as though she did it every day, Erin marched around the desk, dropped her purse into the bottom drawer and took her seat.

Picking up the papers covered with a bold scrawl, she pretended to study them. Max didn't move, and she looked up to find him staring at her quizzically, one dark brow cocked. "Was there something else?" she inquired politely.

"Yes. Buzz Wilma and see if Sam is back from lunch yet. If he is, tell her I'd like to see him."

Wilma? Wilma who? Oh, Lord, what do I do now? Stalling for time, Erin shuffled the papers on the desk and flipped the calendar to the current date, but her dithering earned her an impatient look from Max.

"Will you stop that nonsense and make the call?" he commanded. "I need to discuss the new contracts with Sam."

When that produced only a blank stare he turned to sarcasm. "You *do* remember Sam, don't you, Elise? Sam Lawford, that big guy across the hall who happens to be my partner?"

Erin groped for an intelligent response, but nothing came. Frowning, Max waved his hand in front of her face. "Good God, woman, what's the matter with you? Are you sick or something?"

"No, I...I'm sorry. I guess I was woolgathering." She picked up the phone.

After giving her another hard look, Max grunted, turned on his heel and stalked back into his office.

The moment the door snapped shut behind him, Erin replaced the receiver and let out a gusty sigh, her shoulders slumping.

It had been years since she'd switched places with her twin, though of course they'd done it often when they were growing up. But in those days they'd known the same people. She was going to have to bluff her way through her little deception.

Erin cast a disgruntled look at the closed door. For a man who was supposed to be in love, Max had a strange way of showing it. Or perhaps he was one of those dedicated types who never let his personal life interfere with business. Either way, she felt sorry for her sister.

Erin ran her finger down the typed list of names and extensions taped to the desk beside the phone. Wilma Crenshaw was the fourth one, and as she picked up the receiver and punched out the three digits, Erin mentally crossed her fingers. Halfway through the second ring the phone was picked up.

"Lawford."

Expecting a woman to answer, Erin was taken aback by the masculine voice at the other end of the line. It took her a moment to realize that she had somehow reached Sam Lawford, not his secretary. "Uh...Mr. Lawford, this is Elise. Max would like to see you when you have time."

"Certainly."

He hung up, and Erin replaced the receiver, her brows arching. Obviously Mr. Sam Lawford was a man of few words.

Dismissing Max's partner from her mind, she looked around, intent on investigating her sister's disappearance. Elise had said something about coming back to the office to check the vault. Right now, that was the only lead she had.

Erin started pawing through the meticulous desk like a dog digging for a bone. No doubt Elise had committed the combination to memory, but knowing her sister's thoroughness, she would also have it written down and filed away somewhere. The vault was probably off Max's office, but he had to leave sometime, and when he did she was going to be ready.

Ten minutes later Erin was working her way through the files when the outer door opened. She started guiltily, whirled around and found herself looking into a pair of pale gray eyes so cold and remote they looked dead.

The rest of the man was just as austere. He was tall and rangy, with glossy blue-black hair swept ruthlessly back from a face that betrayed not the slightest hint of emotion. There was nothing in the least handsome about him, although his rugged masculinity might have been appealing had it been tempered by a bit of human warmth. But this man had the look of hardened steel. If he had any feelings behind that cold face, he kept them well hidden.

The silvery gaze ran over Erin from the top of her short, curly red mop to her bright yellow pumps. The man's expression did not alter one whit, but she sensed his mocking disapproval.

When he'd finished his inspection he looked her right in the eye, and she shifted under that glacial stare.

"You're getting brave, aren't you?"

The voice was as cold and hard as the rest of him, but at least it told Erin whom she was facing. Although he'd spoken only two words to her over the phone, there was no mistaking that voice; it belonged to Sam Lawford.

Then his words sank in, and a frisson of alarm skittered down her spine. Erin watched him warily. "Wh-what do you mean?"

"Changing your image," he said in that same flat voice, flicking a hand toward her stylish outfit. "It might work. Max likes a bit of dash in a woman. Personally, I prefer the soft, feminine look."

Without another word, he walked into Max's office, leaving Erin puzzling over the cryptic statement.

She stared after him. Shivering, she rubbed her arms. Erin knew now why her sister rarely mentioned Sam Lawford in her letters. When he'd leveled those cold gray eyes on her, she'd experienced an insane desire to turn and run. And if he had that effect on her, Erin thought, he probably terrified Elise.

When he left Max's office fifteen minutes later, Sam gave her another hard look, but, much to Erin's relief, he didn't stop to talk. She turned her attention back to the files but had barely resumed her search when the outer door opened again. This time her visitor was a stout woman in her fifties.

"Sam told me you had arrived, but frankly, Elise, I didn't expect to see you here today."

"Oh, really?" Erin replied noncommittally.

She assumed that this was Wilma Crenshaw. The woman wore her gray hair twisted into a tight bun, and except for a dab of lipstick and powder, her plain face was free of makeup. Dressed in a severe gray suit, a tailored white blouse and orthopedic shoes, she looked like everyone's idea of a maiden aunt.

Probably a paragon of quiet efficiency who blends into the woodwork, Erin thought as she met the woman's level gaze. And no doubt suits her somber boss right down to the ground.

"To be honest, my dear, you surprise me. You look so fragile, but it appears that you're a lot sturdier than I thought."

Erin waited, not sure how to reply. Had Elise been ill yesterday?

"I was sure that you would—"

"Elise, is that letter ready?" Max burst from his office like a cannon shot, making Erin jump. "I've been waiting— Oh, hi, Wilma."

"Mr. Delany! I didn't know you were back from Europe." Wilma eased toward the door. "I'm sure you're busy, so I'll just get out of your way."

Watching her scurry out, Max shook his head. "Amazing," he mused aloud. "After working here for two years you'd think the woman would have gotten over her shyness by now, but she practically swallows her tongue every time

I speak to her. I guess the reason she likes working for Sam is that he keeps his distance.''

Returning his attention to Erin, he gave her a demanding look. "And speaking of work, where is that letter?''

"I'm, uh, not quite finished. I'll have it ready in just a few minutes.''

"Well, hurry it up. I have some contracts I want you to type, too.''

He darted back into his office, leaving Erin with no choice but to cope with the computer. In her search of the desk she had come across an instruction manual, and with a sigh she opened the drawer and dug it out.

The day turned out to be one of the worst Erin had ever endured. She was simply not cut out to be a secretary. She was fluent in five languages, conversant in three more, but when it came to deciphering a filing system or mastering a keyboard she was a flop.

Erin knew that her twin liked the stability and security of a nine-to-five job, but she found the routine stifling. More than once, as she struggled with the mundane tasks, she thanked her lucky stars that as a translator she had the freedom and independence to work at a variety of jobs all over the world.

It took Erin almost an hour to finish that first letter. She wrestled with the strange wording in the manual for almost ten minutes before she was able to boot the machine, and, all the while she was typing, the blasted thing kept beeping at her, making her so nervous she wanted to scream. Once she had the letter typed, it took another thirty minutes to figure out how to print it out. Then, when she took it in to Max he hit the roof because it wasn't printed on letterhead stationery.

"Good grief, Elise, how could you do something so dumb?" he demanded.

It was almost more than Erin's frazzled nerves could take. "All right, so I made a mistake," she snapped right back. "You don't have to yell." In a very un-Elise-like manner, she snatched the letter from his hand and stomped out to do it over, leaving Max gaping at her as though she'd suddenly sprouted another head.

Max couldn't believe his eyes. The second letter Elise produced had three typos, the style was off and it was printed crooked on the wrong paper. He couldn't understand it. For six months his secretary had performed her job as efficiently as a machine, and now, all at once, she was hopelessly inept.

What on earth was wrong with the woman? From the moment she arrived she had made one mistake after another. She'd jammed the copy machine, mislaid important papers and bungled half the calls—once disconnecting an important South American supplier. Her typing was atrocious, and she acted as though the filing system were a complete mystery. And when he'd dictated this latest letter he'd had to stop after every sentence to let her catch up.

Puzzled, Max stood and walked to the door that separated his office from Elise's. Folding his arms over his chest, he propped his shoulder against the doorjamb and studied her.

She sat hunched over the computer keyboard, staring at the monitor, frowning and nibbling the tip of her index finger. There was something different about her. Partly it was her clothes. It was unlike Elise to wear bright colors or anything quite so trendy. Yet there was more to it than that. But what?

The computer beeped, and she muttered a colorful oath and raked a hand through her hair.

Max's brows rose. In the six months Elise had worked for him he'd never heard her utter a curse word or seen her even mildly flustered. And, he thought, grinning as his attention focused on the tousled red curls, he had never seen her with a hair out of place before.

She had removed her jacket, and Max's gaze was drawn to the tiny birthmark on the back of her shoulder, visible just above the scooped neckline of her tank top. It resembled a misshapened heart and was about the size of a small button.

Slowly, Max straightened away from the door, his eyes growing wide, then narrowing. And it hadn't been there just last week!

When the computer beeped again Erin gave a frustrated growl, flounced out of the chair and stalked across the room to the credenza that held the coffeepot. Max stared after her in astonishment. Why, that little devil. That's not Elise. That's her twin!

You dope, he scolded himself. You should have known when she called you by your first name. Elise was such a stickler for protocol she never would have done that—at least, not during working hours.

It explained everything: the new look, those flashes of temper, her ineptitude...and most of all, the sudden strong attraction he'd been feeling all afternoon.

Though Elise was beautiful, not once had she aroused in him any feeling stronger than admiration—until today.

He had thought he was losing his mind. All afternoon he'd been aware of her. The slightest accidental touch or whiff of her perfume had sent his senses reeling and made his body throb. And every time he'd looked into those flashing brown eyes or watched her toss that tousled mop of curls and march from the room in a huff he'd experienced an almost uncontrollable desire to grab her and kiss that adorable, impudent mouth until she melted in his arms.

It was strange. The two women were identical in looks, yet there were subtle differences. Elise's was the soft, lustrous beauty of a pearl, but her sister possessed the flash and fire, the sparkle of a diamond. It was there in the directness of those snapping brown eyes, the defiant lift of her chin and the proud carriage of that slender body.

What was it Elise called her? Her adventuresome twin? It fit, Max thought as he watched her fill a Styrofoam cup with coffee. She fairly crackled with vibrant energy, audacious zestfulness. It was probably just his imagination, he knew, but even her hair seemed redder than Elise's.

Max grinned. Oh, yes. She was a bold little minx, all right, and probably the one who'd hatched this scheme. No doubt she and her sister had been pulling this switch on unsuspecting males since they were in their teens, he thought, amused and annoyed all at the same time.

Narrowly eyeing Erin's slender form, Max started across the room, his grin growing wider. Well, sweetheart, it's time someone taught you a lesson. And I'm just the man to do it.

Chapter Two

A pair of hard, masculine arms slid around Erin's waist. She jumped and let out a squawk, dropping the packet of sweetener she had been about to put in her coffee.

Her heart seemed to jump into her throat. She grabbed the broad wrists that crossed at her waist, but then she stiffened and froze, her eyes widening as she felt the moist caress of lips nuzzling the side of her neck.

"Relax, sweetheart. It's just me."

The murmured words were followed by a lazy chuckle, and Erin's jaw dropped. "M-Max?"

"Mmm?"

His teeth nipped with gentle savagery, and Erin sucked in her breath. "Max, wh—" she stopped to clear her throat "—what are you doing?"

"Lovin' my woman. What did you think?"

"But—"

"Relax, sweetheart. It's past quitting time, so we can drop the boss/secretary routine."

Erin grappled with the implication behind that statement, her mind reeling. Good Lord, she thought with a trace of panic. Elise's romance with Max had progressed a lot further than her letters had indicated. She hadn't bargained on this.

He batted her earlobe with his tongue, then traced a wet circle on the sensitive skin behind it. Erin's breathing grew shallow, and her eyes drifted shut. Unconsciously, her fingers tightened around his wrists. "But . . . someone might come in," she protested feebly.

"So what? Everyone here knows about us."

Erin swallowed hard and wondered just what everyone knew. "A-All the same, I don't think we should be doing this in the office."

Max chuckled again, but after another foray down her neck and shoulder he released her. "All right. You win. I'll save it for later, when we're alone."

Flustered, Erin turned and looked at him warily, and Max smiled. "Are you ready to go?"

"Go?"

"Yes. Have you forgotten? When I called yesterday we made plans to have dinner tonight." His eyes glinted as he reached up and ran his forefinger over her parted lips and added softly, "At my place."

The caressing words and his intimate touch shot through Erin like a jolt of electricity. She barely controlled the gasp that sprang to her lips. Oh, Lord, now what do I do? she wondered, gazing at the sensual expression on Max Delany's face.

Beneath drowsy, half-closed lids, those sexy blue eyes glittered with disturbing warmth, and the hint of a smile that played about his lips was filled with awareness and anticipation and supreme male confidence.

He was standing close—much too close. She could feel the heat from his body, smell his tantalizing clean male scent. Her skin still tingled where he had touched her.

Erin broke eye contact and stared at the cleft in Max's chin. "I, uh, I guess it slipped my mind," she replied with a wan smile, struggling to subdue the panicky sensation that fluttered in her chest. She risked a glance upward and quickly lowered her eyes again when she encountered that simmering gaze. "But... but maybe we should make it another time." She waved toward the desk and backed up a step. "I still have a lot of work to do."

Like distant thunder, Max's chuckle came rumbling up from his chest. Taking a firm grip on her shoulders, he turned her toward the door. "Nonsense. There's nothing there that won't wait until tomorrow."

"Oh, but—"

A quick kiss on her parted lips stopped her cold. Max's lips were warm and firm, and despite its brevity, the kiss was shockingly thorough.

When he raised his head, he grinned into her startled face. "Now get your purse, and let's go. I'm starving."

For what? Erin wondered uneasily as she was bundled out the door and down the hallway.

The young woman behind the desk looked up when they entered the reception area, a stunned look crossing her face at the sight of Max holding his secretary close against his side, his arm clamped around her waist.

"Good night, Peggy," he called to the gawking woman. "See you tomorrow." Max strode past the desk without even slowing down. The woman's dazed "Good night" followed them out the door.

In the parking lot he steered Erin toward a sleek silver Lincoln Continental.

"But what about my car?" she said, looking back over her shoulder at Elise's blue Chevy.

"What about it?"

"I can't just leave it here. Besides, if I take it, you won't have to drive me home later."

This time Max's grin was openly lecherous. "Who said anything about taking you home?"

Erin's heart did a little skip. Good grief! Just how intimate a relationship did her sister have with this man?

Like a sleepwalker, she got into the car when Max held open the door, and she sat staring straight ahead as he circled around to the other side. Her mind racing, she glanced at him when he slid in behind the wheel, and her gaze zeroed in on the slight upward tilt of his lips.

How had this entire situation come to pass? she wondered frantically. Elise simply wasn't the type for an affair. She'd never done anything so reckless. At eight she'd fallen in love with gangly, fourteen-year-old Tommy Holman and had worshiped him from that moment forward, but she'd still been a virgin bride when they married, fourteen years later. It was impossible to believe that her sister would fall into bed with a man she'd known a mere six months.

Even if he was a handsome devil, Erin thought, eyeing Max's chiseled profile with a touch of resentment.

His concentration was on maneuvering the twisting mountain road, but at that moment, as though sensing her scrutiny, he shot her a lazy, come-hither glance and another of those devastating grins. In spite of herself, Erin felt her insides give a little flutter.

"What are you doing sitting way over there?" Without waiting for a reply, Max reached out, cupped his broad palm around the back of her neck and urged her closer.

Reluctantly, Erin scooted across the seat, since it was obvious that Max was accustomed to a display of affection from Elise.

He tucked her against his side, but his hand remained where it was, his fingers tunneling into her short curls and massaging the taut muscles in her neck. "There, that's better, isn't it?" he said with blatant self-satisfaction, darting her another caressing look that shimmered with promise and sent panic skittering through Erin.

"Hmm," she mumbled.

He released his hold on her neck and picked up her hand, placing it on his thigh, palm down, before gripping the steering wheel once again.

Staring straight ahead, Erin tried to will away the flush that suffused her body like a warm tide. From elbow to fingertips she could feel the heat and hardness of that muscled thigh beneath her arm, while all along her side her body was molded to his. The slight jostling motion of the car increased the intimate contact and sent a prickly sensation rippling over her skin, leaving goose bumps in its wake. The scrub-covered landscape flashed by largely unnoticed as Erin wondered, a bit desperately, how on earth she had gotten herself into such a fix and, even more important, how she was going to get herself out of it.

She didn't dare tell him the truth—not until she was positive he wasn't involved in whatever was going on.

Erin eyed Max out of the corner of her eye. He didn't seem dangerous—not in a criminal way. And it appeared he knew nothing about last night. Of course, he'd been out of town. It was possible that the others simply hadn't had time to fill him in.

Or perhaps they had, Erin thought, her eyes narrowing. Maybe he was just playing a cat-and-mouse game, waiting to see what Elise knew and whether she'd confide in him.

Elise. Her jaw tightened, and Erin shifted her gaze to the arid mountains in the distance. Her search for her sister was getting nowhere fast. Darn it, she had to find her! But how? Max Delany and Global Imports were her only leads.

The car hit a bump, jarring Erin even harder against Max, and her arm slipped off his leg and into the V of his crotch.

She snatched it back as though she had been burned and clasped her hands together in her lap.

Grinning wickedly, Max pried her fingers apart and returned her hand to his thigh, covering it with his own.

When Max turned into a curving driveway and brought the car to a halt, Erin was torn between profound relief that the ride had ended at last and dread over what was yet to come.

Though the drive had seemed interminable, it had actually taken only a few minutes. Max's home was just a few miles up the mountain from Global Imports. Like the warehouse, it sat alone on a level plateau with a commanding view of Santa Fe and the surrounding mountains. It was a sprawling, multileveled adobe structure, with many of the rear rooms climbing up the mountain face in step fashion. A few trees shaded the front corners of the house, and another sprouted in the center from what Erin assumed to be a courtyard or open atrium. Most of the landscaping, however, was a carefully tended rock garden containing hardy native plants.

Assuming that Elise had been there before, Erin tried not to appear too curious. Max slipped his arm around her waist, and she accepted his touch with a polite smile as he led her up three shallow stairs toward the massive oak door.

Inside, the tiled entrance hall was cool and dim. Erin would have liked to look around, but the moment the door closed behind them Max hauled her into his arms.

The move so startled Erin that she resisted instinctively. She opened her mouth to protest, forgetting for an instant that Elise would probably melt in his arms, and felt his lips cover hers.

She froze, eyes opened wide, hands splayed against Max's chest. Her heart thumped, and her mind went utterly blank. She couldn't have moved if the house had caught fire.

Then her shock began to fade, and she realized that never in her life had she been kissed quite so masterfully...or so thoroughly.

Max's lips were firm and warm, tender and demanding. They rocked against hers with a slow, savoring hunger that was wildly exciting. His tongue delved and stroked, laying claim with bold sureness; his hands roamed up and down her back, cupped the rounded fullness of her bottom and kneaded with embarrassing familiarity.

"Mmm, you taste delicious," Max murmured against her cheek. He returned to her mouth, nipping, his tongue gliding over her parted lips. "So sweet." His bold hands pulled her closer, rotating her hips against his. "And you feel so damned good," he whispered in her ear.

So do you, she thought in a flash of panic. That was the problem. Max's kisses, the feel of his hard body against hers, made her dizzy with need. And his scent was so wonderfully male, so intoxicating. It surrounded her, filled her senses and created a delicious woozy feeling in the pit of her stomach.

Erin's mind and body were sending out conflicting signals. The temptation to relax and respond was almost irresistible.

So why don't you? a traitorous inner voice whispered. You're supposed to be Elise, remember? It's what she would do.

But the thought of her sister and of Elise's feelings for Max brought both honesty and guilt to the surface. Idiot, she chided herself. It's Elise he thinks he's kissing.

Wedging her arms between them, Erin broke off the kiss and leaned back within his embrace. She gave a shaky laugh and flashed him what she hoped was a coy look. "Max, we're still in the foyer."

"So?"

"Well, you did say we were going to have dinner, didn't you? I'm starving." It was true. She hadn't had a bite since that cardboard breakfast she'd only nibbled at on the plane that morning.

With a chuckle and another quick kiss, Max released her. "All right. First things first, I suppose. You know where everything is. While I change, why don't you start dinner?" He gave her bottom a swat and started up a short flight of stairs, stopping on the landing to call back, "Just make a salad and that special dressing of yours, and throw a couple of potatoes into the microwave. I'll grill the steaks."

Erin stared after him. Salad dressing? Potatoes? Oh, Lord. She was really in trouble now. Elise was the domestic one. Her own culinary talents were limited to opening cans and adding boiling water to packets of instant mix.

She looked around, her brain working furiously. Well, she had no choice; she was just going to have to fake it. She was stuck on a mountaintop with a man who had amorous intentions. It was either keep him in the kitchen and feed him or run the risk of finding herself in the bedroom, appeasing another appetite.

But first she needed to get the lay of the land.

Erin swept through the rooms on the first level at nearly a run and was surprised to find only a large living room, a powder room, a library and what appeared to be a home office.

Where the devil was the kitchen?

She returned to the entry hall and listened at the bottom of the stairs for Max. Emboldened by the distant sound of a shower running and an off-key baritone raised in song, she raced up to the landing. From it the stairs branched off and upward in several directions, and hallways stretched out on each side.

Erin nibbled briefly at the end of her index finger, then took off down the right hall. Four doors opened onto it. The first two were large closets, the others a bathroom and an enormous game room.

Gnashing her teeth, Erin raced back to the landing. She took the first set of stairs two at a time, then zipped right back down again when she discovered that they led to the master suite.

Working her way across the landing, she ran up and down, exploring at breakneck speed, finding several more bedrooms, each with its own bath, several private terraces tucked between the wings, and a solarium. She also discovered that by building his house in steps up the side of the mountain, Max had ingeniously provided each room with a breathtaking view.

By the time she located the kitchen, which, along with the dining and breakfast rooms, occupied the three-level wing to the left of the landing, she was thoroughly confused. There were countless nooks and steps and interconnecting passageways.

She'd never find her way around, Erin fretted as she washed her hands at the kitchen sink. The place was a regular rabbit warren.

She poked through the refrigerator until she found a bottle of salad dressing. She dumped the contents into a bowl and hid the bottle in the garbage pail under the sink, burying it under a wad of paper towels, then pulled a half dozen cans of likely looking herbs and spices from the cabinet and placed them beside the bowl.

When Max walked into the kitchen, a large salad of lettuce, spinach and tomato wedges sat in the center of the breakfast table, and Erin was standing at the counter, industriously whipping the dressing with a wire whisk.

"What's this?" he asked, peering over her shoulder.

His hands settled on either side of her waist. He buried his face in her hair, and she felt his warm, moist breath filter through the silky curls and feather over her scalp. Then his lips touched her neck. Erin's hands stilled. She gritted her teeth, trying to quell the delicious quiver that rippled through her.

"It's . . . salad dressing."

"It doesn't look like your usual," he whispered into her ear.

"I decided to try a new recipe."

Reaching around her, Max picked up a spice can. "You use *cinnamon* in salad dressing?"

"Uh . . . well . . . just a little."

He dipped a finger into the bowl and brought it to his mouth. "It tastes okay, I guess, kind of like that stuff I buy at the store. But I like your other recipe better."

Erin held her breath, but Max let the subject drop and resumed his affectionate nuzzling. He blew in her ear and kissed the tender flesh behind it while his hands roamed her hips and abdomen.

Erin hunched her shoulder against his marauding mouth and scolded with a shaky laugh, "Max, will you stop! You're supposed to be cooking steaks, remember?"

"Okay, spoilsport. You win." Then his voice changed from long-suffering to suggestive as he added, "For now."

Straightening, he grasped the lapels of her jacket. "Here, why don't you take this thing off."

He eased the garment from her shoulders, and Erin sighed when he moved away to hang it on a hook beside the door. The brief period of relief was shattered an instant later when, while crossing the kitchen, he paused long enough to kiss her neck and trail the tip of his tongue down her spine all the way to the edge of the scooped neckline of her tank top.

"Max!" Erin gasped, but he had already walked away, whistling and grinning as he opened the refrigerator and withdrew the package of steaks. She closed her eyes and shivered, feeling the cool air strike the thin line of damp flesh down her back.

It was amazing, Erin thought an hour or so later, watching Max as she pretended to relax with an after-dinner drink. He barely seemed like the same man who had had her jumping through hoops that afternoon at the office.

Back at Global Imports it had quickly become obvious that Max was a dynamic, forceful man with an agile mind and an enormous capacity for hard work, traits that made him a demanding, exacting boss. He had run her ragged within an hour, and Erin's admiration for her sister's ability and patience had taken a quantum leap.

Max piled on enough work for three people, then expected perfection and growled like a bear when he didn't get it. By the end of the day Erin had been tired and irritated and out of sorts. She had even begun to wonder what Elise saw in the man.

Well, now she knew. When he turned on the charm, Max Delany was lethal.

As they had worked together in the kitchen, and later during the romantic candlelit dinner on the terrace, Max had grown more and more amorous. Passion and promise had been inherent in every look, every word, every touch.

And he had touched her constantly, brushing against her whenever possible, stroking her hand and bare arms with his fingertips, trailing his knuckles down her cheek. He'd made love to her with his eyes and murmured endearments and shockingly intimate remarks that had unnerved her to the point that she'd barely been able to think.

Once, she bit into a roll, and melted butter had dribbled onto her fingers. Before she could wipe it off, Max had captured her hand. Holding her gaze, he'd licked the golden liquid from her skin, running his tongue over her palm and between each finger with slow, sensuous strokes that sent fire streaking from the point of contact to the core of her femininity.

Oh, yes, the man was definitely dangerous.

Hunched down in front of the fireplace, Max jabbed the blazing logs with a poker, sending a shower of sparks shooting up the chimney. The fire hissed and popped, and Erin jumped.

Cursing under her breath, she dabbed at the drops of wine that had sloshed onto her slacks.

Her nerves were eating her alive. From that eerie moment just before Elise's frantic call, the dreadful, uneasy feeling in the pit of her stomach had been growing. Call it intuition, telepathy, ESP—whatever—that strange, mystical communication that had always existed between her and her twin was working full throttle. Every instinct Erin possessed was screaming "Find her! Find her!"

But how? Global Imports, and Max, had seemed her best leads—her only leads—but she was no closer to locating her sister now than when she had walked into the office.

And to add to her worries, she hadn't the faintest idea how she was going to handle Max.

The scene was certainly set for seduction, Erin thought with a wry grimace, glancing around the large living room. The lights were so low that she could barely make out the massive Spanish armoire by the entrance, and the wrought-iron étagère filled with Indian artifacts set against the far wall was just a hulking shadow. The wine was crisp and cool and the small fire romantic, casting a mellow glow over the polished tile floor and the scattering of Navaho rugs. Music drifted from hidden speakers in the dim corners of the room. Ravel's *Boléro*, Erin registered—soft, sensual, soul-stirring, the building strains so subtly, relentlessly arousing.

The niggling doubt that had been worrying Erin all evening grew stronger as she watched Max rise and return the poker to its stand. He stretched, flexing his shoulders and arching his back in a slow, sinuous movement that made his muscles ripple beneath the pale blue knit shirt. Erin's mouth went suddenly dry. Could Elise have resisted a man with that potent combination of charm, good looks and sex appeal? Tommy Holman had been a great guy, and nice looking in a clean-cut all-American way, but he couldn't hold a candle to Max. It was like comparing a tabby cat to a mountain lion.

Max turned and caught her staring. Hooking his thumbs into the waistband of his low-riding jeans, he sauntered toward her with loose-limbed grace. Even in the dimness there was no mistaking the warm, intent look on his face.

You're in trouble, Erin, she told herself shakily. This is the man your sister loves. Even if he weren't, you barely know him, for heaven's sake. You've got to call a halt, somehow, before things get out of hand.

Max sat down beside her and turned at an angle, draping his arm along the sofa back. With one finger he touched her upper arm, drawing a tiny circle on her bare skin. "I missed you," he murmured, and the finger trailed upward, skimming over the narrow tank top and leaving a line of fire across her shoulder and the side of her neck.

A delicate shudder rippled through Erin, and her breathing grew shallow. Maybe she should just tell him the truth, she reflected. Surely Max couldn't be involved in anything nefarious. He hadn't done or said anything in the least suspicious all evening, and it was obvious that the only thing on his mind was seduction.

She had herself halfway convinced when his next words brought her doubts flooding back.

"What did you do while I was gone?"

She looked at him sharply, her heart beginning to pound. "Do?"

"Hmm. Anything I should know about?" He traced the velvety rim of her ear, then twined a bright curl around his finger. "Anything you want to tell me?"

"Why..." She paused and licked her lips. "Why do you ask?"

Inclining his head, he brushed his open mouth back and forth over the curve of her shoulder, dewing it with his breath. "Well," he murmured against her skin, "I could say that as your boss, I need to keep abreast of what's going on...but actually..." With intense concentration, he worked his way up over her shoulder and neck. "...the real reason is..."

Erin held her breath and waited, unconsciously arching her neck to give him better access as he nibbled along her jaw. When he reached her chin he turned her head with one finger, bringing her mouth even with his, and looking into her eyes, his own glittering beneath half-closed lids. "...I was hoping you'd say you'd been thinking about me."

The tension whooshed out of Erin like air escaping a balloon.

Max brushed her lips with a butterfly kiss. And then another. And another. So great was her relief, she accepted the tiny salutes with an eagerness that would have appalled her had she been thinking clearly.

Max pulled back a few inches and looked at her again. "I was also hoping that you'd thought over what we discussed and were ready to give me an answer."

Erin blinked, her muscles growing taut again as his words soaked in. Answer? Oh, Lord. An answer to what?

"I, uh..."

"Come on, honey. It can't be that difficult a decision," Max prodded. "Surely by now you know how you feel."

About what? Erin wanted to scream. Then her eyes widened as it occurred to her that Max could have proposed to Elise. The thought produced a queer little stab of pain that surprised and dismayed her. Adding to her confusion was the strange hint of a smile that twitched at the corners of his mouth.

"I . . . I'm just not sure."

She expected annoyance or disappointment, but, oddly, her answer seemed to amuse him. Max's gaze dropped to her mouth, his lids lowering until his eyes were mere slits. "Well, maybe I can help you make up your mind," he whispered as his head lowered once again.

Erin's heart banged against her ribs. She tried to force her mind to go blank, to will her senses to feel nothing, but it was impossible. The kiss was pure seduction.

With warm lips and nimble tongue, Max tempted and tantalized and sweetly cajoled until at last she shuddered and, with a little moan of surrender, slid her arms around his neck.

Instantly the kiss grew bolder, deeper. Sensations poured through Erin, sweet, hungry sensations that made her throb and burn and shiver all at the same time. She had to stop this, she thought dazedly, even as she parried the rhythmic thrusts of his tongue.

Max applied gentle, relentless pressure, and Erin could only cling to him as she felt herself being lowered, felt the nubby material of the sofa cushion tickle her skin, felt her back and shoulders sink into its softness. He lay over her, his body pressing her deep into the cushion, a delicious warm weight that made her yearn for something more.

She clasped his head with both hands, her spread fingers plowing through his hair, massaging restlessly, learning the shape of his skull. He tasted of coffee and brandy, and his delicious male scent made her head spin. His dark curls twined around her fingers and flowed against her skin like warm silk.

Max kissed her cheek, her chin, her eyes, her ears. His hand stroked her sides. "Oh, sweetheart, I love the way you writhe beneath me," he whispered. "Yes. Yes, that's it. Oh, God, you feel good. I've wanted you here from the moment we met."

Easing to one side, he braced himself up on an elbow and cupped her breast. He flexed his fingers around the soft mound and brushed his thumb across her nipple, and Erin moaned, her back arching.

"Sweet. So sweet." Max stared down at her, his eyes a dark, glittering blue. "And so responsive." His thumb brushed again, and her restive movement brought a look of satisfaction to his face. "You like that, don't you, Erin?"

He lowered his head and took her nipple into his mouth. Moisture and heat seeped through her knit top and fragile lacy bra as he drew on her.

"Max. Oh, Max!" Erin gasped and closed her eyes, lost for a moment in the incredible sensations streaking through her.

Then her eyelids drifted open. "Wh-what did you call me?"

Max raised his head and met her confused gaze. He smiled. "Erin. Elise's globe-trotting sister I've heard so much about. You *are* Erin, aren't you?"

Chapter Three

His words hit Erin like a bucket of ice water. She stared at him, numb with shock.

Then, as it sank in, embarrassment washed over her, and she burned from the soles of her feet to her scalp.

Erin thought of how Max had touched and held her, of his sexy glances and the outrageous things he had whispered in her ear. And his kisses! Oh, Lord, she'd responded to him shamelessly!

And it was no use pretending that she'd merely been faking, behaving as she'd thought Elise would have. She knew it wasn't true. What was worse, she was certain that Max knew it, too.

At that moment Erin would have given ten years of her life if only the earth would open up and swallow her.

Just when she thought she'd reached the peak of embarrassment, Max shifted his weight up onto his elbows, and the movement brought her a sharp awareness of their position.

He lay cradled between her thighs, his aroused manhood pressing against her with shocking intimacy. Chest to breast, belly to belly, their bodies were molded together, separated by only thin layers of clothing. Short of actually making love, they were as close as two people could get.

With a moan of distress, Erin closed her eyes and covered her face with both hands.

Max's deep chuckle vibrated through her. "What's the matter? Cat got your tongue?"

"How long have you known?" The question was muffled against her palms.

"Since before we left the office, though I was aware almost from the moment you walked in that something was a bit out of kilter."

She moaned again as a fresh wave of humiliation washed over her. He'd known for hours!

Erin grew still, a frown forming behind her hands. Which meant . . . he'd been stringing her along all evening!

Embarrassment gave way to anger, and she snatched her hands away from her face. "You knew! All this time, you knew!" she spat accusingly.

Max answered with a slow, smug smile that sent her temper soaring even higher. "Oh! You . . . you're . . ." Erin shoved at his shoulders. "Off! Off! Get off me, you jerk! Right now!"

"Why? I find this position quite comfor—" He stopped, gave her a salacious look and amended slyly, "Well . . . maybe *comfortable* isn't the word. Shall we say . . . uh . . . enjoyable."

Erin made an infuriated sound. She bucked her hips and began to pummel his back and shoulders, his head, anything she could reach.

Chuckling, Max absorbed the rain of blows for several moments without so much as flinching. Finally, taking his time about it, he sat up.

The instant Erin was free of his weight she scrambled off the couch. Flustered, she backed away several steps, snatching at her rumpled clothes and glowering at the grinning man on the sofa.

The amusement in Max's face maddened Erin almost to the point of explosion. Not trusting herself to stay within striking range and too incensed to speak, she made a low, wrathful sound, spun on her heel and stalked toward the door.

Max's taunting laughter followed her.

Erin gritted her teeth and kept going. Ignore him, she instructed herself. Don't let him get to you. That's exactly what he wants. Just use your head and ignore him.

It was good advice but impossible to heed. Before she was halfway across the room her fury boiled over, and she whirled around and stomped back.

"I suppose this evening's charade was your idea of a joke," she accused him, glaring down at him, fists planted on her hips.

Max lazed back and stretched his arms out on either side along the top of the sofa. "More on the order of a salutary lesson."

"*Lesson!* You've got some nerve, mister! Just who do you think you are?"

"Your sister's employer," he shot back with the mocking satisfaction of a man who has the upper hand and knows it. "And frankly, I'm surprised that Elise would be a party to such a juvenile trick. It was unnecessary, you know. If she wanted time off, all she had to do was ask."

His voice held traces of both annoyance and reluctant amusement, but it was the latter to which Erin reacted.

"What? You can't be serious! You actually think my sister would ask me to take her place just so she could have an unearned vacation?"

Max shrugged. "You're here, and she's not. That pretty well says it all."

"All it says is that you have a nasty, suspicious mind and are good at jumping to conclusions. You couldn't be more wrong."

"Uh-huh, sure. Then suppose you explain why you just spent several hours pretending to be Elise?"

"I . . . well . . ." Too late, Erin realized she had backed herself into a corner. Fool! she scolded herself. Now what could she do? It would have been smarter to go along with his assumption. She groped for an excuse, but nothing she thought of sounded remotely plausible.

"What's the matter? Can't you come up with a good enough story?" Max taunted. He laughed as a guilty flush colored Erin's face.

"No, no. It's not that. I . . ." Erin bit her lower lip and watched him warily. She could only hope that Max was as innocent as he seemed, because she had no choice but to tell him the truth.

"I came here looking for Elise. Or at least, I was hoping to discover where she'd gone. You see, last night she called me." Quickly, Erin told him about the mysterious call she'd received from Elise and the hysterical fear that had permeated her sister's incoherent babbling. "I tried to get more out of her, but she just warned me to stay away and hung up." Erin shrugged and spread her hands wide. "I was worried about her. I caught the first flight I could, but when I arrived she had already gone. From the looks of her apartment, she left in a hurry. The place is a mess."

Max gave her a long, steady look, then slowly clapped his hands. "Very good. A bit farfetched, a tad melodramatic, but not bad for spur of the moment."

Erin's face went slack with astonishment. "You don't believe me!"

"Oh, come on, Erin. You didn't honestly expect me to swallow that tale, did you? That someone is trying to kill Elise because she stumbled onto some sort of skulduggery?" He laughed and shook his head. "Surely you can do better than that."

"It's true!"

"Look, she told me that you two pulled this stunt all the time when you were growing up. I think you hatched this scheme between you to give Elise a few days off. From what I've heard about *you*, you probably looked on it as another adventure. Though how you expected to pull it off, I don't know. You're really a rotten secretary, you know."

"You're not exactly a candidate for boss of the year yourself," she retorted, stung. "But for your information, I am *not* making this up. My sister is out there somewhere, terrified and fleeing for her life."

When Max merely continued to look at her with patent disbelief, Erin dragged a hand through her hair and snapped, "All right. All right. If we planned this whole thing, then why was Elise gone when I arrived? Explain that, if you can."

Max laughed and shook his head. "Look, she knew you were coming to fill in for her, right? So...she decided to take off early, that's all. If you'll look around her apartment, you'll probably find that she left you a note, explaining. My guess is that at this very moment Elise is sharing some romantic hideaway with the man in her life."

"That would be a bit difficult, don't you think," Erin charged with angry sarcasm, "since *you* happen to be the man in her life."

"What!"

Max bounded off the sofa and stared at her as though she'd lost her mind. Erin stared right back, daring him to deny the statement.

"Now look here. There's nothing like that between Elise and me! My relationship with your sister is purely professional. She's my secretary. That's all!"

"I don't know how you have the nerve to say that. Not after the way you've behaved all evening."

"That was just to shake you up. It had nothing to do with Elise. I knew all along which sister I was kissing."

The statement sent a little thrill racing through Erin, but she squashed it. "Very good, Delany, for spur of the moment," she taunted, throwing his words back at him.

Max narrowed his eyes. "You don't believe me."

"Do you believe that I'm here because Elise is in trouble?"

"Not a chance, lady."

"Then I guess we're even."

He gave her a long intent stare. "I guess so," he said finally. A hint of laughter glittered in his eyes, and he leaned forward, his lazy self-confidence returning. "But since you brought it up, you sure responded passionately...for a woman who thought she was kissing her sister's lover."

Erin tilted her chin, her jaw tightening. Already riddled with guilt, she had no intention of letting him pile on more. "I was pretending to be Elise."

"Sure you were."

"Oh, what's the use? You're determined not to believe a word I say, so there's no point in continuing."

"Where are you going?" Max called after her when she hooked her purse strap over her shoulder and headed for the door.

"I'm leaving."

"It's two miles to the warehouse."

"I've walked two miles before."

"Down a mountain road in the dark?"

"I'll manage."

Max caught up with her in the entrance hall. He grasped her upper arm and tightened his hold when she tried to wrench away. "I'm sure you would, but as a gentleman, I insist on driving you back to your car. That is, to your sister's car." Ignoring her venomous look, he pulled a jacket from the closet and bundled her out the door and into the Continental.

Deep down, Erin was relieved. The thought of running afoul of a mountain lion or stepping off a precipice in the dark had already begun to send little shivers of fear down her spine. Nonetheless, she would have bitten off her tongue before admitting that to Max. Gentleman, indeed!

For the first minute or so they rode in silence. Erin sat as far away from him as she could get and stared straight ahead. Silently, she called Max Delany every dirty name she could think of. That he had tricked her and made her look like a fool was bad enough. His denial of any personal relationship with her sister really infuriated her. Poor Elise. She had given her heart to a shallow, callous charmer with a roving eye. Erin's hands curled into tight fists in her lap, every protective instinct she possessed aroused as she thought of the ease with which he had dismissed her sister, and of how hurt Elise would be if she knew.

Then she cursed herself and her impulsive nature, which had landed her in the awkward, utterly humiliating situation. Concern for Elise already had her nerves stretched taut as a bowstring. She didn't need this added complication.

Max glanced her way, and from the corner of her eye Erin saw the flash of his white teeth. "Aren't you uncomfortable, squashed up against the door like that?"

She shot him a quelling look, then turned to stare out at the twinkling lights of Santa Fe, below in the distance.

"Brrrr. It's cold tonight," Max said with a thread of laughter in his voice. "Even colder than usual. Maybe I should turn up the heater."

Pretending he wasn't there, Erin maintained her stony silence.

It took only a few minutes more to reach the warehouse. In that time Max made several more teasing attempts at conversation, all of which she ignored.

He turned into the parking lot, but before he could bring the car to a complete stop Erin had the door open and was swinging her legs to the ground.

"Since you're filling in for Elise, I'll see you in the morning. Office hours start at eight, so don't be late."

The words, addressed to Erin's back as she was about to bolt out of the car, stopped her cold. With her hand still on the door handle, she turned her head and gave Max a long, level look over her shoulder. In a soft but precise voice she said, "Go to hell, Delany."

She climbed out and slammed the door with enough force to tear it off its hinges.

An amused smile twitched about Max's mouth. Amazing. Who would have thought that Elise—gentle, soft, serene Elise—would have such a firebrand for a sister. Daring, intelligence, spirit, plus his secretary's vivid coloring and lush beauty—it was a potent combination, one he found wildly attractive and exciting.

He studied the provocative angry sway of her hips as she stalked away, his eyes glittering with masculine appreciation. Yessir, Erin Blaine was one hell of a woman.

Common sense told him he'd be foolish even to think of getting involved with her. She was his secretary's sister, for Pete's sake. Things could get sticky in one big hurry, he cautioned himself.

Besides, how could you have a relationship with a woman who not only didn't live in the same town as you, but who was seldom even in the same country? According to Elise, Erin maintained an apartment in Houston, but it was little more than a place she visited between assignments.

Any way he looked at it, he'd be asking for trouble if he gave in to the attraction. It was ill-advised, impractical, maybe even downright stupid. Max's lips twitched again, and he expelled a wry, self-deprecating sigh. And . . . it was irresistible. It might not rank as the smartest move he ever made, but he was going to do his damnedest to get to know Erin Blaine.

Erin reached the blue Chevy, jerked open the driver's door, climbed in and slammed it shut.

Max winced, his smile growing into a grin. But first, he decided prudently, he'd give her time to cool off.

Of course, there wasn't a hope in hell of her coming to the office tomorrow. He'd known that. But the temptation to needle her, to see that captivating flash of fire again, had simply been too strong to resist.

Well, he could wait. At least until tomorrow evening.

Erin gunned the engine, and the car shot backward out of the parking space. She slammed on the brakes, bringing the vehicle to a shuddering halt, gunned the engine again and went careering across the lot, tires squealing and rubber burning. Barely reducing speed, she made a fishtail turn onto the road, sending dust and gravel flying, and headed toward Santa Fe.

Max laughed. On second thought, maybe the day after tomorrow would be better.

He eased the big car toward the exit at a more sedate pace. He had every intention of returning home, but at the last moment, acting on impulse, he swung the Lincoln in the opposite direction and followed the rapidly diminishing taillights. I'll just see that she gets home safely, he told himself as he closed the gap.

He caught up with the blue compact easily, but it meant driving faster than he cared to on the narrow mountain road. Keeping up with her was not much better, he discovered. A quick glance at the speedometer had his smile dissolving into a frown. "Damn fool woman," he muttered. "Driving like a flatlander on a mountain road. Dear God! Doesn't she have any better sense?"

The downgrade wasn't too bad at that point, but he knew that very soon it would be. If she didn't slow down, she was going to be in real trouble. Grimly, Max trailed her. His gaze flicked again to the speedometer. To his horror, he saw that she was accelerating steadily.

"Slow down. Slow down, for God's sake!" he muttered helplessly. His jaw clenched. His hands tightened around the wheel. Guilt over the way he had goaded her twisted his stomach into a sickening knot. Fear made his skin crawl. "There's a curve up ahead, dammit!" he shouted, as though he could make her hear him. "Slow down!"

He glanced at the speedometer again and spat an obscenity. His balled fist struck the horn and gave it three long blasts. "Hit the brakes, damn you! Hit the brakes!"

Erin pumped the brake pedal frantically. Instead of meeting resistance, she felt as though she were stepping on a sponge. And the Chevy was still going fast.

She willed herself to stay calm, but her heart began to pound. Panic crept over her like icy fingers. Licking her lips, Erin clutched the wheel and fought down the terror. Her breath came in short, labored pants.

She pumped the brake again. On the third push it went all the way to the floor.

"Oh, dear Lord!" Erin whimpered. For an instant her mind went blank with fear. Eyes wide, she sat frozen, staring through the windshield. All she saw was the road rushing toward her in the beam of the headlights—the road and the dark chasm beside it.

Finally she began to shake off the paralyzing fear. Think. Think, she commanded herself shakily, getting a tenuous grip on her emotions. You've got to do something.

The brake. The emergency brake. It had to be there somewhere. Keeping her gaze fixed on the road, Erin groped along the floorboard with her left foot. Her heart leaped when her ankle struck the small pedal. There it was!

She stomped on the emergency brake with all her might and grappled with the steering wheel.

The car slowed but didn't stop. Erin down-shifted into second gear. The engine roared with the increased RPM, and her speed dropped still more.

"Stop. Stop, damn you," she commanded through clenched teeth.

But she was headed down an incline, and the car's momentum was stronger than the auxiliary brake.

Behind her, Max was honking like a madman.

"I'm trying! I'm trying, you idiot!" she screeched at him, one hand letting go of the wheel long enough to return the blast.

The road wiggled in a shallow S curve. Erin let out a choked scream and wrenched the wheel to the left, then back to the right. "God help me. Help me. Oh, please, *please*, help me," she chanted as she fought a desperate battle to avoid going over the edge. The car skidded around both curves with only inches to spare.

When at last she hit a stretch of straightaway, she swerved into the oncoming lane. Hugging the mountainside as closely as possible, she prayed she wouldn't meet another car.

Up ahead a road sign came into view, and Erin's heart jumped into her throat when she saw the inverted U-shaped arrow. "Oh, Lord no! No!"

Erin reacted instinctively. Putting her right foot on top of her left one, she arched her body like a taut bow and applied every ounce of her weight against the emergency brake pedal. At the same time she held her hand down on the horn.

The car's speed continued to drop slowly. Erin gritted her teeth and strained to keep the pressure on. The acrid smell of burning brakes filled the car.

In the beam of her headlights she could see where the road curved out of sight around the mountain, the black emptiness beyond. She kept her gaze fixed on the latter. "Stop. Oh, please stop."

The downgrade of the road increased, and the awful burning smell grew intolerable.

Helpless, Erin gripped the steering wheel, her eyes wide with horror as the car began to build up speed again and hurtle toward the abyss.

"Turn into the mountain! Turn!"

Having seen the blue Chevy reduce its speed with no brake lights, Max had figured out that Erin's brakes were gone, and he'd been shouting instructions at her ever since.

Terrified, he watched the small car slue around the double curve. Sweat popped out all over him on the first turn when the Chevy skidded dangerously close to the edge. By the time Erin had negotiated the second, his thundering heart was nearly suffocating him. For a moment he hadn't been able to breathe at all.

When she hit the straightaway Max groaned his relief. She'd made it by the skin of her teeth.

But he knew the next curve was a switchback, and there was no way in hell she'd get around it.

"Get over! Get over! Ram into the mountain!"

As though she'd heard him, Erin pulled into the inside lane. "Yeah! Yeah! That's it!" Max shouted, hope surging inside him. It fizzled a moment later when he realized that she was just avoiding the edge. "Dammit to hell!" he roared in frustration. "Can't you see you don't have any choice?"

The telltale smell of burning brake shoes reached him as the two cars started down the incline toward the switchback. Cursing, Max stepped on the gas and pulled alongside the Chevy. With grim determination, he jerked the wheel a quarter turn to the left and slammed into the smaller car.

The impact jolted through Erin and flung her against the door. The compact's left front fender scraped rock, sending out a shower of sparks. She screamed and wrested the wheel back to the right, veering away from the wall of mountain.

The Continental crashed into her again, and the screech of metal grinding against metal was horrendous. The larger car refused to give ground, and the deafening high-pitched sound went on and on as she was forced inexorably closer to the mountain.

Panic-stricken, Erin glanced at Max. He was so close that he seemed to be in the car with her. His face was grim and set. As she watched, he wrenched his steering wheel hard to the left again. Erin's eyes widened.

In a flash of understanding she grasped his intent, and hope quickened within her. Instantly she stopped fighting him and angled the car into the face of the mountain.

The world was reduced to a cacophony of sickening sounds and terrifying flashes of unyielding rock. Glass shattered. Metal rent and crumpled. Just inches from Erin's face a wall of roughhewn stone scraped by with a bansheelike shriek, sending more sparks flying. On the other side, Max's car grated against the passenger door. Its squealing brakes added to the earsplitting din.

The little car rocked and bucked, shuddering with each jarring blow. Pitching mercilessly against her taut seat belt, Erin held on to the wheel for dear life.

Fear elongated time, playing out the nightmare in slow motion so that it seemed to go on forever. In reality, it was all over in seconds. The car had begun to slow from the moment of impact, and it ground to a halt within a number of yards, wedged between the mountain and the powerful bulk of Max's Continental.

Chapter Four

The sudden cessation of noise was deafening.

Dazed, Erin sat motionless, gripping the wheel. For a moment a strange feeling of unreality prevailed. There was nothing but utter quiet, absolute stillness.

Steam began to rise with a hiss from beneath the sprung hood of the Chevy. A second later a crumpled scrap of metal groaned and clattered to the pavement. The sounds shattered the magnified silence, and Erin closed her eyes and slumped over the wheel, her breath whooshing out of her.

Vaguely she felt the car rock, heard the screech of metal and the pop of loose gravel beneath tires as Max moved his car away from hers, but she was too weak to move...or care.

Then he was there, frantically prying open the compact's passenger door and reaching for her.

"Erin! Erin, are you hurt?"

Strong hands gripped her shoulders and eased her back against the seat. A callused palm tenderly brushed her hair away from her face. Blunt fingers smoothed down her neck and found the throbbing pulse at its base.

She heard his sigh of relief, felt it in the warm puff of moist breath that struck her face.

"Erin, can you hear me? Are you all right?"

The desperate entreaty brought her eyelids fluttering open. She blinked once. Twice. Max, his handsome face distorted with worry, hovered over her. "I...I think so," she managed in a quavering voice.

"No broken bones?" His hands skimmed over her, probing and testing with brisk efficiency even as he asked the question.

"No, I...I don't think so."

At her wrist he encountered a sticky wetness, and he lifted her arm to inspect it in the dim glow from the dashboard. "You're cut."

Erin glanced at the injury disinterestedly. Blood oozed from the three-inch gash. It seemed trivial—ridiculous, even—that such a close brush with death had resulted in nothing more than a minor scratch.

"It's not deep. I'll live." The profoundness of the off-hand statement struck her, and a giggle bubbled up in her throat. Another followed, and another, each longer, less controlled, until they ran together in a high-pitched trill that edged into hysteria. "I'll live. Oh...Max!" she choked around peals of laughter that quickly turned into sobs. "I...I'm going to live."

Max released her seat belt and hauled her up against him. "Yes. Yes, I know," he crooned against the top of her head. "You're going to be fine now. Just fine."

Erin wrapped her arms around his middle and clung to him as though he were the only source of safety in the world. Racking sobs tore from deep inside her, making her whole body jerk. She buried her face against his chest and gave in

to them. Within minutes her hot tears had melded his shirt
to his skin.

"That's it, honey, cry it all out." With one arm wrapped
around her, his other hand cupping the back of her head, he
held her close and rocked her, murmuring a steady stream
of soft reassurances.

They remained that way for several minutes, until at last
Erin quieted.

She drew a shuddering breath and sniffed, then pulled
back. Meeting Max's concerned look, she swiped at her wet
cheeks with her fingertips and attempted a smile, but her lips
were quivering so badly that she couldn't manage it.
"I . . . I . . ." Emotion squeezed her throat, choking off her
words. Her chin wobbled as a freshet of tears spurted, and
she almost started crying again.

"Come on. Let's get out of here." Max staved off the
crying jag by hauling her bodily from the car.

Erin wobbled on legs that felt like rubber, but when Max
attempted to pick her up she stopped him. "No, please. I
can walk. Really."

"All right. But here, lean on me." He looped his arm
around her waist and clamped her against his side, and Erin
clung to his reassuring bulk as he half carried her around the
big silver car to the passenger side.

He eased her down onto the seat but left her turned sideways with her feet still on the ground. Then he squatted on
his haunches before her in the wedge of space created by the
open door. As he withdrew a first-aid box from beneath the
seat and snapped it open, Erin sighed and slumped sideways against the seat. The cool mountain air stirred her hair
and feathered over her wet cheeks in an icy caress.

"This is going to hurt," Max warned a second before he
swabbed her arm with alcohol.

Erin flinched, but she really didn't mind the small sting,
or the greater one that followed when he daubed the cut with

iodine. The minor discomfort was reassuring proof that she was still alive.

Alive. The word seeped through her like a benediction, and she grew limp. Weakly, she laid her cheek against the soft velour and gazed over Max's shoulder while he bandaged her arm.

Gradually though, as the nightmare receded, an awareness of their surroundings crept over her, banishing the sweet feeling of relief.

The Continental sat diagonally across the road at a protective angle in front of the mangled Chevy, its headlights bouncing off the wall of rock and casting a yellow glow several yards in all directions. Muscle by muscle, Erin's body grew tense, her eyes widening. She straightened and stared down the road in fascinated horror.

They had come to a stop not more than thirty feet from the hairpin curve.

A clammy coldness gripped her. She began to shake. Erin drew a deep breath and tucked her free arm tightly around her rib cage, but the violent tremors continued, and her teeth began to chatter.

Max's head jerked up. "What—" He stopped when he saw her stricken look. Following the direction of her gaze, he glanced over his shoulder and frowned.

"Don't think about it. It's over." He snapped the first-aid kit closed and shoved it back under the seat.

He stood and, with brisk efficiency, swung her legs into the car, then stripped off his jacket and tucked it around her. Erin tried to protest, but he wouldn't listen.

"Hush, now. You've had a shock, and you need this more than I do." Reaching across her, he flicked on the heater. As he pulled back he paused and stared at her chalky face. Slowly, he ran the backs of his knuckles over her cheek and smiled. "Now then, you sit tight. I'll only be a minute."

Before Erin could reply he backed out of the car and slammed the door.

In moments he returned. "I put the keys in your purse," he told her, tossing the leather bag and her suitcase into the back seat.

The silver car was caved in all along the driver's side, and it took several hard yanks to get the door open. When he finally succeeded and slid in behind the wheel, Erin rolled her head on the seat and looked at him, her expression regretful. "Oh, Max, your beautiful car. It's ruined."

"Don't worry about it. A car can be fixed. Or replaced. The important thing is that you're safe."

"For now, anyway."

Max's hand halted in midair halfway to the gearshift, and his head snapped around. "What's that supposed to mean?"

Erin huddled beneath the jacket, pulling it up tightly against her chin. Above the charcoal suede her face was a pale oval, her eyes dark and haunted. "Surely now you believe that Elise is in danger?"

"Oh, come on, Erin. Don't tell me you're still sticking to that crazy story."

"Yes. Because it's true. After what just happened, I don't know how you can doubt it."

"Why? Just because your brakes failed?" Max gave a surprised little laugh and shook his head. "Look, Erin, you're upset. Overwrought. It was a freak accident, that's all. These things happen."

"No! No, it wasn't an accident. Don't you see? Someone saw me arrive and mistook me for Elise, just as you did, and sometime today they sabotaged the car."

"You mean while it was parked in the Global lot?" Max asked, incredulous.

"Yes. That's exactly what I mean. Someone there is trying to kill my sister."

Max sighed and raked a hand through his hair. "Look, Erin . . . this is crazy. No one would—"

"Max, the brakes on that car were working perfectly when I arrived this afternoon."

The insistent tone of her voice stopped him, and he stared at her, his expression a mixture of exasperation and understanding. She returned the look steadily, willing him to believe her.

For an instant Erin thought she saw a flicker of doubt in his eyes, but then it was gone.

"All right. I'll concede that maybe, just maybe, Elise did see something, or at least *thought* she saw something, and took off in a panic. Given that, and what just happened, it's understandable that you're feeling a bit spooked, but believe me, you have nothing to fear. There's nothing clandestine or sinister going on at Global. And to set your mind at ease, I'm going to prove it to you."

He pulled a cellular telephone from beneath the dash and punched out a series of numbers.

"What are you doing?"

"You'll see." When she started to speak again he silenced her with a raised hand.

"Charlie? Max Delany," he said into the receiver. "Listen, Charlie, the brakes on Mrs. Holman's car failed, and it's wrecked about a mile down the road from the warehouse." He paused, listening. "No, no one was hurt, but I want you to tow the car into the shop and check it over for me. Yes, right away. And when you've found what caused the problem, call me back immediately."

"Are you crazy?" Erin demanded when he hung up the phone. "I just told you. Someone at Global is trying to kill Elise. It could be the man you were just talking to."

"Erin, for Pete's sake! Charlie has been our chief mechanic since I started the business twelve years ago. Before that he worked for my father. I've known him since I was a kid, and I'd trust him with my life."

"Fine. You do that. But I don't trust him with mine. Until I know what's going on, I don't trust anyone connected with your company."

"Not even me?"

The softly worded question brought her up short. Erin's eyes widened, and she gazed at him, conscience-stricken. "Oh, Max, I'm sorry. You saved my life, and I haven't even thanked you. Please forgive—"

"Shh." He placed two fingers over her lips to stop the flow of words. "I wasn't asking for thanks. What I want to know is, do you trust me?"

"I..." A niggling doubt lingered still, all mixed up with guilt and gratitude. Erin nibbled on the tip of her index finger and met his steady look with uncertainty.

For heaven's sake! The man saved your life, her conscience prodded. You're being paranoid. And a prize ingrate to boot. If it hadn't been for Max, by now you'd be just a charred lump at the foot of the mountain.

"I... I'm sorry, Max. Of course I trust you," she said finally, pushing aside her uneasiness.

Max's mouth quirked in a lopsided smile that held a touch of sadness. Very slowly, he trailed his knuckles down her cheek.

Another tremor rippled through Erin, and she shivered beneath the suede jacket, clutching it more closely to her. As though the brush with death had shocked her system into a heightened awareness of her circumstances, she was acutely conscious of every minute detail, her senses tingling with a keen sensitivity. The softness of the night, the quiet darkness that surrounded them, were palpable things. Through the cushioned seat, her body absorbed the rumbling idling of the car's powerful engine. Against her cheek, she could feel the crisp hairs on the back of Max's hand, and with every breath she smelled the sharp, enticing masculine tang of his skin.

"Now I wonder why I get the feeling that statement lacks conviction," Max mused, watching her.

"I . . . that is—"

His fingers slid beneath her chin and tilted it up. His thumb gently brushed the fullness of her lower lip. "Never mind. I suppose that, after what you just went through, you're entitled to a few doubts."

Releasing her, he straightened and put the car in gear. With care, he pulled away from the wrecked Chevy. "Anyway, when Charlie calls you'll realize that there's no reason to mistrust anyone. By morning this whole episode will be just a bad memory. But in the meantime, what you need is a stiff shot of brandy and bed." Max glanced at her and cocked one brow. "I suppose you'd object to spending the night at my place?"

Erin shot him a dry look. "You suppose right. I'm sure I'd rest a lot easier at Elise's apartment, if you don't mind."

"Ah, I see. You trust me with your life but not with your delectable body. Is that it?"

"How perceptive of you, Delany."

Max chuckled. "Just one of my many attributes. When you get to know me better you'll find I'm a terrific guy. Trustworthy. Perceptive. Sensitive. Kind. Witty. Intelligent. I'm also a good dancer, a scintillating dinner companion and, so I've been told—" he paused to slant her a devilish look, and his voice dropped to a husky murmur "—a fantastic lover."

"Hmm. Don't forget modest."

"That, too."

Erin faced forward again and gazed out the windshield, fighting back a grin. She was no longer shivering. Miraculously, the teasing banter had lightened the mood and calmed her overwrought nerves. Erin wondered if that had been Max's intention.

A short distance down the road they passed a truck going in the opposite direction. Max honked and waved, and the driver returned the salute.

"That was Charlie. It shouldn't take him long to go over the brake system. We'll probably be hearing from him within an hour."

Erin slanted Max a skeptical look, but this time she said nothing.

At the bottom of the mountain road Max paused before turning onto the highway. "Which way?"

Surprised, Erin looked at him. "You don't know?"

In answer, Max gave a sigh and drummed his fingers on the wheel. "No, I don't know," he said with exaggerated patience. "I told you, my relationship with your sister is a business one. Nothing more. I've never been to her apartment, and I've certainly never been out with her."

Narrowing her eyes, Erin tipped her head to one side. "What about the times you've taken her to dinner? According to Elise's last letter, you took her to a nice restaurant just a couple of weeks ago."

"She wrote to you about that?" Max looked taken aback.

"Among other things."

"But that was just my way of thanking her for working late," he insisted. "Two, maybe three times in the past few months we've had a rush order or a problem of some kind, and she worked straight through until after eight without a complaint. So...to show my gratitude, I bought her a meal and sent her home in a taxi. That was all there was to it. Hell, I don't even remember what we talked about."

Erin gnawed the inside of her cheek and studied him. Either he was an excellent actor, or he was telling the truth. Either way, her heart ached for her twin.

Dear Lord, she groaned inwardly. Had Elise built up this whole romance in her mind out of nothing more substantial than wishful dreams and a few duty dinners?

It was possible. Her sister was a dreamer, an incurable romantic. And, in her gentle, sweet way, she could be frighteningly resolute and single-minded. Elise believed that if you wanted something badly enough and were patient enough, eventually it would be yours.

When she had set her cap for Tommy Holman, Erin recalled with an uneasy feeling in the pit of her stomach, Elise had been a mere child, he a callow teenager.

Faced with Elise's serene implacability, their mother had gently explained that loving someone didn't guarantee that they would love you back. Erin herself had scoffed at the very idea of wanting to marry the creep next door. Even David, who had been Tommy's best friend, had tried to dissuade Elise.

Nothing had worked. Over the years Tommy, in the offhand, thoughtless way of young males, had teased and tormented Elise, unknowingly breaking her heart on those numerous occasions when he'd been besotted with other girls. But mostly he'd been oblivious to her. To him, she had just been one of the Blaine twins, one of those skinny, redhaired little pests who'd lived next door to him all his life.

Through it all, Erin's sister had remained steadfast in her devotion and had waited patiently for Tommy to notice her as a woman and realize that he couldn't live without her.

To everyone's shock, it had finally happened. When the twins had come home for spring break during their junior year in college, Tommy had taken one look at Elise's sweet smile and soft brown eyes and been instantly enslaved. During the entire two weeks he had followed her around, wearing an adoring, dazed look, and by the time the sisters returned to school Elise had a diamond engagement ring.

After that, nothing and no one could convince her that patience and wanting didn't make dreams come true.

Gazing at Max Delany's set face, Erin fervently hoped her suspicion was wrong. She had a gut feeling that, one way or another, her sister had set herself up for disillusionment and heartbreak if she had developed the same sort of romantic fixation on this man.

Then again, Erin thought, feeling guilty and disloyal, maybe the whole thing wasn't a romantic fantasy. Maybe Max *had* been stringing Elise along and was merely feigning innocence.

Even as her mind formed the thought, doubt came creeping in.

Impatient with herself and the whole situation, she shot Max a disgruntled look and snapped out terse directions to Elise's apartment. At this point it hardly mattered, Erin told herself, staring straight ahead in stiff silence. The important thing now was to find Elise.

When they reached the apartment complex Max insisted on seeing her to the door and carrying her bag. As Erin let them in with Elise's key, she frowned and tried to recall if she had locked the door before leaving that afternoon.

Reaching inside, she felt along the wall for the switch and flipped it on. Light flooded the room, and Erin stepped across the threshold, then came to an abrupt halt, sucking in her breath.

"Holy hell!" Max exclaimed behind her in a low, incredulous voice. "You weren't kidding when you said Elise left this place a mess."

Erin's heart began to thud, and her scalp crawled. The apartment was in shambles. Books littered the floor as though an impatient hand had swept them from the shelves flanking the fireplace. Every closet and cabinet door was open, the interiors in disarray. Empty drawers, the contents dumped on the floor along with the scattered books, lay strewn topsy-turvy everywhere.

"Max." Erin's voice quivered with fear. Unconsciously seeking support, she groped behind her for Max's hand, her fingers closing tightly around his on contact. She stared at the jumbled mess, unable to tear her gaze away, and slowly shook her head. "It wasn't this bad earlier. Someone has been here."

Max grew instantly alert, his body braced as though for battle. He dropped Erin's suitcase and pulled her behind him. "Stay here." His sharp gaze darted about the room as he gave the terse command.

"Where are you going?"

"To search the rest of the apartment. Whoever did this might still be here. If you hear anything, I want you to run like hell."

Erin leaped forward as though someone had touched her with a cattle prod. "Oh, no you don't!" she cried. "You're not leaving me behind." She scuttled up as close to Max's back as she could get, grabbed a handful of his shirt and hung on tight.

"Erin, do as—"

"Forget it, Delany. Where you go, I go."

Max glared at her over his shoulder, but Erin stuck out her chin and met the look with stubborn defiance. After a moment he bit off a curse and, muttering something under his breath about willful women, led the way.

A thorough search produced nothing other than the discovery that the rest of the apartment was in the same state of chaos as the living room.

"Whoever did this was looking for something."

"But what?" Erin asked shakily, still hovering close to Max as they surveyed the wreckage in the bedroom.

Max shrugged, his expression grim. "Who knows? Could be they're afraid that Elise got her hands on some incriminating evidence. Or maybe they were just looking for a clue as to where she's gone.''

"Then you do believe that I told you the truth? That Elise saw something she wasn't supposed to, and her life is in danger?''

"Yeah, I believe you. Finally,'' Max said in a voice that was harsh with self-condemnation. "And so will the police when they get a look at this mess.''

He started for the bedside table and the phone, but Erin grabbed his arm with both hands, stopping him. "No! You can't call the police!''

Max looked astounded. "Erin! What the devil's the matter with you? We have to report this,'' he insisted, waving his arm at the wreckage. "And once you tell them your story, they'll find Elise for you.''

"That's what I'm afraid of.''

"What?''

"Max, when I suggested to Elise that she go to the police, she became hysterical. She insisted that someone on the police force was involved, and she made me promise not to contact them.''

Max hesitated, frowning.

"Please, Max,'' Erin pleaded, clutching his arm. "We can't. Elise was terrified. Don't you see? If she's right, we'll only be making things worse for her.''

Expelling a heavy sigh, Max raked a hand through his hair and dragged it down the back of his neck. Looking up, he scowled at the ceiling as he massaged his taut muscles. "All right. We'll do it your way. At least, for now. But we're getting the hell out of here. And don't argue,'' he commanded as he took her arm and marched her toward the door. "If you think I'm going to leave you here, think again. This place isn't safe. Whoever did this might decide to come back for a second look.''

It gave Erin the creeps to think about some faceless criminal invading her sister's home, going through her things, and she didn't argue when Max hustled her out of the apartment.

In the car it was a different matter.

"I have to find her," Erin stated the instant Max turned the key in the ignition.

"We'll talk about it in the morning." He glanced over his shoulder, then pulled away from the curb. "After you've had a good night's sleep we'll discuss this whole thing with clear heads and decide on the best course of action."

"No, Max, I—"

"If you're going to tell me to take you to a hotel, think again. You're coming home with me."

"You don't understand. I don't want to go to a hotel. I have to start looking for Elise. Right now."

Max shot her a hard look. "I assume you're talking about hiring a private detective," he said cautiously. "Please tell me I'm right."

"No. I'm going to find her myself. The fewer people involved, the better."

"Oh, God."

This time the look he flashed her was one of extreme irritation. "Dammit, woman—" he began, but when Erin responded with a quick, defensive tilt of her chin he bit off the tirade. Gripping the steering wheel more tightly, he stared straight ahead, his jaw clenched. She had the uneasy feeling he was grinding his teeth.

At the next intersection Max turned onto a side street and pulled over to the curb. He doused the lights and shifted the car into Park but left the engine running. Turning sideways, he crooked his knee on the seat, draped one arm along the back and the other over the steering wheel and fixed his gaze on Erin. In the dim light from the street lamp she could see that his handsome features were etched with concern, his blue eyes intent beneath a worried frown.

"Erin, you can't be serious," he said in a more reasonable tone. "Whatever's going on, these people aren't playing games. You could find yourself—"

The buzz of the car phone cut him off. He snatched it up with a terse "Yeah. Delany."

He listened intently to the person on the other end of the line, and as she watched his expression harden, Erin grew more and more tense.

"I see. Okay, thanks for the information. Oh, and keep this under your hat until I check it out, okay?"

Max hung up the phone and gave Erin a long, thoughtful stare. "That was Charlie. It seems that the brake line on Elise's car had been cut."

Erin felt suddenly weak and cold, as though all of the blood had been sucked out of her body. She'd had a hunch, of course, that the near tragedy had been no accident, but to have her suspicion confirmed was chilling.

"Not quite all the way through," Max continued. "But close enough so that the first time you stepped on the brake you ruptured the line. After that, all it took was a little more pressure to empty it. By the time you got to the first curve all the fluid was gone."

Clasping her hands together in her lap, Erin struggled to subdue the quivering sensation in the pit of her stomach. "I see," she said in a shaky voice that was little more than a whisper.

"You have to give up this idea of finding Elise yourself," Max insisted. "It's just too dangerous."

"No," Erin replied at once, shaking her head. "No, I can't do that."

"For Pete's sake, Erin! What does it take to convince you? There's already been one attempt on your life because someone mistook you for Elise. Don't you realize that that's why she called and warned you to stay away? Because she was afraid this very thing would happen?''

"Of course I realize it. But that doesn't change anything. I still have to find her and help her if I can."

Frustrated, Max sighed and looked at her in amazement. "Lord, woman, do you always rush in where angels fear to tread?''

A weak smile claimed Erin's mouth. "So my family tells me.''

When Max made a harsh sound she placed her hand over his, where it lay knotted in a tight fist on the back of the seat. "Oh, Max, don't you understand? Elise isn't just my sister. She's my identical twin, and she's very dear to me. She's also soft and...well...fragile. The thought of her alone and terrified is more than I can bear. I have to do what I can to help her.

"It will be all right, I promise you. I left a message for my brother, explaining what was going on. He was with the FBI for years. When he catches up with us he'll know what to do.''

Max did not look reassured. "I don't suppose there's anything I can say that will make you change your mind?''

Gazing at him regretfully, Erin shook her head.

"That's what I thought." Max looked away and stared into the darkness beyond the pool of light spilling from the street lamp, then turned back to her and heaved a sigh. "I probably need my head examined, but...okay. Where do you suggest we start?''

"We? But—''

"If you think I'm going to let you handle this alone, you're crazy.''

Erin was touched, and a part of her—the cowardly part— very much wanted his help and support. Still, she couldn't in good conscience involve him, especially since he claimed to have no personal relationship with Elise. "Oh, Max, that's very sweet of you. But, really, there's no reason for you to get involved in this.''

Max raised his hand and cupped her cheek. Warm and caressing, his gaze moved over her face, lingering a moment on her lips before returning to delve deeply into her eyes. Holding her gaze, he touched the corner of her mouth with his thumb and smiled a crooked little smile. "Oh, yes," he said in a strange, soft voice. "I'm afraid there is."

Chapter Five

The sharp surge of excitement caught her off guard.

One moment they had been arguing, and the next, without warning, the air was charged with electricity, a taut, quivering awareness that pulsed between them and made every nerve ending in her body stand at attention.

His nearness, the warmth in his gaze, the husky timbre of his voice, all had a devastating effect on Erin. Her heart beat faster; her chest tightened. She was acutely conscious of the light touch of his hand against her cheek. Beneath it, her skin grew flushed as a tingling heat radiated outward from each tiny point of contact.

Her breathing was suddenly shallow, almost painful, and as she gazed at him in the shadowy dimness, she felt an insane desire to turn her face into his palm and kiss it, to run her tongue over that ridged, sensitive flesh and taste him.

The thought shocked her, and she swallowed hard, thrusting it away. The attraction was strong—she felt it humming between them—but she knew that she couldn't, she *mustn't* give in to it. No matter what Max's feelings were, Elise was in love with him. She had to remember that.

Erin edged back just enough to pull free of his hand. "Well, since you insist, I have to admit that I'm grateful for your help," she said, striving to keep her voice polite and friendly, unaffected. "To tell you the truth, I'm not sure where to start."

Max allowed the retreat, but the look in his eyes promised that the matter was far from forgotten.

He settled back against the door, drummed his fingers on the seat and pursed his lips thoughtfully. "That would depend on whether or not you think she left town."

"I'm almost certain she did," Erin replied, relieved that the moment of sensual tension had passed. "Elise avoids stress or trouble of any kind. Something like this would send her—or anyone, for that matter—running, just as hard and as fast as she could go."

"Well, at least she didn't take her car. That was a smart move, and it shows she's not so panicked that she can't think straight. If someone on the police force *is* involved, it would be a simple matter to run a check on it. She'd probably have been picked up before she made the city limits."

Erin shivered, recalling the trouble she had attracted by using Elise's car.

Determinedly, she pushed the chilling memory aside and forced herself to think. "Which means she must have left by bus. Even if she managed to get on a flight, she would have taken a bus to the Albuquerque airport."

"Not necessarily. She could have taken a taxi or rented a car, or had a friend drive her." Max shrugged. "She may have even hitchhiked, for all we know."

Erin gave a startled little laugh. Then, realizing he wasn't kidding, she cocked her head to one side and studied him curiously. "You really don't know Elise very well, do you?"

"That's what I've been trying to tell you all evening."

"Yes, well, believe me, it would never occur to my sister to stand by the side of the road with her thumb out, not even in a dire situation like this one."

Max grinned, his teeth a flash of white in the dimness. "No, that'd be more your style."

"That's right," Erin replied with a wry grimace. "If someone were after me, I'd light out of here any way I could."

"Then let me remind you that, indirectly, someone *is* after you. With that face, you're in just as much jeopardy as Elise."

Erin drew in her breath and clamped down on the spasm of fear that rippled through her. She could sense a lecture coming and was determined to dodge it. "All the more reason to hurry," she said briskly. "The sooner we discover where Elise went, the sooner I can get out of here. I think we should start at the bus station. I have a hunch she would have felt safer traveling in a group of people rather than being by herself in a rented car."

Max fixed her with a hard look. She could feel his anger and exasperation simmering just below the surface, and she braced herself for an argument, but after a moment he heaved a sigh and straightened in the seat. "God, you're a stubborn woman," he muttered as he flicked on the headlights and put the car in gear.

She chose to ignore the remark, and after a moment Max said, "You do realize, don't you, that this will probably be a wild-goose chase. She could have caught a bus for the airport at any of a dozen or so hotels."

"Yes, I know. But we've got to start somewhere. If we don't have any luck at the bus station, then we'll try the airlines."

"Okay. Whatever you say. Just don't get your hopes up."

Falling silent, Erin turned her head and looked out the window. Hope was all she had at the moment. Since she'd arrived in Santa Fe her concern had grown steadily into worry with the passing hours. Now, knowing that someone out there was intent on harming her sister, that worry had burgeoned into outright fear. Without hope, it would overwhelm her.

A car darted in front of the Continental. Max cursed and slammed on the brakes, throwing them both forward against their seat belts. Erin looked at him out of the corner of her eye. He was staring straight ahead, intent on negotiating the narrow congested streets, but as Erin studied the grim set of his profile she felt a fresh rush of guilt.

She knew that Max was concerned for her safety and still not convinced that they were doing the right thing. She felt guilty for having involved him. It wasn't his problem.

But even more, she felt guilty for being attracted to the man her sister loved, guilty for the way she responded to him, for the feelings she couldn't seem to control. For those reasons alone she should have refused to let him help her.

It was strange, really, when she thought about it. She and Elise had never been attracted to the same type of man before. Erin smiled to herself as she recalled her brother-in-law's sandy-blond hair and all-American wholesome looks. Tommy Holman had been an easygoing, loving, uncomplicated man with an endearing boyish charm. Even she, once she had stopped thinking of him as the nerdy boy next door, had realized that he was the perfect mate for Elise. But he'd been a far cry from Max Delany.

Erin had always been the one with a weakness for good-looking devils. The kind with that intriguing air of recklessness about them. Once again, she cut her eyes toward Max. Yes, he was definitely of the breed—a bit wild, a bit dangerous, a man of unbridled masculinity and passions. It was there in the roguish gleam in his eyes, the honeyed, slightly wicked drawl and that devil-may-care smile that played havoc with a woman's breathing and scattered her common sense to the winds.

André was such a man, Erin thought with a touch of sadness. Or at least, he had been in the beginning, when love was new. But he had changed, had become more and more conservative. Rigid. Demanding. What he had once found exciting and delightful had become an irritant, an intolerable flaw.

Erin had thought that her marriage and its demise had cured her of her penchant for dashing devils. Even for men in general. Since her divorce she hadn't been in the least attracted to any man . . . until Max.

And her sister had first claim.

A small, bemused smile tugged at the corners of Erin's mouth as she gazed past her own reflection in the side window at the darkened storefronts flashing by. In all honesty, she wasn't sure whether she should curse the fates or count her blessings.

Max pulled into a parking space by the curb and cut the engine. Erin glanced around and saw that they were stopped in front of a nondescript, darkened building. "Where's the bus station?"

"A couple of blocks down the street. Do you have a picture of Elise with you that I can show to the ticket agent?"

Erin gave him a dry look and reached for the door handle. "I don't need a picture. I've got this," she said, tapping the side of her face with her forefinger.

"You're not going in," Max stated. However, Erin was already climbing from the car, and the words bounced off her back.

"Oh, yes I am."

"Dammit, Erin! Will you— Oh, hell." The damaged door gave a protesting groan as he shouldered it open, and another when he slammed it shut. Max skirted the hood of the car at a lope and caught up with her before she reached the corner.

He stepped in front of her to block her way, but Erin kept going, and he found himself backpedaling as he argued. "Erin, listen to me. It would be better if you stayed out of sight. Can't you see that? What if whoever is looking for Elise is watching the station? Why do you think I parked so far away?"

"I am not going to sit in a dark car like a frightened little mouse while you do everything, so just forget it, Delany. Besides, I doubt that they would still be watching the station. It's been hours since Elise took off."

Grim-faced, Max accepted defeat. "All right, you win. I just hope you're right," he muttered as he took her arm and fell into step beside her.

Despite her brave words, Erin's stomach muscles tightened as they stepped inside the brightly lit terminal, and when Max slipped a protective arm around her she didn't object. Alert and wary, he held her close against his side, his hard gaze making a continual sweeping search of the waiting room as they made their way to the ticket counter.

At that hour the terminal was not crowded, though it was far from empty, containing the usual assortment of weary travelers and people awaiting arrivals. Some were milling around, but many were reading or attempting to nap, while others passed the time in desultory conversation. A few just sat slumped in their seats, idly watching the ebb and flow of humankind around them.

A piercing wail rose above the low hum of voices. Erin felt Max's body tense as his head snapped around in the direction of the sound, then relax fractionally when he spotted a harried young mother struggling with an infant and two restive older children.

Ragged nerves and apprehension, both her own and Max's, put a fine edge on Erin's sensory perception, making her aware of every minute detail. The click of her heels against the floor, the staleness of the air, the rumble of engines and the hiss of air brakes beyond the glass doors, the ringing of the phones—each sound, each smell, each individual movement around them imprinted itself on her consciousness with sharp clarity.

A Marine, looking serious and young in his spit-and-polish uniform, paced slowly in front of the wall of lockers and glanced at the clock every now and then. In a corner a pair of lovers held hands and stared into each other's eyes, their faces somber and sad. Two elderly ladies sat side by side, nimble fingers working and knitting needles clacking, never missing a stitch as they chattered away. Across the aisle from them a derelict hunched down in his seat, trying to make himself invisible to the policeman standing by the door.

Three yellow Caution signs marked off an area where a custodian was swinging a wet mop across the floor in lazy arcs, and with each swipe the caustic odor of disinfectant rose from the damp surface to mingle with the other smells of cigarette smoke, cold coffee, diesel fuel and human bodies.

There were several ticket agents behind the counter, all of them busy with customers. Max steered Erin toward the shortest line, and while they waited he turned sideways and kept up his cautious surveillance. Finally their turn came, and they stepped forward. At the same time the clerk looked up.

"Good evening. Can I help—" He stopped, his eyes widening when they fixed on Erin. "Well, hello there, young lady," he said in mild surprise. "What are you doing still here? I thought you'd be halfway to San Francisco by now. Don't tell me you missed the bus?"

Erin's heart leaped with excitement, and she glanced at Max hopefully before answering. "No. That is...that wasn't me. It was my sister who caught the bus. Which is why we're here.'' She glanced around, then leaned closer and continued in a lower voice. ''You see, it's important that I find her. Very important. Obviously she bought a ticket to San Francisco, but could you please tell me when she left, and what time she will arrive?''

''Well, I don't know. I'm not sure I should give out that kind of information.''

Max made an impatient sound and reached for his wallet, but before he could get it out Erin leaned over the counter and placed her hand on the man's arm. ''Please. This is a matter of life and death,'' she said, gazing at him beseechingly. ''You have to help us. Please.''

The man frowned, hesitating. He looked down at the delicate hand on his arm, then into her eyes, and apparently he read the desperate entreaty in her face. At last, coming to a decision, he glanced at his co-workers on either side and began to flip through the schedule book. ''Well, now, let's see. If you were to take the 6:25 a.m. bus, you'd arrive in San Francisco—'' he ran his finger down the timetable ''—the following morning at 9:20.'' Keeping his face deadpan, he looked up and gave them a conspiratorial wink. ''How's that?''

Erin's answering smile was brilliant. ''Fine. Just fine. Thank you very much. You've been most helpful.''

Max added his thanks and took Erin's arm. As they were about to leave he turned back to the man. ''One more thing. Has anyone else made inquiries about a woman fitting the same description?''

Once again the man glanced at the people on either side of him. ''Not that I know of. But then, I just work the night shift. And there are a lot of other ticket agents.''

''I see. Thanks.''

As they hurried from the terminal Erin could hardly contain her excitement. ''Can you believe our luck?'' she crowed. "We picked the right agent on the very first try. And he remembered her! Without our even asking!"

"It's that red hair," Max muttered, glancing at the short mop of curls that glittered in the artificial light. "It makes you stand out in a crowd." Plus, a man would have to be half blind or senile to forget a face like that, he added to himself, unreasonably irritated.

He hustled her toward the door so fast that Erin practically had to skip to keep up. Just before they reached it she dug in her heels and hung back.

"Max, wait! I want to use the phone to call the airport. If I can get a flight out right away, I can get to San Francisco in time to meet Elise's bus."

"Not here." Max looked around. His gut had been eating him alive ever since they stepped into the terminal. "C'mon. We'll find someplace less public," he urged, but Erin was already tugging him toward the row of pay phones.

Left with no choice, he stood beside her, facing the waiting room and impatiently tapping his foot as she made the call.

When she hung up the phone she was beaming. "There's a flight to Las Vegas with a connection that will put me in San Francisco hours before the bus arrives. If I leave right now, I'll just be able to make it. As soon as I get my bag out of your car, I'll take a taxi to the Albuquerque airport." She sighed and closed her eyes for an instant. "I can't believe we found her."

Erin looked up at Max with a polite little smile, and he stiffened as he sensed her withdrawal before she even spoke. "Max, I want to thank you for all you've done for me. And for Elise. Especially for saving my life. I'll never forget it. I want you to know that."

Max simply stared at her, unable to believe his ears for a moment. Or his eyes. She was actually standing there with her hand stuck out for him to shake!

Fury swept through him. He wanted to throttle her on the spot, shake her until her teeth rattled. To keep from doing just that, he rammed his hands into the pockets of his suede jacket and balled them into fists.

All evening he'd been consumed with a desperate, almost obsessive need to protect this courageous, willful woman, to take her someplace isolated and quiet where she'd be out of harm's way until this whole mess was over. And now, here she stood, trying to give him the brush-off with a few mealy-mouthed platitudes. He couldn't believe it!

And he sure as hell wasn't going to stand for it.

He stared hard at her outstretched hand until it began to tremble and she withdrew it self-consciously. Then he looked her right in the eye. "Save your breath. *You* are not going anywhere. *We* are."

"Max, I couldn't ask you to fly all the way to San Francisco. You've done so much for me—for Elise and me—already and—"

"You're not asking. I'm telling. And don't bother to argue. This time you're not getting your own way. Now could we please get the hell out of here?" he ground out tightly, casting one last anxious look over his shoulder as he grasped her elbow and marched her toward the door.

"This is really unnecessary," Erin protested, trotting along beside him. "I assure you I can handle things from here on."

A low sound rumbled from Max, and this time he did give her a little shake. "Shut up, Erin," he hissed. "I'm warning you, you've pushed me right to the limit."

Outside, he steered her away from the lighted entrance. When they reached the shadows he stopped in the middle of the sidewalk and turned her to face him. Erin felt a little thrill of fear shiver down her spine at the harsh anger in his face.

"Now listen, and listen good, because I'm only going to say this once. Until we have Elise safe and sound and this whole mess cleared up and the people responsible behind bars, I'm not about to let you sashay off on your own. No matter how long it takes or where we have to go, I'm sticking to you like glue, lady. You got that?"

Erin opened her mouth to reply, but before she could utter a sound, he continued in the same clipped, no-nonsense tone. "And furthermore, if at any time we find ourselves in what I consider to be a dangerous situation, you are going to do exactly what I tell you, when I tell you. No backtalk, no questions. If you don't, so help me I'll...I'll..." He groped a moment for a suitable punishment, failed to find one and, with another growl of frustration, hauled her against him and crushed her mouth with his.

It was a stunning kiss, hot, hard, demanding, full of male aggression and possessiveness. At first Erin was too shocked to resist, and then she was too caught up in the heat and the magic to even think of it.

Legs braced wide, he held her close, fitting their bodies together like two pieces of a puzzle. His mouth rocked hungrily over hers. His tongue delved and stroked with a sweet, erotic rhythm that sent shimmering waves of fire straight to the core of her femininity. He was strong and masterful, yet it was the heady touch of desperation beneath his ardor that thrilled—and frightened—Erin the most.

The kiss ended as quickly as it had begun. Max grasped her shoulders and held her at arm's length. His breathing was labored, his face flushed. Erin couldn't tell if it was from passion or anger.

"I mean it, Erin. We're in this together, okay?"

Breathless and a bit shaken, her heart pounding, Erin stared up at him. A gentle breeze stirred her hair, and she felt its crisp coolness against her flushed skin. Dimly, she was aware of the derelict from the bus station stumbling by, the flash of headlights and the rumble of the passing cars. Mesmerized by the glittering look in his narrowed eyes, she nodded and replied in a meek voice, "Yes, Max."

They broke all speed limits getting to Albuquerque. Max drove the powerful Lincoln full throttle, nearly burning up the pavement and covering the sixty odd miles in just forty-five minutes. If Erin hadn't been so keyed up and anxious, she would have been terrified.

Even so, they barely had time to buy their tickets and check Erin's bag, arriving at the gate after half the passengers had already boarded.

Relieved and breathless, Erin hurried to the end of the line. She had edged up to within fifteen feet of the boarding tunnel, where a flight attendant was taking tickets, before realizing that Max was not with her.

She whirled around, her anxious gaze darting in all directions. Finally she spotted him at the bank of phones. For a moment she dithered, looking back and forth between the diminishing line of passengers and Max. Gritting her teeth, she dashed over to him.

"What are you doing?" she demanded. Max raised a hand, silencing her.

"Sam, this is Max," he said into the phone, and Erin felt her heart skip a beat. "Listen, I won't be in the office tomorrow morning, so handle that meeting with Jacobsen for me, will you?"

There was a moment's pause, and though Erin strained to hear what Sam was saying, all she caught was a faint murmur.

"No, I'm not sure when I'll be back. I'm going to San Francisco to help Elise. She's in some sort of trouble. I have to make it there in time to intercept a bus."

Another pause followed, longer this time. Listening, Max glanced toward the boarding tunnel and frowned when he saw the last passenger going through. "Look, Sam, I don't have time to explain it to you right now, okay? I'll tell you all about it when we get back tomorrow."

Erin tugged at his sleeve as the voice on the PA system announced the last call for boarding their flight. "Max, c'mon."

"Dammit, Sam! I've got to go or we'll miss the plane. I'll explain tomorrow." He slammed the receiver down and grabbed Erin's hand.

"Let's go," he said, and sprinted toward the gate.

They made it—barely. Max shouted for the flight attendant to hold the door as they tore down the boarding tunnel, and the moment they ran in she closed and locked it behind them. Mere seconds after they had collapsed in their seats the plane started taxiing out onto the runway.

Gasping for breath, Erin leaned her head against the high seat back and closed her eyes. "Why on earth did you do that?" she asked after a moment when her chest stopped heaving.

"I know, I know. I cut it close, but I had to tell Sam something. I couldn't just disappear without a word. We're partners, remember? We've got a business to run."

Again Erin felt a twinge of guilt for involving Max, but then she reminded herself that he was the one who had insisted on coming with her. She looked at him. "But couldn't you have made up something? Did you have to tell him where you were going and why? How do you know that your partner isn't the one behind all this?"

Max's head swiveled sharply. "Because I know Sam," he said with a touch of annoyance. But then, as he studied her, his expression softened. He shifted almost sideways, facing her, and took her hand. "If that's what's worrying you, forget it. Sam's been my best friend since we were three years old. I promise you, there's no one straighter."

Erin wanted to believe him, both for Max's sake and her own peace of mind, but it was difficult. Even now, the memory of Sam Lawford's pale, lifeless eyes sent a shiver through her.

Unable to meet the tender, tolerant look on Max's face, she lowered her eyes and watched his thumb rub slowly back and forth across the back of her hand, feeling guilty and defensive. "I still think it's safer if no one knows where we are," she muttered stubbornly.

Max's thumb stilled, and his hand tightened around hers. "Erin, you realize, don't you, that we might be too late? It's possible that whoever is after Elise might have already found her." Erin's stricken gaze flew upward, locking with his, and Max grimaced. "I just think you should be prepared for the worst. Remember, if we could trace her movements, so could someone else."

Before he'd even finished Erin began shaking her head. "No. No, I don't believe that," she insisted. "If Elise were hurt, I'd know it. I'd sense it. I know I would."

"Erin—"

"No, really. You see, we've always had a special kind of communication between us. A kind of ... well ... I guess you'd call it telepathy. We often know what each other is thinking, and many times, even with great distances separating us, we pick up on what the other is feeling."

"Are you serious?"

"Yes, I swear, it's the truth. It often happens that way between identical twins. Our parents noticed it when we were small. As we were growing up we even took part in a university study on the subject."

She looked at Max earnestly, needing the reassurance his believing would give her. "So you see, if something had happened to Elise, I'd know it. I'd feel it."

"Fine." Max gave her hand another squeeze. "If you say so, that's good enough for me."

"Thank you," she said quietly, and though it made no sense at all, she felt the knot of tension in her chest ease.

A flight attendant came by with the drinks cart, and both Erin and Max asked for coffee. As they sipped it Max said, "Tell me more about this study. It must have been fascinating."

"It was. It was all done under very controlled conditions, and the results were amazing. They always separated us so there'd be no eye contact, no body language or anything like that to pick up on. In one experiment, I remember, they gave Elise a pad and pencil and me a piece of paper with a word written on it. I was told to concentrate on the word very hard. After only a few minutes, three doors down the hall, Elise had written the word down on her pad."

"No kidding?"

"Honestly. They even reversed the experiment several times, sometimes giving me the pad, sometimes Elise, but the results were always the same.

"And sometimes they'd have one of us watch a movie, and the other one would always know if it was funny or sad or romantic. Whatever. Once, when I was watching a real tear-jerker, Elise actually cried."

"Amazing," Max murmured, gazing at her, his chin propped on the heel of his hand. "You two must be very close."

"We are. Sometimes it seems as though we're one person who has been split in two, as though we're two halves of a whole."

"Yet, except in looks, you're very different."

Erin gave a little chuckle. "Oh, yes. Very. We're like the opposite sides of a coin. Elise is...well, I guess *special* is the word," she said, her voice softening. "She's patient and sweet and gentle. There's a wonderful kind of sereneness about Elise, a calm contentment and a warmth that draws people to her. When we were kids she was the angelic one who never got into mischief. Yet every time I landed in trouble, she always tried to cover for me, and she cried harder than I did whenever I got spanked.''

"From what I've seen so far, my guess would be that that happened fairly often," Max commented, making no effort to hide his amusement.

Erin wrinkled her nose at him in feigned annoyance, but then she sighed and rolled her eyes. "I hate to admit it, but you're right," she confessed ruefully. "I was as restless as Elise was content. Ever since I can remember I've had a burning desire to know what was beyond the next hill. I was always getting into trouble for wandering off."

"Didn't you ever get lost?"

"Oh, sure. Countless times. It got to be a joke among our neighbors, who always joined in the search. I'd end up scared and getting the tar walloped out of me, but that never cured me of the wanderlust. A week after Elise and I graduated from college she married the boy next door, and I took off for Europe."

"And you've been seeing the world ever since."

"Mostly," Erin said with a self-conscious shrug. "But what's really strange is, even though Elise put down roots and I roamed, our lives have always run parallel."

"How so?"

"The major events and turning points in each of our lives have always occurred at about the same time. When we were kids Elise broke her right leg one day, and I broke my left one the next. We had emergency appendectomies within thirty-six hours of each other. In college we majored in different fields, but we always had the same grade-point average. I thought that when Elise married Tommy the pattern had been broken, but I met André Meleaux on the plane to Paris, and a month later we eloped."

Max had no ready reply this time; and that surprised Erin. She looked up to find him frowning, his eyes a sharp, glittering blue.

Chapter Six

I didn't know you'd been married," Max said finally. His voice had taken on a sharp edge, startling Erin.

"Yes, for three years. The same as Elise."

Max was still staring at her strangely. Not knowing what else to say, she lifted one shoulder in a dismissive shrug.

"Your sister is a widow," he said a moment later. "Does that mean you are also?"

"No. But my divorce from André became final two weeks after Tommy died," Erin replied with a sad smile. She tried to keep her voice neutral, but some of the old pain had crept in. Uncomfortable, she turned and stared out the window at the darkness.

The flight attendant came by and took their cups, and when she'd gone Max reached up and clicked off the overhead lights. The resulting dimness added a touch of intimacy that seemed to separate them from the other passengers, enclosing them in a tiny, private world of their own.

"So what happened?" he said in the gentlest of voices.

Erin started to tell him that it was none of his business, but when she met his eyes and saw the tenderness there, the caring, she succumbed to his coaxing.

"I'm not sure, exactly." She looked down, fixing her gaze on her fingers, which were pleating and unpleating the lower edge of her jacket. "In the beginning we were very happy. We were young and in love. André was charming and gallant, perhaps as only a Frenchman can be. He made me feel so...so...special."

The words hit Max like a fist in the gut, but clenching his teeth, he strove to keep his expression impassive. Jealousy was an emotion he had never experienced before, and it was damned uncomfortable. He found he hated the thought of any other man touching Erin, of her being bound in any way to someone else. And though it was less than praiseworthy, Max admitted to himself that he was fiercely glad the marriage had ended. Yet, at the same time, seeing the hurt and regret she couldn't hide, he ached for her. André Meleaux was a fool, he decided, studying Erin's pensive expression.

"When he proposed I told him that I didn't think I was cut out for marriage, that I doubted I could ever be content in one place forever," Erin continued. "But he swore that was no problem, that I could work as much as I wanted, travel as much as I wanted. He claimed he found my restless spirit captivating. Certainly he was proud of my ability with languages. I know that."

Max looked at her, saying nothing, and after a moment she went on.

"After we were married I continued to free-lance, though I did cut back on the number of jobs I took. I translated industrial manuals and instructions for companies who exported products, acted as interpreter for visiting diplomats and occasionally took tour groups on short trips, but I was never gone for very long at a time."

Erin gave an ironic little laugh. "But apparently my husband wasn't as modern as he thought. Gradually his delight in my 'uniqueness' dimmed to a sort of grudging acceptance, and even that turned to outright resentment after a couple of years."

"Couldn't you compromise?"

"I tried that. I took fewer and fewer jobs, until I was hardly working at all. I knocked myself out, trying to be the kind of wife he seemed to want; I gave parties, redecorated our apartment, tried to get interested in domestic things." Eyes cloudy with bewilderment, Erin looked at Max and lifted her hands, palms up, then let them fall back into her lap. She shook her head slowly. "Nothing worked. André wasn't interested in compromise; he demanded complete capitulation. It became more and more obvious as time passed that what he really wanted was what his mother had wanted for him all along: a proper 'French' wife."

"Hmm. Do I detect mother-in-law trouble?" Max drawled.

This time when she glanced at him her brown eyes crinkled with a touch of self-derisive humor. "Actually, the whole thing was probably my own fault. If I had given it enough thought, I would have realized that having a Frenchman for a husband also meant having a French mother-in-law."

"I take it she didn't approve."

Placing her hand over her heart, Erin gave him a look of feigned shock, then lifted her nose haughtily and sniffed. *"Pour l'amour de Dieu!"* she exclaimed, giving an excellent imitation of her ex-mother-in-law's disdainful tone. "A liberated, footloose *American* woman for André Phillipe Jean Louis Meleaux?" She closed her eyes and shuddered.

Erin met Max's amused look and made a wry face. "Hardly. From the moment we met, Heloise made it quite clear that I was not at all suitable for her son. Although—" a faraway, wistful look came into Erin's eyes "—I'm sure if I'd been more like Elise, she would have accepted me. Everyone loves Elise, and she, other than not being French, is exactly what both André and his mother wanted."

Erin sighed and lifted her hand in a helpless gesture. "I tried to be like her. I tried very hard, but it wasn't enough."

Max's chest tightened as he watched her struggle with painful recollections, accept them, then square her shoulders and push the memories away. When she turned to him with a determined smile he felt a sharp stab of emotion in the vicinity of his heart, and it was all he could do not to yank her into his arms.

"But I learned something from it all," she said brightly. "I learned it's impossible to be something you're not, or to make yourself over to suit someone else. I wish I could have been what André needed and wanted, but I couldn't. Any more than I could be like my sister. I'm me, and people are going to have to take me as I am, warts, weaknesses and all."

Max leaned closer, took her chin between his thumb and forefinger and turned her face this way and that. "Funny, I don't see any warts," he said, peering at her through narrowed eyes. "All I see is a fascinating, beautiful, desirable woman. One I'm finding more and more irresistible."

Her eyes widened, and she swallowed hard, and Max smiled tenderly as he felt a tiny shiver ripple through her. He cupped her jaw and brushed his thumb over the hint of a cleft in her chin, then touched one corner of her mouth. Against his palm her skin was soft and silky smooth. Her scent drifted to him, tempting, intoxicating, a heady blend of lilacs and sweet warm woman.

Longing shimmered in her brown eyes—he was too experienced not to see that—but there was wariness, too, and because of it he put a tight rein on his own desire, ignoring the throbbing in his loins and the odd constriction in his chest. "This may come as a shock to you, Erin," he murmured, "but, though I think your sister is beautiful and sweet, I find you infinitely more appealing."

Beneath his fingers he felt her pulse leap, saw the excitement and pleasure that flared in her eyes for an instant before it was firmly doused.

"Max, don't. Please." It was half protest, half plea, her voice low and shaky. Max watched her as she pulled free of his touch and lowered her gaze to her interlaced fingers.

"What is it, Erin? What's wrong? Look, if you're still worried that I've been stringing your sister along, I promise you it's not true. There is nothing between us. I'm not interested in her in a romantic way, and I swear that I've never done anything to make her think otherwise. Hell, I've never even kissed her! You've got to believe that."

Erin believed it. From what she knew of Max, he was not the sort of man to lie about something like that. No, she could well imagine her sister weaving dreams around him, getting her hopes up over nothing more substantial than a few words of praise and a friendly smile. No doubt Elise was convinced that all she had to do was be patient and make herself indispensable to him as a secretary, and sooner or later he would begin to notice her as a woman.

She looked at Max and smiled sadly. "No, it's not that, Max. I believe you. But it still wouldn't work. I can't get involved with you."

"Why not? If you know there's nothing between Elise and me, then what's the problem?"

"Don't you see? Whether or not you feel anything for Elise is not the issue. The fact is, she's in love with you. Can't you imagine how she'd feel if you and I..." Erin waved away the rest of the statement and shook her head. "No. No, I couldn't hurt her that way."

"And what about us? What about you? You'd ignore your feelings? And don't you dare try to deny the attraction between us," he said quickly when she opened her mouth to speak. "I know what I'm feeling, and something this strong can't be one-sided." The corners of his mouth twitched in a hint of a smile, and his gaze grew warm and caressing. "Besides, you have very expressive eyes."

Frowning, she opened her mouth, hesitated, then snapped it shut. "All right. I admit it. I find you attractive."

Max cocked one brow.

Erin squirmed under the silent skepticism and shot him a sour look. "All right, *very* attractive," she corrected grudgingly. "But that's beside the point. I still can't get involved with you."

"So that's it? Just like that, you close the door on the what could be, without even giving us a chance? All because of your sister's romantic fantasies?"

Erin turned her head slowly and looked at him, her eyes pleading with him to understand. "Max, don't you see? Elise is like a part of me, my other half. If I hurt her, I hurt myself. Much, much worse."

Max simply stared at her. He couldn't remember ever feeling so helpless or frustrated. How the devil did you argue with that?

You don't, you fool, he berated himself, seeing the weariness and worry in her eyes. At least not yet. Not without coming off like a self-centered, insensitive clod. Besides, she's got too much on her mind right now to deal with this, so back off.

"All right," he said on a resigned sigh. "We'll let it ride for now." He reached out and captured a bright curl, his eyes flaring as he watched the silky strand coil about his finger as though it had a life of its own. Meeting her gaze, his mouth quirked in an ironic smile. "But I'm warning you, Erin. I'm not giving up."

She bit her bottom lip and gazed back at him uncertainly, and for the first time Max noticed the violet smudges beneath her eyes, the faint look of fatigue about her mouth. Against the halo of fiery curls that surrounded it, her face was a pale oval.

Hell, she's dead on her feet, you idiot, he scolded himself.

"Come here, woman," he commanded in a tough yet tender growl. He flipped up the armrest between their seats, put his arm around her and hauled her close, pressing her head against his shoulder. "You look as if a puff of wind would blow you over. How long have you been up, anyway?"

"Since about twelve-thirty this morning," Erin murmured, snuggling her face against his shirt.

"Almost twenty-four hours. No wonder you're exhausted. Well, we've got about an hour before we land in Las Vegas, so why don't you get some sleep while you can?"

"Hmm" was Erin's drowsy reply, and even that faded as Max cradled the back of her head with his hand and tucked her more securely against him.

Her breathing began to slow and deepen. Max stroked her arm from wrist to elbow to shoulder and back again, carefully avoided the bandaged cut. Absently, he rubbed his chin against her crown, inhaling the sweet, clean fragrance of her hair, oblivious to the way the silky strands clung to his beard stubble. "Erin?" Max whispered.

She made an inarticulate sound, and he smiled and dropped a kiss on the top of her head. "I meant it. I'm not going to let you turn your back on what we could have."

He waited for her reply, but none came. After a few seconds he leaned back and looked down at her and smiled tenderly when he saw that she was fast asleep.

God, she's beautiful! he thought, feeling his chest swell with a sudden rush of sweetly painful emotion. Her face was soft in slumber, her lips slightly parted. He marveled at the smoothness of her skin, the fragility of her eyelids and the delicate tracery of blue veins just beneath their surface, the way her lashes lay against her cheeks like thick fans. Max stared at her, overwhelmed by the feelings that washed through him.

It amazed him that he had ever mistaken her for Elise, even for a moment. It was a mistake he'd never make again. Probably the only reason it had happened at all was because he hadn't been expecting the switch.

Physically, Erin and her sister were as alike as two people could be, but there were differences—subtle differences that weren't apparent at first glance. Erin's mouth was just a bit wider than Elise's, and the tilt of her eyes just a bit more marked. And if he wasn't mistaken, her hair seemed a shade redder.

Max grinned as he studied the freckles scattered across the bridge of her nose, only faintly visible beneath her make-up. Tiny flaws her sister didn't share, but he found them endearing. Like gold dust on porcelain, he thought fondly, then chuckled at the fanciful thought. Lord, Delany! The next thing you know, you'll be spouting poetry.

But the truth was, there were a great many things about Erin Blaine that he found endearing. And exciting. Things that had nothing to do with her physical appearance: the way she had of looking a person right in the eye, her quick mind, the belligerent thrust of her jaw when she was angry. She possessed a sort of energy, a spark, that drew him as surely and as irresistibly as the moon pulls the tides. He loved her adventuresome spirit, her feistiness, her courage, the way she embraced life with open arms, her resilience when it dealt her a blow. Even her impulsive willfulness delighted him, Max realized a shade ruefully.

Such little things, he thought. Tiny, subtle differences, Erin and Elise were equally beautiful, each in her own special way, and yet it was those small dissimilarities that stirred him and created a chemistry that made him desire one sister while merely admiring the other.

Would Elise have stuck her neck out this way for Erin if their positions had been reversed? Max wondered. He stroked the silky hair at Erin's temple and tucked a curl behind her ear. Knowing what he did of the two, he didn't doubt that his secretary would have been just as concerned and would have enlisted whatever help she could to save Erin. But somehow he doubted that she would have knowingly rushed into a dangerous situation. She didn't have Erin's kind of spunk, her impulsive nature.

Though he found it delightful, it was that very same impulsive nature that worried Max the most. It could get Erin killed. It nearly had already. A cold fear clutched at Max, and his arm tightened about Erin as he relived those terrifying moments when he'd watched, helpless, as she'd careered down that mountain road. He hoped to God that he never had to witness anything like that again.

His gut told him that whoever had caused that "accident" wasn't going to give up. Until the perpetrator was caught and this whole mess cleared up, both women were going to be in danger. Which was why he intended to stick to Erin like ugly on an ape.

Max looked down at her, sleeping peacefully against his shoulder, and smiled. Actually, he would have preferred to stash her away somewhere safe, maybe under Sam's watchful eye, while he made this trip alone, but he had known better than to even suggest it. Furthermore, he shuddered to think what she might have taken it into her head to do in his absence.

Her ex-husband was right about one thing: Erin was unique. She would lead a man a merry chase, and give him a few gray hairs in the process, but he had a feeling that life with her would never be dull or ordinary.

No, Erin wasn't a woman for hearth and home and fireside dreaming, Max thought with a wry smile, trailing his fingers down the velvety curve of her cheek. But then, what the hell? He'd never hankered for a pipe and slippers anyway.

Erin didn't want to wake up. She was lost in the mists of a delicious, incredibly erotic dream. Firm male lips rocked softly over hers, the very gentleness of the kiss making it so exquisitely sensual that every cell in her body tingled. A large hand cupped her breast, fingers flexing about her sensitive flesh, making it burgeon and ache. She could feel her nipple pushing against the warm, hard palm, a tight, turgid button of desire. With every shallow breath she drew in a heady masculine scent.

The lips withdrew, then returned to nibble again.

Erin sighed and pressed closer.

"Erin." A nimble tongue outlined her eager mouth and probed the corners. "Erin, we're about to land."

Lips rubbed in lazy seduction, breaths mingled. Teeth nipped her, and Erin moaned at the sweet savagery, then moaned again when her lower lip was caught by that wonderful, marauding mouth and sucked gently.

When released, she protested, but the sound turned into a purr of feminine delight as a line of kisses was strung across her cheek. Hot, moist breath filled her ear, sending rivers of fire through her, making her nipples ache and throb, her womanly core burn. Erin shivered deliciously.

"Erin. Sweetheart, wake up," the husky voice said in her ear. "We're in Las Vegas. We have to change planes."

She frowned and tried to ignore the voice that seemed intent on dragging her from the pleasurable dream, but in the next instant a bump and a screech jarred her rudely awake.

Erin started. Her eyes flew open and darted around in confusion. It took her a moment to realize that she was in a plane, and it was hurtling down a runway, engines whining under the reverse thrust of power. It took another second before it registered on her muzzy brain that she was practically lying in Max's lap, *and* his hand was massaging her breast while his lips roamed greedily over her neck.

She hadn't been dreaming at all!

"Max! What on earth do you think you're doing?" Erin shoved at his shoulders and scrambled to sit up. Flustered, she hastily straightened her clothing and patted her mussed curls, shooting Max an accusing look out of the corner of her eye and trying her best to ignore the way her body still tingled.

Max grinned. "Sorry," he said guilelessly, although there wasn't an ounce of repentance in those dancing blue eyes. "I tried shaking your shoulder, but you only snuggled closer. Actually, it was nice, but the way you were climbing all over me, I had to wake you up somehow, before it got embarrassing."

"Very funny, Delany." Pretending not to notice her cheeks burning, Erin pulled a compact from her purse.

By the time she had powdered her nose and repaired her lipstick the plane had taxied to the gate and the passengers had begun departing.

Although they had arrived a bit behind schedule, they made their connecting flight with no hitch. This time, though, Erin made sure she stayed awake all the way to San Francisco.

They were even further behind schedule when they landed, and a mechanical problem with the luggage conveyor caused another delay. It was after five in the morning when they arrived at the bus station, and by then Erin was so exhausted that she could barely hold her head up. They had four hours until the bus arrived, and Max suggested that they check into a hotel and get some rest while they waited. Erin, however, stubbornly refused to budge.

"I'm not leaving here until I can take Elise with me," she said, collapsing onto a seat close to the door where arriving passengers entered.

Max sighed and sat down next to her. "All right, hardhead, have it your way. It doesn't matter anyway. At this point I'm so tired that I could probably sleep sitting up."

Slipping an arm around her, he pulled her close, pressed her face against his shoulder and laid his cheek against the top of her head. After what had happened in the plane Erin knew she should object, but she was simply too tired. She had one last coherent thought as she snuggled against him and sank into oblivion. After all, what could he do in a lighted bus station?

She soon found out.

For a while they both dozed fitfully, waking every few minutes with a start when arrivals and departures were announced over the public address system, but after a short time even that failed to penetrate Erin's comalike sleep.

It seemed to her that she had barely closed her eyes when she was once more coaxed awake by Max's exhilarating kisses. He toyed with her lips, mouthing them ever so softly, and when her heavy lids lifted he pulled back and smiled down at her.

"Good morning," he whispered, and dropped another quick kiss on her mouth. Erin blinked owlishly, and his smile grew. "Wake up, sleepyhead. They've just announced the bus."

"Mmm, that's nice," she mumbled, turning her face back into his shoulder. A second later his words registered, and Erin sat up with a jerk. "It's here? Elise's bus is here?"

"It's just pulling in."

"Well, what are we waiting for? C'mon." She shot out of the chair as though it were spring-loaded, leaving Max to follow with her bag.

The strong scent of diesel fuel and the deafening rumble of powerful engines hit Erin the moment she pushed through the door. Muttering a distracted "Excuse me, excuse me," she darted through the people milling around, keeping her eye on the bus that was rolling into the loading area. The driver tapped the horn as he brought the bus to a stop, and the sound reverberated through the terminal, along with the hiss of air brakes. Before he could shut off the engine Erin was standing by the front of the bus, anxiously watching the door. Max joined her a moment before the first passenger stepped off.

People poured out in a steady stream, all looking tired and rumpled and not in the best of moods after traveling all night. Erin's anxious gaze darted to the face of each passenger emerging. Ten people stepped off the bus. Twenty. Thirty. Gnawing her lower lip, Erin looked up at Max.

"Don't worry," he said, giving her shoulder a reassuring squeeze. "She'll get off in a minute."

Erin fiddled with her purse strap and tapped her foot. Finally she stood on tiptoe and craned her neck, trying to see into the bus. All she could make out through the tinted windows were vague shadows, but she could see that there were only a few passengers left inside. More poured out, but finally the flow dropped to a trickle as the last few stragglers came stumbling off. Then nothing.

Erin and Max looked at each other, their eyes wide with disbelief.

After a moment of stunned silence he grasped her elbow. "Let's look inside."

It was empty, except for the driver, who was making his way up the aisle, checking each seat and the overhead storage racks for forgotten items.

He glanced up and saw them, then did a double take. Before he could speak Erin said, "Excuse us, sir, but we're looking for my sister. She got on this bus in Santa Fe. Her ticket was for San Francisco, but we didn't see her get off." She leaned to one side and looked beyond the driver to the rear of the bus. "Is there a rest room on this bus? Perhaps she's in there."

"Nope. She ain't in there." The driver grinned as he approached them. "You gave me a start there for a minute, little lady. I couldn't figure out how the devil you'd gotten here."

"What do you mean, she's not in there?" Erin demanded with an edge in her voice, ignoring the last part of his statement. "She has to be."

"Nope. She got off a ways back."

"She got off? When? Where?"

The man shrugged. "Sometime yesterday. In...let's see...Las Vegas, I think. No...maybe it was Flagstaff. I don't remember exactly."

"You don't *remember*!" Erin's voice had risen to a shrill pitch that brought a frown to the driver's face. Before she could say more Max put his arm around her, his hand tightening in warning against her waist.

"But you are sure that she got off, and that it was in a large city?" he interjected calmly.

"Yep. We were at a busy stop, right in the middle of loading luggage and taking on new passengers, when she got off and asked for her cases."

"Did you at least find out why she was getting off before reaching her destination?" Erin asked.

"Look, lady, it ain't my job to question the passengers," the driver snapped, becoming annoyed at her tone. "She didn't ask for a refund. So she bought a ticket to the coast, then got off before we get there. So what? It's no skin off my nose. It's her money." He pulled a clipboard from the rack next to the dash, then turned to them, making a shooing motion with his hands. "Now, you folks are going to have to get off. This is the end of the line for me, and this bus is going to the barn."

Dispirited, Erin and Max reentered the waiting room and in silence made their way to the front entrance. They stepped out into a mild San Francisco morning of watery sunshine, stiff breezes and high, billowy clouds in a pale sky. By mutual consent, they walked along the curving entrance to the city sidewalk and stopped in front of the building. They looked at each other, their faces filled with worry, frustration and weariness.

"I'm sorry, Erin. It looks as if we're back to square one," Max said, propping one shoulder against the gray granite wall.

Even in July there was a nip to the wind. It swirled around them, whipping Erin's rumpled pants against her legs. She crossed her arms in front of her and huddled deeper into the thin jacket. "I know," she responded in a listless voice. "Oh, Max, I'm so worried. Where could she be?"

She looked so forlorn and downhearted that it wrung Max's heart. One side of her hair was flattened, and her face still bore crease marks from sleeping with her head on his shoulder. What little makeup she'd had on was almost gone, and she was so pale with fatigue that the freckles on her nose stood out like splatters of gold paint. Even her bright curls seemed to droop. But it was the sheen of moisture in her eyes and the slight quiver in her chin she was trying so hard to control that got to him the most.

He reached out and fluffed her hair, then cupped the side of her face and rubbed his thumb back and forth across the hollow beneath her cheekbone. Against his dark hand her skin looked parchment white and unbelievably fragile. "Don't worry about it, sweetheart. This is just a temporary setback. We'll find her."

Actually, Max had serious doubts on that score, but at that moment he would have promised Erin anything.

Erin lifted her chin and gave him a wavering smile that squeezed his heart even more. "Yes. I know. So . . . I guess we'd better get started."

"Whatever you say." Max pushed away from the building and took her arm. They had taken only a step when suddenly Erin stopped, gave a little cry and put her hand up to her cheek. Puzzled, she looked at Max, then drew her hand away and stared at her fingers.

Max chuckled. "What's the matter? Did a bird get you? Here—let me," he said, reaching for his handkerchief.

His hand froze halfway to his pocket.

A thin line of blood oozed from a scratch on her cheek, and there was more smeared on her fingertips. Caught in a curl at her temple was a tiny chip of granite.

Max's head snapped around, his gaze sweeping over the street and the traffic flowing by. As he looked back at her he heard a *thunk* and saw a second chip fly from the wall, leaving a white pockmark in the surface.

His gaze shifted to Erin in horror.

"My God! Someone is shooting at us!"

Chapter Seven

The small amount of color that was left in Erin's face promptly disappeared.

"Wh-what?"

"Run!" Snatching up her suitcase, Max grabbed her hand and took off, jerking her along with him.

"Hey!" Erin shouted, almost yanked off her feet.

Another *thunk* sounded behind them. Max glanced back over his shoulder. When he saw that Erin wasn't hit he gave her arm a hard tug. "Run, dammit. Come on!"

Towing her at top speed, Max zigzagged through the pedestrians on the sidewalk. Erin stumbled along behind him, gasping and straining to keep pace with his long stride, her feet barely touching the ground.

"Hey! Watch it, buddy!" a man shouted when Max slammed into him.

Without sparing him so much as a glance, Max shouldered his way past. As Erin was tugged by, her purse slapped the man in the side.

"Hey!"

They skirted around an elderly woman pulling a two-wheeled shopping cart and pushed their way through three sailors walking abreast.

More angry shouts followed, but Max didn't slacken the pace.

Behind them tires squealed and horns honked. Max glanced back over his shoulder and cursed under his breath as he saw a dark blue Camaro, across the street from the bus station, pull away from the curb. Forcing his way into the traffic, the driver made a sharp U-turn, tires screaming, and headed in their direction.

Max poured on another burst of speed, and behind him Erin let out a wail.

The signal light was red when they reached the intersection. Max slowed just enough to gauge the traffic before dashing out into the street. With his arm around Erin's waist he held her against his side and turned and twisted and darted among whizzing cars and trucks, drawing shouts of abuse and angry horn blasts.

The light turned green as they reached the far curb. He grabbed Erin's hand again and kept going. They were halfway down the block when, from the corner of his eye, Max saw the Camaro draw alongside them in the center lane. The car slowed, and Max cursed. His eyes darted frantically around for cover while his feet pounded the sidewalk. They were not in the best part of town, and the rundown buildings they passed did not offer much hope. Inside they could be cornered. But there was nowhere else to go.

He was on the verge of shoving Erin to the ground and throwing himself on top of her when a bus pulled into the inside lane, blocking the blue car from view. Max ran for all he was worth, straining to keep the barrier between them and the two men in the Camaro, but the long silver bus steadily eased ahead.

The traffic light at the next intersection turned red, and the bus began to slow. Glancing back, Max saw that cars were stacked up four deep behind the bus in both lanes. He skidded to a stop and reversed directions.

"M-Max! What...are you...doing?" Erin panted.

He didn't waste his breath on a reply but pounded back the way they had come. His lungs were on fire, and his heart felt as though it were about to burst, but he didn't slacken his speed.

Erin stumbled and jerked back on his arm. "Max, wait! I've g-got a s-stitch."

He tightened his hold on her hand and kept going. They made another death-defying dash across the street and raced back around some of the same people they'd passed only moments before. Behind them they heard wild honking, and Max made a quick calculation. Until the light changed the Camaro wasn't going anywhere, and when it did it would still have to circle the block. With luck, they would make it.

"Max! Please!" Erin cried. She stumbled, and her knees hit the sidewalk. Max dragged her a few steps, then scooped her up and half carried her clamped against his side.

When they reached the bus terminal he burst through the doors and tore through the lobby, weaving in and out among the milling crowd, bumping into people and sending luggage flying. He spotted a bus getting ready to pull out, and he shouldered their way past a portly man and out the door.

"Stop! Hold it! Wait for us!" Max shouted. Racing alongside the rolling bus, he banged on the door with Erin's suitcase, and after a few seconds the air brakes hissed.

"You folks almost didn't make it," the driver said when the door swished open.

Max tossed Erin's bag inside, then jumped aboard, hefting her with him.

Standing on the bottom step in the well, he eased her down on the one just above him, then straightened to face the driver, his chest heaving. "We don't have...tickets," he gasped out. "But I'll give you...fifty bucks to let us...ride with you for a mile."

The driver looked startled, then dubious. "Well, I don't know," he said doubtfully, but Max saw the calculating gleam in his eye as he glanced back at his passengers.

"Okay...make it...a hundred." Max pulled out his wallet, removed several bills and held them out to the man, fanned out so that he could see each one. "One hundred dollars for...one mile. That's all we ask."

The driver stared at the money, then at Max. He hesitated only a second longer before snatching the bills from his hand and stuffing them into his shirt pocket. "Okay, you got a deal."

"Good," Max replied tersely. "Now shut this door, and get the hell out of here."

As they pulled out of the terminal Max crouched down in the stairwell in front of Erin. She sat bent over, clutching her side, sucking in deep gulps of air. Max touched her hair and laid his hand against her neck. "Are you all right?"

She looked up at him. "Yes. Yes, I'm fine," she managed shakily as her labored breathing began to slow. "Just winded."

It wasn't the truth, and Max knew it. His worried gaze ran over her. The scratch on her face was caked with dried blood, and more was smeared up under her eye. Her slacks were dirty and torn from her fall, revealing two badly skinned knees, and the palm of one hand was abraded and red, with little bits of grit embedded in the angry flesh. But even more than her physical injuries, Max was concerned about her emotional state. He could feel her shaking, and now that the flush of exertion was beginning to fade, her complexion was whiter than before, almost pasty. Sweat-dampened curls clung to her pale face, and her brown eyes were huge with barely restrained panic.

It was the latter that tore at his heart. Fury moved through Max. Whoever had done this to her was going to pay, he vowed.

No, she was far from fine. Max cursed silently, resisting the urge to take her in his arms. She was hurt and frightened and exhausted, but dammit, at the moment there wasn't time to deal with any of those things. First he had to get her away from there, to someplace safe.

Gritting his teeth, Max gave her shoulder a squeeze and straightened up slightly. The bus stopped at the corner and waited for the light to change. From a half-crouched position, Max peered through the windshield. Scanning the street that ran in front of the station, he spotted the Camaro cruising toward them, not twenty feet away.

He ducked and went rigid, waiting. Hell! Had they seen him?

"What is it? What's wrong?" Erin grabbed his arm and started to rise.

Max shoved her back down and held his hand on her shoulder. "Sit still," he commanded in a rough whisper. "Don't move. The last thing we need is for them to get a glimpse of that red hair."

Erin's eyes went wide. She stared at him like a trapped fawn, and beneath his hand he felt her trembling increase, but to her credit, she clamped her lips together and said nothing.

The driver gave them a sharp look, which Max ignored. He held Erin's hand in a tight grip and waited, tensed and braced, expecting to hear someone bang on the door at his back at any moment.

Instead, the driver swung the bus out into the street, turning in the opposite direction from the blue Camaro. Max held Erin's gaze and waited, but after a while he slumped back against the door, all the air rushing out of him. Until that moment he hadn't even known he'd been holding his breath.

"Do you think they saw us?" Erin asked, looking at him hopefully.

"I don't think so. But they may figure it out. Sit tight. I'm going to have a look."

Max climbed past her into the aisle and made his way to the back of the bus, ignoring the curious glances of the other passengers. He bent over and looked out the rear window, and his mouth curved in a tight, satisfied smile.

The blue car was still going in the opposite direction at the same slow speed.

It didn't take long to go a mile, but to Max's relief, the driver took a winding route out of the city, making several turns before stopping to let them off.

When the bus pulled away from the curb, Erin gazed after it longingly, the brief sense of victory she felt fading. Panic fluttered in her chest. Determined not to give in to it, she squared her shoulders and looked around.

The driver had deposited them on a quiet corner of a hilly street in what appeared to be a prosperous area of town. The buildings were old but well cared for, many of red brick with crisp white trim. Farther up the hill the street was lined with tall, narrow Victorian houses. The general appearance was orderly, sedate and affluent.

"Well, at least this is a better neighborhood," Erin said with a halfhearted attempt at a smile.

"Yeah, but not necessarily safer." Max looked around, frowning. He took her elbow and started to lead her down the hill, his eyes constantly scanning their surroundings.

A block away they heard a trolley bell, and at the next intersection they turned the corner and saw the car rumbling away. "C'mon, let's catch it," Max said, urging her into a trot. "I feel like a sitting duck out here on the street."

After the footrace they had just run, Erin barely had enough energy to move, and by the time they hopped onto the trolley she was drained. Breathing hard, she collapsed on the center seat, and when Max put his arm around her and pulled her against him she went willingly, resting her head on his shoulder with a sigh.

The lady opposite them stared. Her expression grew wary and slightly appalled as she took in Erin's skinned knees, scratched face and torn, dirt-smeared clothing. Too exhausted to care, Erin ignored her. She leaned against Max and let her mind go blank. For the moment she was simply grateful to be alive.

Max massaged her shoulder, his hand rotating in slow, soothing circles, but when Erin glanced up at him she saw that his face was set, his eyes hard and piercing. Swiveling his head back and forth, he scanned the traffic around them constantly.

His vigilance reminded Erin that they were far from safe. Whoever had shot at them—or more precisely, at her—was still out there somewhere, searching for her at that very moment.

Erin pulled away from Max and sat up straight. Her worried gaze met his, then joined in the surveillance.

They rode in silence, the proximity of the other passengers making it impossible to discuss what had happened, but every now and then their eyes met and held. Though Max's gaze reflected the same worry and anxiety she was feeling, she also saw reassurance and solid strength there, both of which she sorely needed.

The trolley steadily put more distance between them and the bus station, but after a while the aimless riding began to grate on Erin's overwrought nerves. Finally she could take it no longer. Leaning close to Max, she muttered, "Max, we can't ride this thing forever."

"I know."

"Well, what are we going to do?"

The bell clanged, and the trolley slowed. Max made a quick search of the street. Grabbing her hand and the suitcase, he stood up and pulled her along with him. "We're going to get the hell out of here."

They had no sooner hopped off the trolley than Max flagged down a taxi and bundled Erin inside.

"Take us to the St. Francis Hotel," he instructed the driver as he climbed in after her.

Erin looked at him sharply. "Why are we going there? We need to get out of this town."

"We're going to. But those guys are probably watching the airport, so we can't risk going there. And we can forget taking the bus. That leaves only a car. We can rent one at the hotel."

"Oh, I see."

"And while we're there we're going to check in to get a few hours' rest."

"What?" She looked at him as though he'd lost his mind. "Max, we can't do that! We still have to find Elise!"

"I know. And we will. But, dammit, Erin, neither of us is in any condition to go on. We're both about ready to drop. For the past couple of hours we've been running on adrenaline and willpower."

"But Elise—"

"Has to rest sometime, too," he finished for her.

Erin's face remained stubborn. Raking a hand through his hair, Max looked away, then back again. His expression held both understanding and exasperation. "All right, I'll make a deal with you. It's—" he glanced at his watch "—almost eleven. We'll get a room, sleep until about six, then drive as far as Bakersfield."

"Why not Las Vegas?"

"Because it's too far. Even if we had the energy to make the drive, which I doubt, we'd arrive in the wee hours. This way we can get some rest, then get up early tomorrow morning and be in Las Vegas before ten."

Erin looked at him resentfully, knowing he was right but hating the thought of delaying the search so much as an hour. She was terrified—and *she* had Max with her. Imagining what her twin must be going through, all alone, with no one to turn to, made her cringe.

Still, she had no choice. All the will in the world wouldn't take her bruised and battered body much farther. She ached to the marrow of her bones, her eyes burned and her head felt like a fifty-pound block sitting on her shoulders. Seven hours wouldn't be nearly enough, nor would seventeen. The way she felt, she could probably sleep around the clock.

"All right. We'll do it your way," she agreed with weary reluctance. "Except we'll get two rooms, not one."

Max gave a snort of laughter, but when he spoke there was steel in his voice. "Forget it, sweetheart. After two attempts on your life, I'm not letting you out of my sight for a minute. Anyway, if it's your virtue you're worried about, you can rest easy. I'm too beat to seduce you."

A half hour later, Erin stood in the middle of a luxurious room, dazed and glassy-eyed, swaying on her feet. Her purse strap slipped from her shoulder, and the bag hit the thick carpet with a plop, but she was oblivious to it. She didn't even notice that there was only one bed in the room.

After closing the door behind the bellhop, Max checked the lock and shoved the safety bolt home. When he turned and saw her his face softened.

"Here, love, let me help you. You're about to drop."

Erin stood, docile as a lamb, as he unfastened her slacks and pushed them and her ruined panty hose down over her hips. After seating her on the edge of the bed he dropped onto one knee, removed her shoes and carefully eased the torn slacks over her scraped knees and slipped them off.

Max felt a touch at his temple and looked up to find her watching him groggily.

"Mr. and Mrs. M.M. Pierce, huh?" she mumbled. "That was quick thinking." A lazy little chuckle drifted from her as she sifted her fingers through the hair at his temple and lightly traced his ear. "Or is it just that you've had lots of practice taking women to hotels and checking in under an alias?"

Her words were slurred and run together, and her eyelids were so heavy that she could barely keep them up. Max could tell that she was giddy with fatigue and didn't know what she was doing, but the gentle touch sent fire streaking through him. Even pale, scraped and so worn out that she had dark circles under her eyes, she looked adorable and sexy as hell, sitting there slumped in a tired little heap, wearing only her rumpled jacket and tank top and those tiny white bikini panties.

To his chagrin, he was discovering that exhaustion was not as hard on the libido as he had thought.

The smile he gave her held wistful regret. "Actually, it's not an alias. My full name is Maxwell Morgan Pierce Delany," he explained. "My mother's maiden name was Pierce."

"Maxwell Morgan, huh? I like it." She ran the back of her fingers over the stubble along his jaw; then her hand dropped limply into her lap. "I like you, too," she managed over a huge yawn.

Ignoring his body's yearnings, Max forced his gaze back to her injured knees. "I'd better clean these scrapes before infection sets in," he said, frowning as he picked out a tiny piece of embedded gravel.

"Don't bother," she told him drowsily. "I'm going to take a shower. I'll do it then." But even as she said the words her eyelids dropped and her head lolled forward. When her chin hit her chest she jerked it up and blinked, but almost at once her head began to sway again.

Max smiled. "Fine. But I'll get the worst of it first. Why don't you just lie back and relax for a minute while I go get a washcloth?"

He gave her shoulder a little nudge that sent her toppling, and Erin sighed as her back sank into the mattress. "Okay," she murmured. "Just for a minute."

Scant seconds later, when Max returned with a warm, wet cloth, she was sound asleep. He stopped beside the bed and looked down at her. He knew his expression was probably sappy as hell, but he couldn't help it; he'd never met a woman like Erin before. She's such an exciting, vibrant creature, Max mused. Beautiful. Intelligent. Courageous. And she was fiercely loving and loyal to her sister. Would she give the same depth of devotion to a husband? he wondered.

The thought produced a startled chuckle. Whoa! Hold it, Delany. You've only known the woman twenty-four hours, for crying out loud. She's special, yeah, but it's a bit early to be thinking in those terms. Yet, as he gazed down at her pale, tired face, he felt his chest tighten with a strange mixture of passion and tenderness.

With a sigh, he bent and carefully cleaned the scratch on her cheek and her scraped knees. When done, he turned back the covers, swung her legs up onto the bed and shifted her onto the clean sheets. About to turn the covers back over her, he hesitated, debating. Finally he swiftly stripped off her jacket and tank top and tossed them aside. He hesitated only a moment longer over the lacy bra before removing it also.

He stared down at her, his breathing growing shallow as he drank in the sight of lush breasts and exquisite slender curves. Jaw clenched, he closed his eyes. Then he pulled the sheet over her and tucked it under her chin.

Max shook his head. His eyes glinting with self-mocking amusement, he bent and placed a kiss on her sweetly parted lips. "Sleep well, sweetheart."

A sharp thwack on her behind awakened Erin. Almost.

"Haul that luscious body out of the sack, babe. It's quarter to six."

The second thwack drew a groan. Lifting her head an inch off the pillow, Erin opened her eyes partway. The first thing she saw was Max, sitting on the bed beside her. She buried her face back in the pillow and moaned, "Go away. I need sleep." Muffled by the cushion of down, the slurred protest was almost inaudible.

"Erin, wake up." This time he took her by the shoulders and turned her over, giving her a little shake. "You wanted to start after Elise today. Remember?"

Erin blinked and peered up at him. "What time is it?"

"Almost six."

"Already?" she grumbled. She started to sit up, but when the sheet began to slither down her naked breasts she made a grab for it and slid lower in the bed, her eyes widening.

Max grinned as he watched her tuck the cover under her arms. "I thought you'd sleep more comfortably without your clothes," he said in answer to her silent accusation.

Erin glanced around the room and then at the dented pillow beside her. She had slept in the same bed with Max, nearly nude. The thought created a strange quivering sensation in her lower belly. She told herself that she was being foolish. It had been a necessity, and anyway, all they'd done was sleep. Nothing had happened.

It didn't help.

"I see," she said, striving for nonchalance. "Well, I suppose you're right."

It hit her then that Max was wearing a fresh pair of jeans and a blue-and-brown plaid shirt. "Where did you get those clothes?" she asked, frowning.

"I sent the bellhop out for them after you conked out. I also had our clothes laundered, although I'm afraid your slacks are beyond repair. I don't know about you, but I'm starving, so I had room service send up some sandwiches. We can eat them while we drive." He gave her leg a pat and stood up. "As soon as you're ready we'll leave."

Max smelled of soap, and she noticed that his hair was damp and his bristly stubble was gone. The sight of him made her acutely aware of how grubby she was, and suddenly her need for a shower outweighed every other consideration, even sleep. "Just give me fifteen minutes," she said, pulling the sheet free and wrapping it around her as she climbed from the bed.

The water stung her knees and grazed palm, but Erin didn't care. She luxuriated in the feel of the hot, needling spray, the creamy lather sluicing down her body like warm, wet fingers. Even after she was thoroughly scrubbed and shampooed she stood there for a few minutes, soaking up the heat, letting the pulsing shower pound her weariness away.

When she finally stepped out she felt revitalized and deliciously clean.

Bandages and an antiseptic cream were laid out on the counter. Smiling at Max's thoughtfulness, she applied the medicine and dressing to her scraped knees and the cut on her arm.

She quickly dressed in a green scoop-necked T-shirt and a green linen wraparound skirt with a border print of seashells in varying shades of coral, then slipped her feet into flat coral sandals. It took only a few minutes longer to apply her usual minimal amount of makeup and dry and fluff her short curls.

When she emerged from the bathroom Max was on the phone. Erin assumed he was making arrangements for a rental car, and she went about gathering their things.

Their laundered clothes were on the dresser, along with a large department store bag. Peeking inside, Erin discovered that Max had purchased another change of clothes and a few basic toilet articles. She debated for a moment, then, with a shrug, added his things to her suitcase.

She found one of the scuffed yellow pumps she'd worn the day before and was down on her hands and knees searching under the bed for the other one when a snatch of Max's conversation registered.

"Look, Sam, I'll keep you informed. Okay?"

Erin jerked up onto her knees and stared at Max over the bed in shocked disbelief.

"Yes, I know you're concerned, but there's nothing you can do. Erin and I will find her. You just hold down the fort."

Erin scrambled to her feet and darted around the bed. She stood in front of Max and gestured wildly, her expression furious. "Max, are you crazy?" she hissed when he paid no attention.

He frowned and held up a hand to shush her. Erin clenched her fists at her sides and snorted in exasperation.

"Dammit, Sam, just who am I supposed to report it to?" he demanded in a sharp voice. "The driver couldn't remember whether Elise got off in Flagstaff or Las Vegas. And even if we knew, what would we tell the local police? We *think* she witnessed a crime, and we *think* she's running for her life? If they did believe us, the first thing they'd do is contact the Santa Fe police, and we sure as hell don't want that. Not until we know who on the force is involved."

"Oh, Lord," Erin groaned, pressing her palm to her forehead, "did you have to tell him everything?"

Ignoring her, Max listened to Sam's reply, then argued, "If we had reported the shooting to the San Francisco police, we would have had to tell them the whole story, and the same thing would have happened. Anyway, what could we tell them? Two guys in a dark blue Camaro tried to shoot us, and we don't know why or who they are? Hell, we'd probably still be at the station answering questions. The important thing now is to locate Elise."

Erin rolled her eyes and gave a long, despairing groan. "I can't believe you're doing this!" she raged in a low, tight voice. "I just can't!"

Her agitation was unmistakable, and Max cast her a puzzled frown while listening to his partner. "Yeah, sure. We'll be careful," he assured him. "And I'll call you when we know something definite." There was another pause, and with a sigh Max said, "Okay, okay. I'll call you tomorrow, regardless. Now I gotta go, Sam."

Erin pounced before he hung up the receiver. "Of all the stupid, crazy, thoughtless things to do! Have you forgotten already that we were nearly killed just a few hours ago?" she demanded furiously.

"No, I haven't forgotten. But what does that have to do with my calling Sam?"

Astonishment widened Erin's eyes, and she stared at him as though he had suddenly turned into a blithering, drooling idiot right before her. "You don't think it's just a bit coincidental that you called your partner last night and told him where we were going, and this morning two men show up outside the bus station and try to kill us?" she asked incredulously.

Understanding dawned on Max's face, and he looked at her in stunned silence. He sighed, and when he spoke both his tone and his expression were mildly reproving. "Erin, you're upset, and you have every right to be, but I know Sam, and I'm telling you, he's not behind this. I would stake my life on it. I swear."

"Fine! You do that!" she shouted, so incensed and frightened that she was shaking. "Just don't stake mine on it!"

Chapter Eight

Remotely, Erin knew the remark was low and uncalled for, but she was far too upset to heed the prickling of her conscience.

Max's head jerked back as though she had struck him, but as she watched, the brief flicker of hurt in his eyes vanished, pushed aside by a quiet, building anger.

He stood up. "I'm going to chalk up that remark to overwrought nerves," he said in a chilling voice. "But just in case you really think I'd play fast and loose with your life, let me remind you, lady, that I've done a damned good job of protecting you so far. As I recall, I saved your butt twice in the past twenty-four hours."

It was the truth, and she knew it, which infuriated her more. "And if you hadn't called your partner last night, this morning's heroics wouldn't have been necessary," she countered.

"That's a matter of opinion."

"Yes. Mine! And if you weren't such a blind fool—"

She stopped, suddenly aware of the shrill pitch of her voice and the growing anger in Max's face. Oh, Lord, what was she doing? Max had done nothing but help her. All through this madness he'd been a rock, the only person she could turn to, and here she was, shrieking at him and hurling useless accusations.

Erin's shoulders slumped. She cupped a hand to her forehead and waved the other one in front of her, palm out. "Oh, Max, I'm so sorry," she groaned. "You're right. I'm upset and worried, but I shouldn't be taking it out on you. Please . . . I'm sorry."

Max stared at her hard. For a moment she was afraid he wasn't going to accept her apology, but at last he relented. His chest heaved as he released a gusty sigh and raked a hand through his hair. "Oh, hell, I'm sorry, too. Look, I know you're under a lot of strain. We both are. But . . . well, I just don't understand why you're so certain that Sam is behind all this."

"Max, we know that it's got to be someone in your company," she said with as much patience as she could muster. "Sam is the obvious one, and after this morning, I don't know how you can doubt it. He's the only person who knew where we were going. At least, where you were going. You didn't mention my name when you talked to him—only you were going to San Francisco because Elise needed your help."

"I don't doubt that those men thought they were shooting at Elise, but that doesn't mean Sam sent them. They could have found out that she got on a bus for San Francisco the same way we did. Besides, I know Sam. There's not a crooked bone in his body, and he hates violence."

Erin's brows rose, and Max shrugged at her skeptical look. "Oh, it's true that under certain circumstances, when someone he cares about is threatened or you push him too

far, he can be lethal. I know I wouldn't want him for an en-
emy. But he's incapable of cold-bloodedly hurting anyone.
Especially someone as soft and gentle as Elise.''

"Sam?" Erin shook her head as though she hadn't heard
him correctly, her expression incredulous. "Are you talking about the same Sam Lawford? The one with the icy gray
eyes and the warmth and charm of a meat locker?"

Max cocked his head to one side, his eyes narrowing.

Erin could have kicked herself. Hadn't she already
learned that Max didn't take kindly to criticism of his
friend? Lord! When would she ever learn to curb her
tongue?

She braced herself for his anger, but when he spoke his
voice was soft and touched with sadness.

"So that's the problem, is it? You're reacting only to what
you see."

"Are you saying there's more?"

Max walked to the window. For a moment he rubbed the
back of his neck and stared out at the evening traffic. When
he turned back to face her his expression was grim. "I have
to believe that there is," he said with a quiet intensity that
bordered on desperation. "That somewhere underneath that
cold shell is the friend I grew up with. That Sam was nothing at all like the man you met. He was friendly and outgoing, warm. In those days everybody liked Sam—parents,
teachers, classmates—and he liked everybody, especially
kids and dogs. He'd even planned to become a pediatrician
someday."

A faraway look came into Max's eye, and as he stared
across the room a sad, wistful smile touched his mouth. Erin
could see that he was lost in memories. She watched him,
touched by his devotion to his friend, and though she fought
to hold on to it, her distrust of Sam began to fade. If the
man could inspire that kind of loyalty, surely he couldn't be
evil or totally unfeeling.

"What happened?" Erin prodded gently when the silence lengthened.

Max pulled out of his trance and flashed her a sharp look. "Vietnam." He spat the word out, his voice cold, bitter. "Rather than waiting around to be drafted, we enlisted together, right out of college, two young heroes full of vinegar and idealism. Of course, Sam could have gotten a deferment had he entered medical school as he'd planned, but we'd always stuck together, so when I decided to enlist, he signed up, too.

"After basic training we got split up, though we were both shipped to Nam. I survived it without a scratch, but five months after he arrived, Sam was taken prisoner by the Vietcong. He spent the next four years as a prisoner of war."

Erin's heart ached for Max. Though his voice remained impassive, she heard the pain beneath the words and knew that he blamed himself. She wanted to go to him and put her arms around him, to hold him close and soothe away all the anguish, to assure him that it wasn't his fault. She forced herself to remain where she was, sensing that nothing she could say would convince him.

"No one knows exactly what happened to him during those years. Sam won't talk about it. But whatever it was, it must have been horrible, because he came back a changed man. The old open, easygoing Sam just seemed to have vanished behind that wall of reserve. He's not hostile or unfriendly, mind you. Just . . . remote."

"Even with you?"

"To a degree. The friendship gets me past some of the barriers, but even so, he lets me get just so close and no closer. It's as though he's drawn an invisible line around himself, and no one is allowed to cross it." He paused. "It's not surprising, I suppose. God knows what horrors he lived through. Then he came home to find that his parents had died and the girl he loved had married someone else."

"Oh, Max. That's awful."

"Yes. It was," he agreed. "Sam took it stoically. It was as though that sort of thing was all he expected of life. I assumed that once he'd had time to grieve and adjust to being back he would go on to medical school as he'd planned, but when I asked him about it he just said that that was yesterday's dream and refused to discuss it further. Instead he took all his back service pay and invested it in the company I had just started. At the time I was in need of capital, but even if I hadn't been, I would have taken him on as a partner. He needed a purpose, something to focus on. He also needed to know that there was someone in his life who would stand by him, no matter what."

The look Max gave Erin was filled with entreaty, a silent plea for understanding. "I don't believe for a moment that Sam would betray my friendship or my trust. Outwardly he may have changed, but not inside. Not where it really counts."

I hope so. Oh, Lord, I hope so, Erin thought. For all our sakes.

She stared at Max, her throat aching with emotion. His explanation had filled her with a melting warmth and added a new dimension to her feelings for him. Max Delany, she was just beginning to realize, was a very nice, very special man.

She had been attracted to him physically since the instant they met; he was, after all, handsome and charming, and he positively oozed sexual magnetism. And in the past twenty-four hours she'd learned that he was also dependable and clever, a good man to have in your corner. But it was his loyalty, his capacity for caring that touched her the most.

Max was secure and comfortable within himself, man enough to give rein to his finer feelings. His sensitivity, compassion and steadfastness, far from making him ap-

pear weak, were traits that enhanced his masculinity and
strength and stirred Erin to the depths of her soul.

She had an uneasy feeling that the discovery would be her
undoing. Physical attraction she could resist. And though
it was nice to have a protector, someone to lean on, Erin was
an independent woman, capable of taking care of herself.
But this glimpse of Max's vulnerable side, of the feeling,
giving inner man, tugged at her heartstrings and drew her to
him in a way that could not be ignored.

As she stared at him, she felt her heart thumping painfully, and lodged beneath her breastbone was a burning knot
of emotion.

If only she could be as sure of Sam's innocence as Max
was. She felt compassion for Sam, and pity when she
thought of all he'd suffered, all he'd lost. She even felt a
certain amount of guilt for the snap judgments she'd made
about him. But absolute faith? No. No, she couldn't quite
manage that. Who knew what shadows those four years had
etched on the man's soul?

But Max trusted him. Max *needed* to trust him, and for
his sake she at least had to give Sam the benefit of the doubt.

"You're probably right," she agreed with a gentle smile.
"Don't pay any attention to my ravings. I'm just frightened and on edge and reacting emotionally. And anyway... you know Sam better than I."

Max grasped her shoulders and gazed down at her.
"Thanks, Erin," he said softly, and she knew that he was
aware of her doubts and understood them.

He tugged her closer. She could have resisted—his gentle
hold gave her that option—but she went into his embrace
willingly, sliding her arms around his lean middle and laying her head against his chest with a soft sigh. At that moment she needed his touch, the warmth of human contact,
to give and receive solace and comfort.

He wrapped his arms around her and held her tight, rubbing his cheek against her head as he rocked from side to side. "Thank you, darling, for understanding."

"You're welcome," Erin murmured. She snuggled against him and gave herself up to the sweet, undemanding pleasure of his embrace. In the haven of his arms she could forget, for a moment, the problems and dangers that awaited them and simply savor the closeness and unspoken feelings that flowed between them. The tension and fear that had kept her wound tight for hours began to drain away as Erin's senses absorbed the essence of Max.

Her palms were pressed flat against his back, and through the thin shirt she could feel the firm, broad muscles that banded his shoulders, the resilience and warmth of his flesh. His body was lean and tough and reassuringly strong. The clean aroma of soap clung to his skin, and mingled with it was his own unique male scent. His cotton shirt had that peculiar new smell and felt scratchy against her cheek as she unconsciously rubbed her face against it. Beneath her ear his heart beat with a slow, heavy thud.

It felt so good, so right, to be held in his arms. He was so deliciously, enticingly male that the urge to taste him was irresistible. Without thought, Erin turned her head and pressed her mouth to his throat. With a soft sound of pleasure, she drew deeply of his scent and touched the tip of her tongue to his skin.

Max inhaled sharply, then moaned. Pulling back, he placed a finger under her chin and lifted it. Desire stamped his features, and his blue eyes were blazing, yet when he spoke his voice was soft and adoring. "In case I neglected to tell you, you're a special lady, Erin Blaine."

He held her gaze. Mesmerized, Erin watched him as he lowered his head, her eyes growing heavy lidded and smoky. Unconsciously she licked her lips, and his breath struck the moist flesh in warm puffs as he whispered, "A very...special...lady."

With excruciating slowness, his mouth settled over hers. Soft. Open. Hot. His lips brushed back and forth, back and forth, the merest touch of flesh upon flesh, but the slight contact sent desire shivering through her.

Max's hand smoothed over her back, his fingertips sensuously rubbing each tiny knob in her spine. His tongue probed the corners of her mouth. With a little moan, Erin pressed closer and slid her arms up over his shoulders, her hands spearing into the thick hair at his collar.

She pulled his lips more firmly against hers, and Max made a rumbling sound of pleasure deep in his throat. Obeying her silent command, he deepened the kiss, his tongue plunging into the wet warmth of her mouth with sure, bold strokes. He drank of her sweetness like a man dying of thirst, his lips rocking over hers. His tongue glided over the roof of her mouth, tested the slickness of her inner cheek, the serrated edge of her teeth, then withdrew... plunged again...withdrew. In. Out. In. Out.

His hands grasped her hips and moved her against him, matching the undulating rhythm.

Erin was a shimmering flame. Her nipples pressed against Max's chest, tight and turgid, aching. Her blood ran hot and searing through her veins to settle and throb in that secret feminine core.

This is crazy and reckless, she thought vaguely. Dangerous. You're playing with fire, you fool. It's time to call a halt.

And I will. I will, she told herself, even as her fingers clutched his broad back and kneaded restlessly. In just a minute.

Oh, Lord, if only she had remained aloof! If only she hadn't let him touch her emotions. The physical attraction between them was strong, but she could have controlled that. But this—this was something more. Much more.

Slowly Max ended the kiss, pulling back just enough to look at her. Erin, still lost in the throes of passion, remained as she was, her head thrown back, lips parted and wet, eyes closed. A flush tinted her skin, and her breathing was labored.

Max smiled and touched her cheek with fingers that weren't quite steady.

"Oh, sweetheart, what you do to me. My heart is pounding like a jackhammer." He pulled one of her hands from around him and placed it on his chest. "Here, feel it."

Erin's lids lifted, and she gazed at him with feverish eyes. "So is mine," she said, giving him a weak smile.

"Good." His look held a blatant satisfaction that made her flush deepen. "We don't have to drive to Bakersfield tonight, you know," he said in a rough voice, glancing beyond her at the rumpled bed. "We could stay here and get an early start in the morning."

Erin stared back at him and swallowed hard. The very air around them crackled with sensual tension, making it difficult to breathe. Implicit in his words, in his blazing eyes was the unspoken promise that if they stayed, they would become lovers.

Erin was tempted. Oh, yes, she was tempted. She would have been lying to herself if she had tried to deny it. Intellectually, physically and emotionally, Max appealed to her on every level, as no other man ever had, not even André. Her heart longed for his love, and her body burned with need, but she knew she dared not satisfy either. Elise was in love with this man, and no matter what her own feelings were, she could not ignore that.

With great effort, Erin pulled out of his arms and took a step backward. Her body still throbbed with desire, and she knew that Max felt the same aching need. She gazed at him regretfully, her wan smile touched with sadness as she shook her head. "No, Max, we can't."

She didn't elaborate, but the look of grim acceptance that settled over his face told her that he knew her reason. Yes, she thought, feeling a painful little stab in her chest. Max would understand loyalty.

"No, I suppose you're right. We'd better be on our way if we're going to pick up Elise's trail before it gets cold."

"Yes. Yes, we'd better," Erin agreed. It wasn't precisely the reason for her refusal, and they both knew it, but she grabbed at the tactfully offered alternative. Whether he had given her the out because he knew that she wasn't ready to cope with the feelings growing between them, or because he feared what her reaction would be if he pushed too hard, she didn't know, but she was grateful for his sensitivity.

"Well, uh..." A bit self-consciously, Max looked around. "If you're all set, I guess we'd better get going."

Just as awkwardly, Erin gestured toward the telephone. "Uh, if you don't mind, first I'd like to call my brother. He'll know what to do, and if he's home, he can probably meet us in Las Vegas."

"Sure. Go ahead." Spotting her yellow pumps, Max scooped them up, dumped them into her suitcase and snapped it shut. He picked up the case and headed for the door. "While you do that I'll go check us out and pick up the keys to the rental car. Why don't you meet me in the lobby in...say—" he raised his left arm and checked his watch "—ten minutes. Okay?"

"Okay."

For timeless seconds after he had gone Erin remained where she was, staring at the closed door. Her chest was tight, and the urge to cry was almost overwhelming. Tears gathered, but she blinked them back furiously.

You little fool! she groaned inwardly. You can't let yourself fall in love with Max. You can't!

* * *

Erin sat sideways, her legs bent and resting on the seat, her back against the car door. Absently, she tugged at her shirt, tucking it more securely around her knees, and glanced over her left shoulder.

"You're going to have a crick in your neck if you don't stop that."

Her head swiveled back, and she aimed a puzzled frown at Max's profile. "What?"

"Looking out the back window every thirty seconds." He glanced at her, his expression wry and mildly chastising. "You've been doing it for the past four hours, ever since we left San Francisco. Don't you think that if those guys were following us you would have spotted them by now?"

Erin grimaced and shifted on the seat. "I can't help it." Her tone was defensive and slightly injured, and as though to prove her claim her eyes darted to the rear window again. "Just knowing that they're out there somewhere, looking for us, gives me the willies. Besides, they could be hanging back, waiting for the right moment."

"I doubt it. If they were back there, they'd have made their move before now. They've had plenty of chances in the past four hours."

"You can't be sure of that," she argued.

The edge to her voice drew Max's gaze again, and his hands tightened around the steering wheel. Even in the weak light from the dash he could see the lines of strain in her face and the stark look in her eyes. And despite her casual posture, he knew that her body was as taut as a wound spring.

He reached over and patted her knee and gave her a reassuring smile. "Relax. There's no point in borrowing trouble."

"I'm sorry. I don't mean to." Erin straightened her legs and shifted to sit facing the front. She stared out the windshield at the arid, moonlit landscape and willed herself to relax, but the prickly feeling down the back of her neck and between her shoulder blades wouldn't go away. Looking down at her lap, she saw that she was unconsciously twisting her fingers together.

Snorting in disgust, she jerked her hands apart and raked one through her hair. "If only I had been able to reach David, I'd feel better about this whole thing," she blurted out.

Assuming a supercilious expression, she mimicked in a nasty singsong, "I'm sorry, I can't come to the phone right now, but if you'll leave your name and number, I'll get back to you as soon as I can." She snorted again. "I swear, if I hear my dear brother's voice giving that canned spiel one more time, I'll scream. Or better yet, I'll leave an obscene message on his damned answering machine."

Max laughed. "That ought to get his attention, although I think it's against the law."

Erin turned her head and shot him a sour look. "Somehow, at the moment that fails to scare me."

She sighed and drummed her fingers on the armrest. "Darn David. Where could he be?"

"Don't worry. He'll show up. And in the meantime we'll keep looking and calling," Max assured her. "Now why don't you do me a favor and check if there are any of those sandwiches left. I'm hungry."

"What, again? You've already eaten four."

Max flashed her a grin. "I've gotta keep my strength up if I'm going to go tearing around the country with a wild redhead," he teased. "Besides, I'm just a growing boy."

"Heaven forbid," Erin remarked dryly, eyeing his large, lean frame.

She half suspected that Max was simply trying to lighten the mood and take her mind off the situation. Nevertheless, grateful for something to do, she rummaged through the sack of sandwiches the hotel had provided. "You're in luck. There are two left. And—" she felt along the floorboard for the soft drinks they had picked up at a convenience store "—one lukewarm cola."

"Great. Divvy it up."

Erin unwrapped a sandwich and handed it to him. After taking a bite of her own she popped the tab off the canned drink and sipped. "Yeecch! That's awful." Shuddering, she shoved the cola into Max's hand.

"Yeah, but it's wet," he said with a chuckle, and chugalugged half of it, washing down the sandwich he had demolished in four bites. Without a word, Erin divided her sandwich in two and handed him half.

For several minutes they rode in easy silence, eating their meager meal and passing the can back and forth between them.

"Unless you want me to fall asleep at the wheel, you'd better talk to me," Max said finally. "That little rest back at the hotel perked me up for a while, but the way I feel now I could use another ten or twelve hours of sleep."

Erin glanced at him, then looked out the side window, smiling into the darkness. Another sidetracking ploy, she thought, feeling a rush of warmth in her chest. Subtle, thoughtful, caring. Of course, it was unnecessary, she told herself. She was a bit on edge, true, but she could cope. Still . . . it was nice.

"Okay. What do you want to talk about?" she asked, playing along.

"Tell me about your work. Elise said that until recently you were working in the Middle East."

"Yes, for a construction firm. They were building a power plant, and I acted as translator between the site manager and the local officials."

"How many languages do you speak?"

"I'm fluent in five—six, if you count English—and conversant in three more."

Max produced a low whistle between his teeth. "Amazing. With that kind of ability, you must have worked in a lot of different countries."

"Yes, I have. Before the Middle East job I spent six months with the U.S. embassy in West Germany, and before that I did some industrial translation in Japan." Erin turned sideways on the seat again and looped her left arm around the headrest. "Currently I'm translating a very hot French novel into English. It's the kind of job I can do anywhere, which is what I take when I want to spend some time stateside."

"Sounds like an interesting way to earn a living." Max glanced at Erin and smiled when he saw her lean her head on the seat back and snuggle her cheek against the soft velour upholstery.

"Mmm, yes, it is." She blinked drowsily, and Max's smile grew at the way her words slurred together. "Very interesting. But the best part is, I get to see the world," she managed over a stifled yawn.

He asked a few more questions. Erin's answers came more and more slowly, until finally her voice trailed away and she drifted off to sleep. Max glanced at her, his face full of tenderness and satisfaction. Very carefully, he reached across the seat, pulled the empty can from her loose grasp and dumped it into the sack.

As Max returned his attention to the highway his expression grew serious. The only sounds were the incessant drone of the engine and the hum of the tires on the pavement. The desert spread out in all directions, silvery in the moonlight, the sparse clumps of vegetation dark shadows against the luminous landscape. In front and behind the car the highway lay like a long narrow blue ribbon floating on the shimmering sand.

Traffic was light and spread out. Ahead in the distance Max could see three sets of glowing red taillights, and the rearview mirror revealed another half dozen vehicles strung out over several miles, moving silently through the night. The scene was peaceful and serene, nonthreatening, yet despite his assurances to Erin, Max kept a close watch on the cars in the mirror and tensed every time one overtook them, not relaxing his death grip on the wheel until it had passed.

Erin was still asleep when they reached Bakersfield. Max was bone-weary himself by that time and stopped at the first decent-looking motel he saw. When he had registered and driven around to the room he shook Erin awake and led her inside.

The room was typical of ten thousand others in chain motels across the country, the determinedly cheerful decor garish, impersonal and showing signs of wear.

Max placed Erin's suitcase on the luggage rack and turned to find her dubiously eyeing the two double beds. Though startling, he knew the bright yellow and turquoise bedspreads were not the cause of the intense scrutiny.

"If you want to use the bathroom first, it's right through there," he said, hiding a grin.

"Uh...no. You go ahead." Sitting down on the edge of one of the beds, she reached for the telephone. "I'm going to call David again."

"Okay. I won't be long."

When Max returned a few minutes later Erin was still sitting on the bed, only now she was frowning and nibbling on the tip of her index finger. It was not, he had learned in the short time he'd known her, a good sign.

"Still no luck, I take it."

Erin glanced up and made a face. "No. I got the stupid answering machine again. I'll try again in the morning before we leave."

Yawning his agreement, Max sat down on the bed opposite her and flopped backward, stretching his arms up over his head.

Erin shot to her feet. ''Well, uh . . . I guess we'd better get some sleep if we're going to get an early start.''

Through slitted eyes, Max watched with interest as she pawed through the suitcase and extracted a cosmetic bag and an intriguingly sheer nightgown.

When the bathroom door clicked shut behind her he rose wearily and stripped down to his shorts. He hooked his thumbs under the elastic waistband to remove them, too, then stopped, debating a moment. Oh, what the hell. He'd be up and dressed before she woke up anyway, he told himself, and peeled off the red bikini briefs, tossing them on top of the jeans and shirt in the chair. Besides, he'd never been able to sleep wearing clothes.

He turned out the lights and slipped into the bed, pulling the sheet up to his armpits. Sighing as his body went lax, he stared up at the darkened ceiling and listened to the small sounds coming from the bathroom.

Fate, he decided wryly, certainly took odd twists and turns. Just a few days ago he'd been wrapped up in his business, dashing around Europe making contacts and setting up deals. A bit restless, perhaps, beneath the frantic activity, but he'd been fairly content with his life.

Until Erin.

With amusement he knew that, just three days ago, if anyone had told him that he'd be jackrabbiting around the country with a ravishing redhead, dodging bullets and playing detective, he'd have called the person crazy. And yet, here he was. And if it weren't for the danger to Erin, there was no place he'd rather be.

Well...on second thought, he amended with a grin, there was that little isolated beach on Antigua. He could picture Erin, lying on the white sand in a tiny bikini...him rubbing oil over her creamy skin...unfastening the top...touching her breasts....

"Oh, Lord." Max groaned and squeezed his eyes shut as the image created a stirring warmth in his loins.

At that moment the bathroom door squeaked. Turning his head at the sound, he opened his eyes, and his breath caught. For an instant before she doused the light Erin stood in the doorway, clad in the short, diaphanous gown, her lovely body silhouetted against the brightly lit room at her back.

Max gritted his teeth to stifle another groan. He lay rigid, his fists clenched at his side, his breathing shallow and painful, and listened to her pad across the worn shag carpet. He caught a tantalizing whiff of scented talc as she passed by and slipped into the other bed.

"Good night, Max." Her voice floated to him in the darkness, soft and warm, a little breathless.

His body throbbed, and his heart pounded. Several seconds ticked by before he gained enough control to answer, and even then all he managed was a hoarse whisper. "Good night, Erin."

He heard what he thought was a sigh, and then her bed creaked and the sheets rustled.

God in heaven, his erotic imaginings had been bad enough, he thought desperately. But knowing she was sleeping in that wispy little nothing, not three feet away, was sheer torture. He might as well have left his shorts on; he sure as hell didn't have a chance of getting any sleep.

Chapter Nine

Barefoot, wearing only a pair of low-slung jeans, Max strolled from the bathroom, vigorously toweling his wet hair. When he caught sight of Erin he came to an abrupt halt. He stood perfectly still with his arms still upraised, and stared, his arrested expression filled with awe and longing.

With the total abandon of a child, she lay sprawled on the bed on her stomach. Her arms were flung wide, as though she had collapsed face forward, and her body was as limp and yielding as a cooked noodle. Her fiery curls were a wild tangle, her face slack and rosy with sleep. Sometime while he'd been showering Erin had kicked the light covers off, and they now lay in a wad across her feet. Her lilac shorty nightgown was bunched up around her shoulder blades, exposing a tempting expanse of creamy skin and the elegant curve of her spine above the sheer bikini panties that cupped her bottom. The gown was askew, one thin strap dropping over her shoulder. Below, the gaping armhole allowed a tantalizing view of the outer curve of her breast.

Max began to pull his gaze away from the tempting sight, but as it drifted downward over the impossibly long legs he released a shuddering sigh.

Good manners demanded that he look away. Plain common sense urged him to at least cover her up, for the sake of his sanity as much as her modesty. Max, to his chagrin, discovered that where Erin was concerned, he possessed neither manners nor the slightest wit of sense.

Slowly his arms lowered, and the damp towel dropped to the floor with a soft plop. Like a man in a trance, his gaze fixed on her supine form, he moved steadily, silently across the flattened shag carpet and sat down on the bed beside Erin.

Up close her skin had the soft luster of silk. As he gazed down at the graceful symmetry of her bare back, it occurred to him that he had never before fully appreciated the erotic appeal of that particular portion of the female anatomy.

Leisurely, his eyes tracked over the narrow back, with its fragile shoulder blades thrusting up beneath the soft flesh, the long, graceful inward curve of the delicate rib cage that led the eye to that tiny waist and, below it, the delicious flare of womanly hips and tight buttocks.

Unable to help himself, Max reached out with an unsteady hand and trailed his forefinger along the shallow trench that marked her spine, from a point almost at her shoulders, down below her waist to the top of the bikini pajama bottoms.

Erin made a small incoherent sound and wriggled sinuously.

The innocent movement sent a hot surge of desire through Max, and he caught his breath. He closed his eyes. When he opened them again his lips tilted in a reckless smile.

Cupping his hands over her hips, with his thumbs he drew light circles around the enticing indentations on either side of her spine, just above the lilac panties.

"Erin," he murmured in a voice husky with masculine desire and just a hint of amusement.

When she didn't respond, his thumbs probed the little hollows. He braced his forearms on either side of her and leaned forward to string a line of slow, wet kisses up her spine. She smelled delicious, a mixture of floral talc and sweet, clean woman, and when he reached her nape he buried his face in the curve of her neck and inhaled deeply. Playfully, he traced an intricate pattern with his tongue, then blew on her wet flesh.

Erin stirred.

He smiled and mouthed the velvety rim of her ear. "Erin, sweetheart, do you have any idea what the sight of you lying here in this little bit of nothing is doing to me?" he murmured as, with a slow, flexing movement, he rubbed his chest across her bare back. "It's nothing short of torture."

Sensations. Erin became aware of them gradually—so gradually, at first, that she thought she was dreaming. A feathery touch...warmth...whispers. Pleasure. Sweet, delicious pleasure.

Against the sheet her nipples puckered into tight aching nubs. A hot, insistent throbbing started deep within her.

The veils of sleep lifted one by one, and the sensations grew sharper.

"Erin."

She heard Max call her name, his voice soft and sensuous, and she smiled into the pillow. Dream and reality overlapped, merged. For a blissful moment Erin lingered there, wavering languorously between the two.

"Good morning, sweetheart."

"Mmm. Mornin'," she mumbled.

Erin frowned and blinked—once, twice—and slowly the world slid into focus. "Max?"

A throaty chuckle sounded in her ear. "Yes. Who were you expecting?" he answered, playfully batting her earlobe with his tongue.

Erin's eyes widened as she came fully awake and her senses sprang to attention. In a rush, she became aware of his scent and heat surrounding her, and the feathery brush of his chest hair against her bare back. Her heart pounded, and for an instant she didn't move, torn between pleasure and panic.

"Max. Oh, Max, that's not fair..." she complained when he began to nibble her shoulder. But her voice was husky and weak and trembled breathlessly.

"You want to talk fair?" he murmured against her skin. "It's not fair for you to lie here in that little scrap of a nightgown—" he nuzzled her neck, his breath skating warm and moist over her flesh "—looking like a gorgeous, rumpled siren. It's not fair—" the tip of his tongue trailed down her spine to the small of her back, and Erin moaned and shivered "—that you smell so heavenly, or—" with gently savagery, he nipped the side of her waist, then soothed the tiny pain with a soft kiss "—that your skin feels like silk."

"Max...Max..." His name was a breathy sigh on her lips.

Gently but firmly, he turned her onto her back. He gazed down at her, his face flushed and rigid with desire, his eyes glittering. When he spoke his voice was a low rasp that caressed her skin like warm velvet, making her nerve endings twang and tingle, her pulses pound. "Nor is it fair to deny what you feel. What we both feel."

Her brief nightgown was twisted and bunched up under her arms, the ecru lace ruffle at the bottom draped wantonly across her breasts, exposing their full lower curves. Through the fragile material her nipples showed an enticing rosy pink.

Max's eyes lowered, and she felt her breasts swell and tighten under his avid gaze. His eyes sought hers once again with searing hunger, and he cupped his palm around the soft flesh.

"Can you tell me you don't like it when I touch you?" His fingers flexed, and he rotated his palm slowly against the engorged bud. Erin gasped and jerked as she felt her body quicken.

Bracing on one arm, Max leaned forward, his gaze fixed on her mouth. "Don't you feel the fire? It's raging." His parted lips brushed over hers and moved from side to side in an excruciating gossamer touch. Erin felt its sensual impact all the way to her toes. "I burn."

It was a raspy, drawn-out whisper, spoken into her mouth. Evocative. Hot. Heavy with need.

Erin reacted to it as to a physical touch. The words, his exquisitely sensual tone, the passion blazing in his slumberous gaze, all fanned the smoldering fires within her. They flared into a raging inferno that made her body throb and burn with a consuming desire that matched his.

Longing was a wild, sharp pain in her chest. It pulled at her relentlessly. She gazed at Max, feeling a need greater than anything she had ever known. He was a beautiful man, handsome and utterly male, but it was more than physical attraction, and her heart knew it. Mind, body and soul—everything in her called out to him. Everything that was Max appealed to her as no man ever had—and, she was very much afraid, as no other man ever would.

Erin knew that she should call a halt, say something, *do* something to break the sensual spell before things got out of hand, but she couldn't. She just couldn't.

Think of Elise, she commanded herself. Her feelings for this man. You know you can't let this happen.

But even as her conscience nagged her, Erin's hands were sliding up Max's arms. Against her palms she felt the tickle of crisp hairs, then the smooth, warm hardness of bulging biceps and broad shoulders.

Max continued his tender, tormenting assault on her mouth. From beneath half-closed lids, they watched each other in silence, their eyes darkened and glazed with passion. Then her hands met behind his neck, and she buried her fingers in his hair. With a sigh, she pulled him closer, and her eyes drifted shut as his mouth settled firmly over hers.

It was a powerful kiss, filled with need and hard demand. They sought assuagement, but the yearning ache grew stronger, bigger. Hunger fed hunger as mouths rocked together and nimble tongues danced and stroked and caressed.

With a groan, Max stretched out on the bed, one leg hooking over hers, his broad chest pressing against her breasts, pushing her deep into the mattress. Erin clutched him, her mindless cry swallowed by his devouring mouth as she felt their bare flesh meet and meld.

He was so warm, his weight a delicious burden. Her restless hands played over his back, flexing against the broad muscles, probing his spine, her fingers slipping beneath the low waistband to press into his firm buttocks. Their legs tangled together, and against her bareness the abrasive rub of his new denim jeans was both frustrating and oddly erotic.

"Oh, Lord, Erin. I want you so." Max kissed her neck, her collarbone, then nuzzled aside the thin strap and gave the same attention to her shoulder. "We belong together. Can't you feel it?"

Still holding her close, he rolled onto his side. He gazed into her eyes, his own smoldering, and slid his hand up over the long curve of her hip, waist and midriff, finally cupping his palm around the firm fullness of her breast. "I want to love you. Right here. Right now." He brushed his thumb

across her nipple and kissed her again, hard. "It's what you
want, too, isn't it?"

Erin stared at him, dazed, achingly aware of his arousal
pressed against her belly, the hollow throbbing in her lower
body...and most of all, the yearning ache in her heart.

"Isn't it?" he urged in a rough whisper.

Erin felt her puny resistance melting, felt herself being
drawn into the deep blue pools of his eyes, felt herself giving in to the wildness and want that raged in them both.

Watching her, Max sensed her weakening, and his eyes
flared with triumph, but as he bent his head to kiss her again
the travel clock on the bedside table started a strident beeping.

Erin stiffened within his embrace.

"Dammit!"

Max muttered the curse in a vicious undertone as he
watched the glaze of passion clear from her eyes, and guilt
and regret take its place. Nevertheless, when she pulled from
his arms he let her go and flopped over onto his back, his
face hard and set with bitter frustration.

Erin sat up on the side of the bed, hastily adjusting her
nightgown as she picked up the clock and switched off the
alarm. She folded it shut and turned the tiny case over and
over in her hands, staring at it, her head bent. The skin between her shoulder blades prickled, and she knew Max was
watching her, waiting.

"It's getting—" Her voice broke, and she stopped to clear
her throat. "It's...getting late. We'd better be on our way."

She waited for a reply, keeping her back to Max and her
gaze fixed on her hands. Silence filled the room, thick and
heavy with emotions and words left unsaid. Erin's nerves
vibrated and hummed. Unable to bear it a moment longer,
she jerked to her feet and started for the bathroom.

Halfway there she came to a halt. She hesitated, standing
rigid, her mouth a straight line. Finally, with her back still

to Max, she said in a soft, sad voice, "I'm sorry, Max. But it...it can't be. Not for us. I...I'm sorry."

Not waiting for a reply, she hurried on toward the bathroom, but Max sprang off the bed and was there before her, stretching a taut, muscled arm across the doorway, barring her way. Erin started and jumped back a step, but he caught her with his other hand and hauled her close. Vitally aware of his bare chest just inches from her nose, she stared at the mat of silky hair covering it, her senses assaulted by his clean male scent, his heat. He leaned close, his face hard and determined, eyes glittering.

"I won't accept that," he growled. "We have something special going for us, and I think you know it. Erin, I like and admire your sister, but I'll be damned if I'll let this chance for happiness slip away just because she's developed some kind of schoolgirl crush."

She looked at him pleadingly, her face full of anguish. "Max, please listen to—"

"No, you listen. We *are* going to be together, Erin. Now I don't know whether this idea you have that Elise is in love with me is actual fact or just something you've read into her letters. And, frankly, at the moment I don't give a damn. But this much you can count on: no way in hell am I giving you up."

His words sent a rush of joy and hope through her, but despair quickly followed. She looked at him sadly and shook her head. "Oh, Max."

His face hardened more at her forlorn exclamation. "I mean it, Erin. I'll back off—for now—but I'm not going to let you shut me out."

He shoved himself away from the door and stomped over to the open suitcase. "Now I suggest you do whatever you need to, and let's get out of here." He snatched up a clean shirt and shrugged into it, his movements stiff and jerky.

She hesitated, staring after him, her chest a painful knot of turmoil. She felt that she should say something more, something to ease the tension and make him understand, but the rigid set of his shoulders discouraged further discussion. Swallowing against the ache in her throat, she stepped into the bathroom and closed the door.

Twenty minutes later Erin emerged to find Max dressed and pacing the floor, raring to go. The emotional intensity had lessened, but there was still constraint between them. They treated each other with wary politeness, saying little, keeping their voices and words neutral.

"All set?" Max asked when Erin had returned her belongings to the suitcase and snapped it shut.

"Just give me a minute to call David, and I will be."

"Sure. I'll meet you in the car."

To her disgust, the call produced no better results than the previous ones, and after leaving a terse message and a caustic, sisterly comment about people who forced you to talk to a machine, then didn't have the common decency to check it, she slammed the receiver down and stalked out.

By sunrise they were twenty miles out of Bakersfield, heading toward Barstow. Erin sipped her coffee and made half-moons in the Styrofoam cup with her fingernail, watching the sky fade from black to gray, then deepen into dusky blue as a warm glow lit the eastern horizon. The colors changed quickly, bleeding one into the other, each growing darker, more intense. Pale yellow became pink, then rose, and finally a molten orange-red. Against the brilliant display, the arid mountains stood out in sharp relief, their rims lined with silvery gold, their slopes abstracts of amber-bathed ridges and deep purple shadows. A moment later Erin caught her breath as shafts of sunlight shot out over a low peak and beamed across the valley floor like giant spotlights, the golden rays hazy and luminous with dust and rising mist.

She glanced at Max to see if he had noticed, but he was staring at the empty highway ahead. With a shrug, she reached into the sack on the seat between them and extracted a sweet roll. Neither had wanted to stop for breakfast. Instead, they had picked up the rolls and a thermos of coffee at an all-night convenience store before leaving Bakersfield. Erin took a bite and chewed thoughtfully.

She felt...strange, a churning mass of raw nerves and emotion. Fear and worry were all mixed up with longing and desire and that sweet, tight ache of euphoria that comes with falling in love.

And guilt. Oh, yes, there was guilt. She hadn't expected this sharp, urgent attraction. Didn't want it. Lord, things were enough of a muddle without her falling for Max.

But want it or not, there it was. Feelings, she was discovering, paid no heed to common sense or whispers of conscience.

Covertly, Erin studied Max out of the corner of her eye. His face was somber and set, a tiny frown creasing his brows, and, unhappily, she assumed he was still chewing over their argument. A second later he proved her wrong.

"Drugs."

Erin jumped at the unexpected pronouncement. "What?"

"Drugs. I'll bet that's it."

"What are you talking about?"

"I've been trying to figure out what we're dealing with. I think we can safely assume that someone is using my company for some kind of illegal activity. Smuggling, probably, since we import goods from all over the world."

"And...and you think it's drugs?"

"Yeah. That would be my guess."

"Why?"

"Because these people are obviously into something very lucrative and very risky." Max shot Erin an assessing look. "Something big enough and dirty enough that they're willing to commit murder to keep from getting caught."

Dear Lord, was that what Elise had stumbled upon? Drug-runners? Corrupt, amoral people who would do anything for money? Fear coiled in the pit of Erin's stomach. With sickening sharpness, she felt again the shock and horror of that moment when they had shot at her, the mindless, gut-wrenching terror.

She shuddered and dropped the half-eaten sweet roll back into the sack, her appetite deserting her.

"I...I suppose you're right," Erin said weakly. "It makes sense."

"God knows the opportunity is there. And the cover. What I can't figure out, though, is if it is drugs, how do they get by customs inspections undetected?"

"It must be sealed inside something. Maybe..." Erin waved her hand vaguely. "Maybe in a hollow chair leg. Or in a false bottom on a vase or pitcher. You import those kinds of things, don't you?"

"Yeah, but they have dogs that can sniff out drugs even in a sealed crate. Also, everything is x-rayed during customs inspection."

"Then maybe you're wrong," Erin said hopefully. "Maybe we're misreading this whole thing."

Max gave her a pitying look. "Erin. Your sister witnessed a crime serious enough to send her running for her life. And remember, these are people who cut brake lines and shoot at you in broad daylight."

Erin's heart gave a little leap at the blunt reminder of how close she had come to being killed. She flashed him an annoyed look, but after a moment her shoulders slumped. "I know, I know. I guess I was just hoping it would be something not quite so...so...vile."

"Crimes usually are, sweetheart," Max said softly.

Erin sighed and took a long swallow of the coffee, hoping its warmth would settle her nerves. Mulling over his theory, she stared pensively out the window, oblivious now to the beauty of the morning.

They rode in silence for several miles until a horrifying thought occurred to her, and she turned to Max. "If it is drug smuggling, those men could be connected with organized crime!"

"It's possible, but I doubt it."

"Why?"

"Because it doesn't fit. Their usual method when they want to make use of a company is to take control of it and put one of their own people in charge."

A picture of Sam Lawford's emotionless face flashed into Erin's mind, but she guiltily pushed the image away. "I see. Well, I hope you're right."

It was a comfort. A small one, to be sure; nevertheless, it made her feel a bit better to think they weren't up against an entire army of men like those two in San Francisco.

After finishing her coffee she tossed the empty cup into the trash sack and turned sideways on the seat. "If these people are using your company to smuggle goods, then they probably work there."

"Yeah. That's occurred to me." A muscle clenched in Max's jaw, and his voice grated with bitter anger.

"Did you get a look at those men who shot at us?"

"Just the one closest to me. The driver." He glanced at her with a hard, crooked smile. "At the time I was too busy hotfooting it out of there to study him in detail."

"What did he look like?"

"Early to mid-thirties, medium brown hair, clean-cut looking. But I didn't recognize him. As for the other one, I caught a glimpse of pale hair, but I didn't see his face. He did seem older, though, and . . . I don't know . . . I got the impression that he was a big man.''

The description nudged a memory, and when it clicked, Erin's eyes widened. "Max, when I arrived at Global Tuesday, there was a man on the loading dock. He stared at me strangely. He was big and burly and had white-blond hair."

"That would be Floyd Shulman, our warehouse foreman." Max frowned, his expression thoughtful. "He logs all incoming and outgoing shipments, which means he's in the perfect position to intercept contraband."

"What do you know about him?"

"Not much. Sam hired him about two years ago."

"Sam?"

Max shot her an exasperated look. "Now don't start that. Sam does most of the hiring. He doesn't like to travel that much, so mostly I make the contacts and do the buying, while he takes care of the domestic end of the business."

It seemed to Erin that the arrangement provided Sam with plenty of opportunity to set up a smuggling operation, but she refrained from pointing that out to Max. It would very likely anger him, and he wouldn't believe it anyway.

"I see. Did, uh . . . did Sam know him before?"

"No, I don't think so. Though, as I recall, Shulman did come highly recommended. Of course, that doesn't necessarily mean that he's not up to his armpits in whatever's going on. Good men have been corrupted by money before. I think it'd be a good idea if I call Sam when we get to Las Vegas and have him check on Floyd. I'd be interested to know if he was at work yesterday."

Erin thought it was a rotten idea, but she held her tongue. While Floyd Shulman seemed a likely suspect, it was inconceivable to her that the shop foreman was the brains behind the whole thing. It had to be someone higher up in the company. Someone with inside knowledge who would know

well in advance what was being shipped from where. Someone in a position like Sam's.

Tactfully, Erin tried to get Max to come to the same con-
clusion. All the way to Barstow, where they stopped to top
off the gas tank and refill the thermos before continuing
across the desert, she asked leading questions and dropped
hints, but her efforts were futile. She didn't know if Max
was being deliberately obtuse or if he simply had a blind
spot where Sam was concerned.

Even so, she did not stop trying. The minute they were on
the road again she returned to the subject.

"Max, there has to be someone in the office. The warehouse foreman can't be the only one. Now think. Who with
access to the firm's records has the brains and the organi-
zational talent, plus the gall, to set up something like this?"

For the next fifty miles, to her utter disgust, Max ticked
off the names of people on the office staff, told her what he
knew of each one's character and speculated at length on the
likelihood of each employee's being behind the scheme. Not
once did he mention Sam Lawford.

When done, he looked at her and shrugged. "I don't
know. There are a few I wouldn't want marrying my sister,
but as far as drug running, I can't imagine...."

He stopped abruptly, his eyes narrowing on the rearview
mirror. "Erin." He said her name in a soft warning tone
that sent a shiver down her spine and made her instantly
alert.

"What? What is it?"

"Sweetheart, I don't want to alarm you, but I think we
have company."

Erin twisted around. "Where? I don't see anyone." The
road was empty both ahead of and behind them. Few people drove the desert during the day, they had learned from
the gas station attendant in Barstow, and for miles it had
seemed as though they were the only ones in the world.

"They dropped out of sight, but keep your eye on the road where it curves by that big butte. They should be coming around it any time."

She kept her gaze riveted to the spot. Her heart pounded, and her palms grew clammy. She barely managed to breathe. Silently, she began to count off the seconds. At eleven a dark blue Camaro came around the bend.

"Oh, dear God." Her eyes sought Max, wide and filled with fear. "How did they find us? They weren't following us last night!"

"I didn't think so."

Her frantic gaze went back to the car. It was about a half mile behind them, moving at the same steady pace. There were two people in the front seat, but the distance was too great for her to tell if they were men. Unconsciously, Erin dug her fingernails into the velour upholstery. "Maybe it's not them. There are probably thousands of blue Camaros on the road."

Max's gaze darted to the mirror again. "Well, there's one way to find out." He gripped the wheel tighter and pushed down on the gas pedal.

The speedometer needle eased up to seventy. Seventy-five. Eighty. The blue car grew smaller, the distance between them stretching out. Just when it began to look as though they would leave it behind, the other driver sped up.

"Here they come," Erin warned.

Grimly, Max tried to coax more speed out of the rented car, but even with the pedal on the floor the Camaro was still gaining on them. Max cursed viciously and struck the steering wheel with his balled fist. "Go, you piece of junk! Dammit, go!"

Sweet heaven, am I going to die in this godforsaken place? Erin wondered, fighting a surge of suffocating panic as her gaze swept over the parched landscape.

There were no houses, no signs of life anywhere, just the empty highway before them and the endless, awesome desert. It stretched out in every direction as far as the eye could see, barren and bleak, unforgiving, veined with dry arroyos and dotted here and there with sparse vegetation that grew bent and hunched over in a futile effort to escape the merciless sun.

They could kill us and dump our bodies in one of those gullies, and no one would ever find us, Erin realized.

She shivered and jerked her gaze away from the desolate landscape. Frantic, she looked back at the trailing car, then turned to the front. Ahead, the highway danced drunkenly in the shimmering heat waves rising from the desert floor. It was empty to the horizon.

With only an occasional butte or flat-topped mesa rising up to break the feeling of limitless space, they were dwarfed by the vastness of their surroundings and seemed barely to be creeping across the great expanse of sun-bleached land.

"Can't we go any faster?" Erin cried. With unconscious body movements she urged the vehicle along, every muscle straining.

"It's wide open now," Max snapped grimly. "I'm just praying the engine doesn't blow in this heat."

"Oh, God." Erin clamped her hand over her mouth, but she could not contain the whimper that bubbled up in her throat.

Her skin was cold, yet even so, perspiration collected in tiny rivulets on her scalp and trickled through her hair. Her bright curls clung wetly to her neck and white face. Eyes wide, she stared at Max, trying desperately to think.

"That's odd." Max frowned at the rearview mirror. "They've slowed down."

Erin's head whipped around, and she stared at the blue car, her mouth hanging open. Her puzzled gaze met Max's. "Do you think they're having car trouble?"

He looked in the mirror again and shook his head. "No. No, they're maintaining a steady distance. Somehow, I've got a hunch...."

"What are you doing?" Erin cried when he let up on the accelerator.

"Testing."

Max kept watch on the rearview mirror. Their speed dropped steadily. Terrified, Erin looked behind them, and her eyes widened when she saw that the blue car was slowing also.

At sixty Max leveled off. So did the other car. He held that speed for a couple of miles, then eased up to seventy-five.

His mouth thinned. "That's what I thought. They don't want to catch us, just keep us in sight."

"But...why? Yesterday they tried to kill me on a busy San Francisco street, and now they have the perfect chance and they're backing off. It doesn't make any sense."

"Unless they now know that you're not Elise. Which means that someone had to have told them."

Max turned his head and looked at her. His face was expressionless, but the grief and utter despair in his eyes wrung Erin's heart. "And besides the two of us, Sam is the only other person who knows."

Chapter Ten

His lips lifted in a travesty of a smile. "It seems you were right all along."

"Oh, Max. I'm so sorry." Erin reached over and touched his arm, her eyes soft with compassion.

"Yeah. So am I."

She gazed at his grim profile, her heart aching for him. She would have given anything to spare him this pain and disillusionment. Oh, Lord, if only she had been wrong.

Erin longed to say more, to comfort him somehow, but Max's expression told her he did not want to discuss Sam's betrayal. And anyway, now was not the time.

She looked back at the blue car. It tracked them as though they were connected by an invisible cord.

"What are we going to do?" she asked hesitantly.

"There's not much we can do until we reach Las Vegas. We can't outrun them, and there sure as hell isn't anywhere to hide. You can see forever in this stinking place."

For the next hour they said little. Erin kept an anxious eye on their pursuers while Max drove in brooding silence. Like ants moving in tandem, the two cars crept across the broiling desert. The only sounds were the whine of the engine, the hum of tires and the rush of wind around the car as it sliced through the scorching stillness.

It was eerie and nerve-racking. Between the heat, the quiet and the ever-present threat of danger, Erin was strung so tautly that she felt as though she would snap and fly apart at any moment. No matter at what speed Max drove, the blue Camaro religiously kept a half-mile distance between them, and after a while she thought she would surely go mad if something didn't happen to break the monotony and suspense.

When the pattern altered a short while later, as they approached the edge of Las Vegas, Erin found it no more to her liking than the game of follow-the-leader across the desert.

"Here they come," Max announced. "I figured they'd close the gap about now."

Checking behind them, Erin saw that the other car was moving up fast. She looked at Max. "But why? Why now?"

"Don't worry. They're not going to overtake us. They just can't take the chance of losing us in the city. They're hoping we'll lead them to Elise. The poor dumb bastards probably think that because they've kept their distance we're not wise to them."

"What are we going to do?"

"Lose 'em."

As the words came out of his mouth, Max stomped on the gas pedal, and the car shot forward, pinning her to the seat. "Hold on!" He whipped around the car in front of them, darted into the right lane just inches ahead of a taxi, passed three more cars and darted back.

A block behind them the blue car began weaving desperately through the traffic.

Ahead, their lane was clear for almost a block, and Max
poured on the gas. They shot down the street, passing an
endless string of gaudy hotels and casinos with flashing
marquees. Even at that hour of the morning the sidewalks
were filled with milling people going from one pleasure
palace to another. They were all so intent on finding another place to lose their money that no one paid any attention to a maniac driver.

Erin held on to the armrest and the edge of the seat for
dear life, expecting them to be hit at any second as Max took
advantage of the smallest breaks in traffic to swerve in and
out among the other cars. Horns blared and the squeal of
tires behind them told her that the two men were still following. A muttered curse from Max when he checked the
rearview mirror confirmed it.

"We're never gonna lose them on this damned straightaway." As they neared the next intersection Max flashed her
a grimly determined look and ordered, "Hold on tight."

He cut in front of an eighteen-wheeler in the outside lane,
drawing an angry blast from the trucker's air horn. Ignoring him, Max jerked the steering wheel to the right. Erin
cried out and closed her eyes as they skidded around the
corner, tires screeching.

For what seemed to her like hours, they zigzagged
through the streets, dodging pedestrians and other cars,
running stop signs and red lights and careering around corners at top speed, with the blue Camaro tracking them like
a homing missile. The wild chase was going full tilt when,
without warning, Max swung into a parking garage.

"What are you doing?" Erin cried. "We can't hide in
here! They'll find us!"

"I don't intend to."

He slowed just enough to snatch the ticket from the machine. The top of the car scraped the lifting cross bar as they shot under it. Tires squealing, they tore up the spiraling ramp at a dizzying speed that made Erin moan and close her eyes. Though a sign at the entrance had said Parking on 6, Max got off on the second level, sped straight across to the opposite side of the garage and onto the down ramp. They were halfway between floors when they heard another car racing upward on the other side of the building.

"If we're lucky, they'll go all the way to six looking for us," Max said as they reached ground level.

There was another car ahead of them at the cashier's booth, and when he pulled in behind it Max cursed under his breath. As the driver fumbled in his pocket for the correct amount Max and Erin exchanged a harried glance, then stared straight ahead, every muscle tense as they listened to the scream of tires coming from above.

When at last the other driver drove on and their turn came, Max shoved the ticket and a five-dollar bill into the attendant's hand and peeled out of the garage before the man could utter a word.

When they hit the street Max drove like a race-car driver on qualifying day. For several minutes neither spoke, their concentration on putting distance between them and the parking garage as quickly as possible.

"What do we do now?" Erin asked when it became apparent that the two men in the blue Camaro were no longer following.

"The first thing we're going to do is ditch this car," Max replied decisively. "Then we're going to get a room somewhere and hole up for a few hours while we make plans."

"But—"

"Sweetheart, you can bet those two guys are going to be cruising this town looking for us. They know we came here to search for Elise and that we're not going to leave until we find her, or at least a clue as to where she's gone. We can't afford to go off half-cocked. We have to think this thing through.'' He spared her a glance that both coaxed and commanded. ''Trust me in this, Erin,'' he urged gently.

Erin gazed at him, her expression troubled, but after a moment she nodded her reluctant agreement.

Max wasted no time. He drove straight to the Strip and pulled up at the entrance to the fanciest hotel. When the parking attendant opened the door Max handed him the keys and a generous tip and said, ''Park this one in the rental agency's lot. I'm turning it in.'' Taking Erin's arm, he hurried her inside.

The paperwork was handled quickly, so quickly that the inside of the hotel was little more than a series of impressions for Erin: plush carpets, greenery, marble, glass and chrome, a strange combination of opulence and glitter; a mélange of people of all ages, dressed in every conceivable garb from Bermuda shorts to sequined gowns. From the casino adjacent to the lobby came the dull roar of voices, the clank of coins, the crank and whir of slot machines, clamoring bells, flashing lights and an occasional shout or groan. There was an underlying sense of feverish excitement, a feeling of endless night and desperate gaiety. Pervading the air were the combined scents of expensive perfumes, old whiskey, crisp new money...and fear.

Erin stood beside Max as he dealt with the rental agency clerk, looking around, wide-eyed, her bemused senses overwhelmed by the myriad sights and scents and sounds.

She had expected them to check into the hotel once they had settled the car bill, but to her surprise, Max paused only long enough to inquire whether an Elise Holman, or a woman who looked like Erin, had rented a car within the past few days. When they received a negative answer he hustled her out and into a waiting taxi.

The motel Max chose was a far cry from the glitter palaces that lined the Strip. The Red Rooster was a garish little place squeezed between a sleazy night spot and a wedding chapel, which bore the name Hitchin' Post in flashing neon over the door. Erin had been surprised when Max instructed the cabdriver to drop them there, but once inside the room she was stunned speechless.

She stood just inside the door, her eyes growing round as they took in the fuzzy red carpet, red flocked wallpaper and red satin spread covering the biggest bed she had ever seen. The only other items of furniture were a bedside table and a television set. No table or chairs graced the room, no dresser, no luggage rack and, unless her eyes deceived her, no closet. Didn't people ever check in here with luggage? she wondered.

As Max set the suitcase on the floor at the foot of the bed a movement overhead caught Erin's eyes. She looked up and gasped, her mouth falling open as she stared at the mirrored ceiling.

"Max?" Wary uncertainty and vague suspicion colored her voice. "What kind of place is this?"

He gave her a distracted look, followed the direction of her gaze and shrugged. "Some sort of hookers' hideaway, probably. Sooner or later those guys are going to start checking hotels for us, and it's my guess they'll probably start with those fancy places on the Strip. I figure by the time they get around to dives like this, we'll be long gone. At least I hope so."

Erin was appalled . . . and fascinated. She'd never seen a place like this except in the movies. She'd certainly never been in one. It was on the tip of her tongue to ask Max if he had, but when she looked at him the words fled her mind.

He was sitting on the edge of the bed, forearms braced on his spread knees, hands dangling loosely between them. His shoulders were slumped, his head bent forward in an attitude of total dejection, and as Erin looked at him pity welled up inside her.

For hours he had pushed aside personal pain, but she knew that was no longer possible. They were safe, for the moment at least, and now that the urgency was past, the enormity of Sam's betrayal had hit him like a blow to the midsection.

How he must be hurting, she thought, watching him rake a hand through his dark hair. He and Sam had been friends since childhood. Max had believed in him, loved him as a brother...as she loved Elise.

"Oh, Max," she said, her voice low and vibrating with feeling. "I'm so sorry."

Slowly he raised his head and looked at her, and Erin's heart constricted at the abject sorrow she saw in his eyes. It drew her to him with an irresistible force and, dropping her purse to the floor, she moved across the room.

"I can't believe it, Erin," he said in a dazed voice. He moved his head from side to side, his eyes glazed with pain and bewilderment. "I can't believe he'd do this. But there's no other explanation for those men finding us. At least none I can think of."

"I know, Max. I know," she crooned as she came to a halt in front of him. Tenderly, she touched his face, then ran her fingers through the hair at his temples. "I'd give anything if there were."

"Oh, God, Erin!" He closed his eyes and reached for her blindly. Grasping her hips, he pulled her forward to stand between his legs and wrapped his arms around her, burying his face against her middle. "Why? *Why?*"

It was a cry from the heart that touched her almost beyond bearing. Erin cradled his head in her arms, holding him close, her throat working with emotion.

She ran her hands over his back, his head, threaded her fingers through his hair. Emotions trembled through his

powerful body. His muscles were rigid with the effort to
hold them in check.

He clutched her to him, his hold fierce, almost brutal. She
felt his pain keenly, and her vision blurred as tears welled.
She looked at the ceiling to hold the moisture at bay, only
to encounter their reflection, and the sight of Max's
hunched shoulders tore at her heart. One by one, her tears
spilled over, and she silently cursed Sam for his perfidy.

It was then that she knew she had fallen in love with Max.

Oh, Erin...Erin. You're such a fool, she told herself,
aiming the scolding lament at her mirrored image. You
should have known better.

She looked down at the dark head nestled against her
breasts, her eyes sad and tender. But how could she not love
him? she wondered. Max was such a good man, a wonderful man, everything she had ever longed for. He was a
complex mixture of strength and gentleness, determined,
ambitious, yet loyal and compassionate. He could be funny
or teasing or bossy or even a bit arrogant when it suited him,
but he was a man who gave of himself completely, a man
who could be relied on utterly.

With a tremulous smile on her lips, Erin laid her cheek
against Max's sable curls and rubbed back and forth. His
hair was soft against her skin, its clean fragrance pleasing.
His breath filtered through her cotton shirt and flowed
warm and moist over her breasts. It had been a stupid,
reckless thing to do, falling in love with Max, she admitted
forlornly, but there was no denying it. Just as there was no
denying him. Not when he needed her so.

Soft endearments and meaningless words of comfort
tumbled from her lips. The need to console, to soothe, to
shield this strong, caring man from further pain consumed
Erin.

For endless moments they simply held each other. Then
Max twisted and stretched out on the bed, tumbling her with

him. Erin offered no resistance, going willingly into his arms when he aligned his body to hers.

He pressed his face to the side of her neck and murmured her name over and over. Erin smoothed her hands over his chest, her fingers flexing against his shirt, feeling the warmth beneath it, the heavy thudding of his heart against her palms. There was something so right, so comforting in human closeness, in touching.

They lay belly to belly, breast to chest, legs entangled. Warmth generated warmth. Max nuzzled her neck, her ear, the underside of her jaw. Easing back, he brushed a wayward curl away from her face. Their eyes met and held. His were stark, hers infinitely soft. Silently he sought. Silently she gave.

When their lips met in a tender kiss, it seemed the most natural thing in the world. It was a balm, solace for a wounded soul, a gift of caring.

One kiss followed another, and another, brief, featherlight touches, lips rubbing, breaths mingling. Moist. Warm. It was a leisurely give and take, relaxed and soothing, making no demands, yet it was incredibly sensual. Each nibbling caress stirred emotions and stoked fires, until, imperceptibly as night easing into dawn, the exquisitely delicate exchange altered.

The need to give and receive comfort became merely need. Pulses began to pound, chests tightened. Heat and anticipation grew.

Still, with quivering restraint, the excruciating kisses went on.

"Oh, Erin. Sweet Erin," Max murmured against her lips. "Your touch is magic. Somehow, when I hold you like this, nothing else seems important."

She felt the same. At that moment nothing and no one else mattered—not her sister, not the danger they faced, not even the need to protect herself from the pain of loving a man she could never have.

"Max." His name was all she could manage, and even that was said in an aching whisper that carried the threat of tears, so overcome with emotion was she.

Rising on one elbow, Max looked down at her, his face dark and intense. With his other hand, he unfastened the top button on her blouse...and then the next...and the next...his gaze locked with hers all the while. When he reached the last one he paused. "I need you, Erin," he said in a voice that shook with raw urgency. "I need you so much."

It was there in his eyes—burning desire tinged with desperation—and in the blue depths there were also shadows of pain he made no attempt to hide.

His grief did what no amount of logical reasoning or masterful seduction could have. Erin gazed up at him, eyes glistening. She touched his cheeks with her fingertips, then his temples, feeling her chest swell and ache. He had suffered a loss so great that it was almost unbearable, and his bereaved heart was asking for the comfort of her love.

And because she loved, she gave. All that was in her, all that was soft and nurturing came rushing up from deep within, pouring through her in a warm tide. She felt as though her heart would surely burst.

Erin slid her hands behind his head and clasped them together, pulling him down to her. "Max, my love, I need you, too," she whispered. Her eyelids drifted shut, and with a soft sigh, her open mouth met his.

The time for gentle exploration and restraint had passed. The kiss was filled with hunger and heat and feverish emotion.

Max tugged the blouse free of her slacks and spread the edges wide. He slid his hand up over her rib cage and cupped her breast, and Erin moaned, her nipple peaking against its lacy confinement as his fingers flexed rhythmically around the soft mound.

Erin shifted against him, a feeling of urgency building within her. Blindly, a bit desperately, her fingers sought the buttons of his shirt. Her hands shook, and her movements were jerky and awkward, making her task harder. When the final button resisted her efforts she whimpered and gave it a sharp yank, and with a pop of thread the tiny disk came off in her hand.

Frantic, she ran her palms over his chest, threading her fingers through the mat of soft hair covering it. She found the flat nubs nestled there and with her fingernails drew circles around them, lightly scoring his flesh. Max stilled, then shuddered as she nipped his lower lip and at the same time flicked the small turgid nipples.

"Oh, God, Erin," he said on a groan. "I can't take much more of this." He rose to his knees and looked down at her, his face flushed with desire, his eyes a burning blue. "I want you too much."

"I want you, too." Erin trailed her hand down over his flat abdomen and slipped her fingers beneath the waistband of his jeans.

Max sucked in his breath. "Come here, love." He pulled her to a sitting position and stripped the blouse and lacy bra from her. She lay back, languid and flushed against the pillow, and watched him with drowsy eyes as he removed her shoes, then eased her cotton slacks down over her hips and legs.

He straightened and hooked his fingers under the top of her bikini panties to remove them, then went still as he took in the picture she made, clad in only the brief wisp of white silk and lace. "Dear Lord, you're so beautiful," he whispered. Tentatively, he touched her breasts. With his forefinger, he traced a blue vein that rivered just beneath the surface. The sight of his dark hand against that pale, delicate flesh was unbearably arousing and, unable to help himself, he bent and touched a pink nipple with his tongue. It tightened at once, and he drew the rose velvet tip into his mouth. Erin cried out, her back arching.

With a growl, Max shoved her panties down and off and tossed them aside. He scrambled from the bed, snatching at his own clothes, his eyes never leaving her as he disrobed. Then he was there beside her, pulling her to him, their sighs blending as warm, bare flesh met and melded. As he kissed her deeply, hotly, he rolled her onto her back, parting her legs with his knee, and eased between her silken thighs.

His mouth rocked over hers as he pressed intimately against her. Erin shifted and moaned. Their lips clung, then parted as Max lifted his head. Looking into her eyes, he whispered, "I love you, Erin," and he entered her with a slow, silken stroke.

The beauty of it wrung a cry of joy from Erin. She clung to him, her hands roaming his bare back in restless passion, her body responding with a thrusting urgency that matched his.

Their joining was intense and powerful, almost frantic. It was the natural coming together of a man and woman in the ultimate expression of love; it was an act of comfort; but, dimly, Erin was aware that it was also a reaffirmation, proof that they were alive, that they could feel and respond, that life in all its beauty and struggle was theirs still. After the past two days of trauma and near disaster, that was something they both desperately needed, and they grasped at it like eager children.

The pleasure was glorious. It spiraled rapidly, fueled by days of pent-up tension and longing. Max rose on his elbows, his face tightening with fierce gladness at the glaze of passion in her eyes. He thrust deeper, harder, and smiled as he watched her rapture grow.

"I knew it would be like this for us," he declared in a ragged voice. He threw his head back, and his jaw clenched as though he were in pain. "Oh, God, Erin! It feels so wonderful to be inside you."

Erin gazed up at him, almost senseless with pleasure. She slid her hands down his sides to his hips and grasped them, her fingers digging into his firm buttocks. "Please, Max," she whispered, her head moving back and forth on the pillow. "Oh, please."

His response to her incoherent plea was immediate. "Yes! Oh, God, yes!" he cried, and he lowered his chest over the soft mounds of her breasts. A low moan rumbled from him as he felt her hardened nipples push up through the mat of hair and touch his flesh, felt her silken legs wrap around him.

The flames of passion raged. Pressure built. Ecstasy grew and grew until it bordered on pain. It swirled around them, within them. It made them breathless and desperate and filled their hearts to bursting. Bodies grew taut, straining for more, still more, until the sweet agony could no longer be borne.

The end came in a cataclysmic explosion of sensation that flung them to the edge of the universe and gave them a glimpse of heaven that shook them to their souls.

The drift back to earth was slow and dreamy. It was several minutes after their harsh cries of completion had faded before their hearts slowed and their breathing approached normal. Erin lay with her head cradled on Max's shoulder, her eyes closed. Savoring the delicious lassitude, she absorbed his warmth, his scent, the feel of his skin against hers.

The aftermath of passion rendered her mindless for a few moments, but too soon, reality began to nibble at the edges of her consciousness. Erin opened her eyes. The first thing she saw was the expanse of damp hair covering Max's chest.

Her hand lay curled in the silky thatch. It stirred with every breath she took.

A heaviness began to grow in the region of Erin's heart. She swallowed and gazed across the room at the garish red wallpaper. Oh, Lord, what had she done?

Erin squeezed her eyes shut, her face contorting with anguish.

The slow rotation of Max's hand on her shoulder came to a halt. "What is it, darling? What's wrong?"

"Nothing. Nothing at all." She spoke with forced lightness, her tone soft and sincere. Hearing her own voice, Erin was amazed that she could sound so convincing when what she wanted to do was cry and wail at her own foolishness.

"Then why are your lips quivering like that?"

Erin wondered how he knew, but before she could puzzle it out he tipped her face up with a finger under her chin, and when her eyes popped open she grimaced. She had forgotten the mirror on the ceiling.

She turned her head aside and fought against tears and guilt.

Max shifted, bracing himself up on an elbow to lean over her. "Ah, love, don't." He would not let her evade him. Cupping her jaw in the V between his thumb and fingers, he turned her anguished face back. He grimaced at the sight of her moist eyes and wobbly chin.

"Sweetheart, I'm sorry. When you kissed me so sweetly, things just got out of hand. God knows, I didn't mean for our first time to be in a dump like this. But I'll make it up to you. I swear it."

His apology made her feel worse. What she had done was bad enough, but to betray her sister in a place like this...

Erin's eyes swept the room with distaste. She was suddenly conscious of the sleazy feel of the red satin against her skin and the smell of cheap perfume that hung in the air. Though she kept her gaze averted from the ceiling, she was aware of their wanton reflection in the mirror, and even the slightest movement of their nude bodies registered in her peripheral vision.

"It's not that," she denied, unable to meet his eyes. "At least . . . not completely."

"Then what? Something is bothering you."

Giving a little cry, Erin rolled away and sat up on the side of the bed. She felt vulnerable and wanted to hide, or at least cover herself up, but her robe was in the suitcase, and she didn't have the courage to make a dash for the bathroom. She kept her back to him and pulled the bedspread across her front, tucking it under her arms. She sat hunched over, head down, arms crossed over her breasts, clutching the quilted satin.

The bed shifted as Max moved closer. Erin sucked in her breath and shivered when he trailed a finger down her bowed spine.

"I think I'm developing a fetish for your back," he murmured wickedly in her ear. His hand explored her shoulder blades, mapping the long inward curve to her waist and the flare of her hips. Once again he drew his finger along her spine, down to that shadowy cleft at its base. "It's easily the most beautiful back I've ever seen. I get all hot and bothered just looking at it." As if to prove his statement, he placed a lingering kiss on her shoulder.

Erin wriggled in a halfhearted protest, which he ignored. Slipping an arm around her waist, Max pulled her into the curve of his body, and she closed her eyes as she felt the feathery brush of his chest hair against her back. He propped his chin on her shoulder, and his moist breath dewed her ear as he said, "Now then, why don't you tell me what's really bothering you?"

"Several things," she admitted. Her mouth twisted in a pained grimace and she shook her head. "For one, I can't believe that I . . . that we . . ."

"Made love?" Max supplied helpfully.

"Yes! Do you realize that we met only a little over two days ago? You may find this hard to believe, but I'm not in the habit of jumping into bed with a man I barely know. Or even with one I do know!" Erin closed her eyes and moaned. "Oh, Lord, I can't believe this!"

Max chuckled and gave her waist a squeeze. "Honey, we know each other, all right. In these past few days we've lived through a lifetime and experienced more together than most couples ever do. There's nothing like stress to cut through all the polite facades and reveal true character. We got to know each other under the worst possible conditions, yet we still fell in love." He grasped her chin and turned her head, forcing her to meet his eyes. "Didn't we?"

"Max, this is crazy—"

"Didn't we?" he insisted.

Erin wanted to deny it, but under Max's direct gaze she could not. Unable to help herself, she reached up and touched his cheek and nodded, her misty eyes filled with love and longing and abject misery.

Something flared in Max's eyes, and he looked at her with fierce satisfaction. Then he leaned forward, and their lips met in a slow, sweet kiss that made her heart pound.

When it ended he drew back and smiled. "Say it. I want to hear you say it."

"I love you."

"Then that's all that matters."

"Oh, Max." Erin looked at him forlornly, her face ravaged with guilt. "It's just not that simple. What about Elise? I don't know how I'm ever going to face her."

Max's mouth firmed into a thin line, and when he spoke his voice was stiff with impatience. "Erin, I've told you over and over, *I am not interested in Elise.* Nor will I ever be. Denying our love won't change that."

"I know. But you don't know Elise. She would never believe that. She would always feel that she'd lost you to me."

"Dammit! She never *had* me!" Max exploded.

He swung his legs to the floor and sat beside her on the edge of the bed. Erin glanced at him and quickly looked away. Despite her feeling for Max, she was still shy. He, on the other hand, seemed not in the least self-conscious about carrying on a discussion in the nude.

"Look, Erin," he said in a more reasonable tone, raking a hand through his tousled hair. "Has Elise ever actually told you that she's in love with me?"

"Well...no."

"Then maybe she's not. Maybe you're assuming something that just isn't there."

Erin looked at him, her eyes full of hope. "Do you really think so?"

"Well, she's certainly never given me any indication that she'd like our relationship to be more than it is. And until we know for sure, I don't think we should borrow trouble."

"Maybe you're right," Erin said, her voice thoughtful and a bit distracted. She was grasping at straws, and she knew it. Given her twin's romantic nature and passive tenacity, the chances that she had misread the situation were slim. But Erin knew that as long as there was the slightest possibility, she had to cling to it. Because, heaven help her, she did love Max so.

"I know I am. It'll all work out. You'll see." Max grasped her shoulders and eased her back on the bed. He leaned over her, his expression full of heat and sensual promise.

Erin's heart began to thud. "Max. Max, listen to me," she said shakily. "I won't hurt my sister." Max's intent gaze was focused on his forefinger as it traced the top edge of the satin spread, leaving a line of fire on her skin. "No...no matter what. I won't hurt her. You've got...to understand that."

Sighing, Max stopped his exploration and looked into her eyes. "All right, sweetheart. I accept that. Okay?"

Erin's body went limp with relief, and when she smiled up at him his eyes glinted wickedly.

"Now then, about this spread..."

He pried her fingers loose from the red satin and, inch by inch, peeled it away from her body.

Chapter Eleven

Now I want you to keep this door locked. And under no circumstances are you to open it for anyone but me. You got that?'' As Max issued the strict instructions he tipped his head forward and gave Erin an insistent look from under his brows. He held her within the circle of his arms, his clasped hands at the small of her back molding their hips together.

"Yes, Max." With her forearms resting against his chest, she needlessly smoothed the collar of his blue cotton shirt. "I still think I should go with you."

"No."

"But, Max, I want to help."

"C'mon, sweetheart, we've been all through this."

Sulking, she fiddled with the top button of his shirt and stared at it in silence.

Max rolled his eyes. "Look, you know I don't want to leave you. Just the thought of your being here alone scares the hell out of me. But we can't chance those two goons spotting you." He glanced at her bright curls, and his mouth twisted in a wry grimace. "And that fiery mop makes you stand out in a crowd. Anyway, you can help by calling all the hotels. Just go down the list in the phone book. You'll cover a lot more ground that way than I would by running from place to place."

"Oh, okay," Erin grumbled.

"Good, girl." Max gave her a squeeze and reached behind him for the doorknob. "And while you're doing that I'll check the airport and bus station and the other car rental places. It may take me a while, so don't worry."

He kissed her goodbye and slipped out. Erin was about to shove the bolt home when the door opened again. With a hungry growl, Max hooked a hand around her neck and hauled her to him for another lingering kiss that made her head spin.

"God, I hate to leave you," he ground out against her mouth. He kissed her again, hard, then stepped back, shaking his head. "But I've got to go. Lock the door behind me. And remember, you don't budge from here unless the place is on fire."

"All right! All right!" Erin placed a palm flat on his chest and pushed him out. As she shut the door and turned the lock, his muffled "And even then, you wait until the firemen chop down the door!" sounded from the other side.

"Go, will you!" she yelled.

His footsteps receded, and Erin leaned back against the door, grinning. Though she hated being left behind, Max's concern made her feel loved and cosseted.

With a sigh, she wrapped her arms around her middle, her expression dreamy as she thought about the past couple of hours spent in Max's arms. His lovemaking had left her replete, satiated. Even now her body felt as though it were glowing. Was it wrong, she wondered, to feel so deliciously fulfilled and happy in the midst of a crisis?

Immediately Erin thought of her twin and experienced a pang of guilt. What was Elise feeling at that moment? Where was she? What was she doing? Closing her eyes, Erin caught her lower lip between her teeth. How would Elise react if she knew about her and Max?

A part of her wanted to know, wanted to get it out in the open and settled, while another part of her dreaded finding out. Erin felt torn in two, hopeful one minute and despairing the next. She could not bear to hurt Elise, but the thought of losing Max, especially now, was too painful even to contemplate.

Impatiently she told herself to stop worrying about it; until they found Elise, there was no way of knowing what her sister felt or what the future held.

A thump from the room next door jarred Erin out of her worrisome thoughts. The sound was followed by a giggle and a groan. Then came the rhythmic squeaking of bed-springs.

Color crept up Erin's neck and flooded her face. She moved away from the door in a flurry of agitated movement, tightening the sash on her robe as she hurried to the bed and sat down.

Gritting her teeth, she snatched the phone book and riffled through it, making the pages snap and crackle noisily. "Let's see…hosiery…hospices…hospitals…hot tubs… Ah, here it is! Hotels!" Determinedly striving to block out the sounds coming through the wall, Erin grabbed the telephone and punched out the first number listed.

"Hello. Will you connect me with Mrs. Elise Holman's room, please?"

Erin wound the coiled cord around her finger and waited. "No? You're sure? Well, perhaps she's registered under her maiden name, Elise Blaine. Or she might even be using an alias. You see, my sister came to Las Vegas to get a divorce, and she doesn't want her husband to find her," Erin lied smoothly. "She's slender, about five-six, with bright red hair and brown eyes, twenty-seven years old. Have you had a guest within the past few days who fits that description?"

"I see. You're sure? Well, thank you for your help."

With a sigh, Erin pushed the disconnect button and checked the phone book for the next number.

Seven hours of dialing resulted in a sore ear and a stiff neck but no leads on Elise. And she was only to the P's.

"Oh, this is impossible! It's like looking for a needle in a haystack!" Erin slammed the receiver down and paced the room, absently rotating her head and flexing her shoulders. After the first couple of hours it had occurred to her that perhaps Max had assigned her the task just to keep her mind occupied, and with every fruitless call the nagging suspicion had grown stronger. "He probably knew we didn't have a prayer of finding her this way," she muttered.

Erin glanced at her watch and then at the door. It was after nine. Max had said he would be late, but she'd thought he would be back by now. She sat down on the bed and nibbled at the tip of her index finger. Had something happened to him?

She sprang up and began to pace again. The bed took up most of the room, forcing her to follow a U-shaped path back and forth around it.

A door closed, and the intimate sounds started up again in the next room. Erin groaned and rolled her eyes. She tried to ignore the noise, but it was impossible. Whoever was over there, they were an extremely physical pair, and from the growls and squeals and pounding footsteps, it sounded as though the woman and her customer were engaged in a game of tag.

Desperate for a distraction, Erin marched over to the television, noticing only as she reached it that there were no control knobs, just a coin slot at the top. A loud squawk beyond the wall sent her scurrying for her purse.

After dropping the requisite coins, Erin sank down on the end of the bed. When the picture filled the screen, at first she couldn't believe her eyes. Blinking, she stared and cocked her head to one side, then the other, her jaw slowly sagging as it dawned on her what she was watching.

"O-o-h no-o-o!" Erin jumped up and slapped her hands across the front of the set, trying to locate a button to turn it off. When she found none she searched in back for the plug, but it was fastened into the wall socket with some sort of clamp, and she couldn't budge it.

Between the noise coming from the next room and the disgusting things happening on the screen, she felt as though she were in the middle of an orgy. Erin tried to keep her gaze averted, but the television, like the mirror on the ceiling, drew the eye like a magnet.

A few minutes later, when Max burst into the room, he found Erin sprawled facedown on the bed.

He skidded to a halt beside her, his heart booming in his chest. When he saw that her hands were clamped over her ears, he knew a moment of relief so great that it almost buckled his knees. Then anger quickly banished the momentary weakness.

"Erin, what are you doing?" he demanded furiously, giving her ankle a sharp tug that made her jump. "I knocked and called your name a dozen times. You scared the hell out of me when you didn't answer."

Erin sat up and scrambled from the bed. To his astonishment, she planted her hands on her hips and glared right back at him. "I'm sorry I didn't hear you, but I had to do something to shut out the grunts and groans. Do you have any idea what goes on in this place? Or the kind of movies they show on that thing?" she demanded accusingly, waving her hand at the television.

Max's eyes widened. "Oh, no. Don't tell me you..." He glanced over his shoulder at the set and groaned. "Good grief, Erin. It never occurred to me that you'd turn the thing on. I assumed you knew what it was for."

"And just how was I supposed to know? *I* have never been in a place like this before."

"Sweetheart, people don't check in here to watch the Disney channel. These rooms are generally rented by the hour, you know."

"So I've learned. They've rented the one next door at least six times since you left."

She tried to shove past him, but he chuckled and pulled her close, clamping his mouth over hers. She struggled at first, but the moment of fright had his adrenaline pumping, and he held her tightly, pouring into the kiss all the ardent longing that had been building during the hours since he had left. Gradually her resistance melted, and she grew soft and yielding in his arms, her body pliant against his. The sweet surrender took Max's breath away, and he moaned, feeling his insides turned to liquid. God, he would never get enough of her. Never!

When the kiss ended they were both breathing hard. Still holding her close, Max grinned down at her bemused expression and shook his head. "Such a little innocent. And I'd always heard that travel was broadening."

"Not *that* broadening."

Max turned his attention to the cavorting pair on the television screen and studied them for several seconds. "Hmm. Interesting." He looked back at Erin, his eyes glinting. "Did you learn anything?"

"Nothing I cared to know," she told him haughtily. "I'm not into Jell-O and plastic wrap."

His eyes widened. "No kidding? Jell-O?" His head whipped back around, but at that instant the time ran out and the screen went blank. "Aw, shoot."

Erin poked him in the ribs. "Max, I'm not kidding. You are not going to leave me alone in this pit of perversion again. I don't care if the entire Russian army is out there searching for me."

"Don't worry, I won't have to." He gave her another quick kiss and a hug, then released her and stepped away to pick up one of the sacks he'd dropped on the floor beside the door. "When we leave you're going to be wearing this." He drew a dark wig from the bag and tossed it to her.

Erin caught it. Astonished, she stared at the silky pelt for a moment, then rushed into the bathroom to try it on. Max followed and stood in the doorway with his shoulder propped against the jamb.

"Oh, Max. It's perfect. I hardly recognize myself," she said in stunned surprise, gazing at her reflection in the mirror above the sink.

The wig was a smooth fall of sable brown that hung to her shoulders, the tips turning under in a soft pageboy. Uncompromisingly straight bangs hid her forehead and most of her auburn brows. Against the dark tresses her skin looked porcelain fair, the sleek style giving her a haughty elegance.

"Very nice," Max commented. "Though, personally, I prefer the fiery-haired beauty I know and love, it ought to give you a certain amount of protection."

His words reminded Erin of why the wig was necessary, and she swung around, her face taut with eagerness. "I hope you had better luck than I did today. I called every hotel and motel through the O's and learned zilch."

"As a matter of fact, I found out that Elise rented a car yesterday morning."

Erin's face lit up at the news. "Oh, Max, that's—"

He stopped her excited exclamation with an upraised hand. "However, at the moment that's all I know. I talked to the manager at their main office, and the rental showed up on their computer. She picked up the car at the Riviera Hotel at about ten in the morning, but the clerk who rented it to her, a Ms. Alma Kent, had already left for the day, and the manager refused to give me her home telephone number. I checked the phone book, but apparently it's unlisted."

"Didn't you explain that it was a matter of life and death?"

"Yep. But it didn't cut any ice. He was bending the rules to tell me what he did. However, he did say that the woman would be on duty tomorrow. We're going to be there bright and early in the morning to talk to Ms. Kent. I just hope to God that she remembers something that might tell us where Elise was heading."

Erin's shoulders slumped. "Oh, Max. Do you think she will? It seems like such a long shot."

"I know. But right now, it's the only lead we've got."

He pushed away from the door and walked back into the bedroom. Erin pulled off the wig and followed.

One of the other sacks Max had dropped by the door contained numerous cartons of Chinese food. They ate on the bed, with Erin sitting cross-legged in the middle and Max lounging across the foot, propped up on one elbow. Though he had brought two of everything, they were both hungry and managed to work their way through the astonishing array of dishes, talking only now and then.

When they were finished, Max gathered the empty cartons and napkins and stuffed them into the sack. Erin stood and flipped back the bedspread to shake off the crumbs. "Good grief. Look at that."

Max glanced back over his shoulder and grinned when he saw her dubiously eyeing the heart-strewn sheets. "Don't worry. The manager assured me that they're changed after each rental."

"I certainly hope so."

Chuckling, Max dumped the sack of garbage into the room's only wastebasket. "By the way, I got us some transportation. I bought a pickup."

"You *bought* a truck?"

"Yeah. And some western duds to go with it. I figure they're not going to be looking for a kicker and his lady."

"Max, you shouldn't have done that! This crazy chase is costing you a fortune, and—"

"Don't worry about it. I can afford it," he assured her, cutting into her worried protest. "It's just a used truck, kind of beat-up looking, but it's got a hot engine. Anyway, I've always wanted a pickup."

Erin's face softened, and she looked at him tenderly, love overwhelming her. Smiling, she walked to Max and looped her arms around his neck. He looked surprised, but his arms automatically enfolded her. "Has anyone ever told you, Max Delany, that you're a very nice man?" Her voice was husky with emotion, her eyes shining.

He laced his fingers together across her lower back, just below her waist, and rocked her against him. "Hmm, let me think. No. No, I don't think so. Though there was this little firebrand of a redhead who once called me a jerk."

"She must have been out of her head at the time," Erin said with conviction. She stood on tiptoe and kissed his chin. Tipping her head, she mouthed the underside of his jaw and nibbled her way down his neck. "It was probably just a case of temporary insanity, brought on by stress," she whispered between nips.

Max closed his eyes and shuddered. His expression was strained. "Well, I suppose she...was a little...a little, uh...overwrought."

"Of course she was." Erin's tongue delved into the hollow at the base of his throat. "Otherwise she would have seen instantly what a wonderful..." She skimmed the rims of his ears with her fingertips. "...caring..." Nuzzling aside his shirt, she kissed his collarbone. "...exciting..." Her hands slid downward over his chest, and with nimble fingers she released his shirt buttons one by one. "...fantastically sexy man you are."

Her hands slipped beneath the open shirt and roamed over his taut abdomen as she rubbed her nose back and forth in the mat of dark hair on his chest, inhaling his scent. Leaning back, she blew ever so softly on the silky thatch. The tender torment wrung a moan from Max, and with a small, knowing smile as old as Eve, Erin closed her eyes and pressed her face into the soft curls, her tongue stabbing through them to trace wet patterns on his flesh.

"Oh, sweet heaven!"

The harsh cry tore from Max as his big hand clamped the back of her head, pressing her tightly to him. For a moment he stood with his head thrown back, eyes closed, his face twisted with fierce pleasure. When he could stand it no longer he curled his fingers into her hair, tugged her head back and kissed her with a force and desperation that bordered on violence.

Erin responded with a matching hunger. What had begun as a gentle seduction exploded into a storm of need. It spiraled within her, hot, frantic need that made her heart pound and her feminine core throb with a hollow, yearning ache. Lips rocked, tongues thrust, bodies strained closer. Her hands clutched at him, fingers digging into the hard muscles of his back.

Dimly Erin knew that fear as well as passion drove her. It was fear born of the helpless, inevitable sensation that for them, time was slipping away. They would find Elise, if not tomorrow, then maybe the next day, or the one after that. Soon. She could feel it.

She loved her twin and wanted to find her, to keep her safe, but no matter how much she wanted to believe otherwise, Erin could not shake the feeling that when they did, Max would be lost to her.

This time together might well be all they would ever have, and she was consumed with a driving compulsion to grab at it with both hands, to live for the moment and store up all the loving memories she could.

Max broke off the kiss and looked at her, breathing hard. "God, I love you! All day I thought of how it had been when we made love, and it's been driving me crazy. Do you have any idea what you're doing to me?" he asked raggedly.

Beneath half-closed lids Erin's eyes held a provocative glitter. Her lips curved up in a siren's smile. "The same thing you're doing to me, I hope."

"Witch," he growled, giving her hair a playful tug before releasing it.

With his hands clasped together in the small of her back, he held her close and maneuvered her backward toward the bed. "We have no choice, you know. We have to wait till morning before we can follow up on that lead. Which means . . . we've got about ten hours to fill," he said suggestively. His mouth quirked, but there was nothing teasing about the look in his eyes. Desire blazed in their blue depths, and Erin felt her bones melt beneath that hot, hungry stare.

"Yes, I know." She smoothed her hand over his chest and coyly wound a curl around her finger as she added in a seductive murmur, "Do you have any suggestions?"

"Well . . . as a matter of fact—" the backs of Erin's legs bumped into the mattress, bringing them to a halt "—I do."

He gripped the lower edge of her blue knit top, peeled it off over her head and tossed it aside. She was not wearing a bra, and his eyes seemed to sizzle as they fastened on her breasts. He touched one pearly mound, trailed his forefinger down the silken slope and circled the nipple with a slow, maddening touch that made it tighten and ache. When at last the pad of his finger brushed that sensitive nub, Erin caught her breath.

A smile of sheer masculine satisfaction tilted his mouth, and in a quick movement Max dealt with the snap and zipper on her crisp tan-and-blue-print skirt, hooked his thumbs beneath the waistband and pushed it down over her hips. The garment fell to the floor and crumpled in a heap around her ankles.

Grasping her waist, Max braced one knee on the bed and toppled her backward, coming down with her. He lay half over her, his gaze drowsy and hot, wickedly sensual, his grin a devilish enticement. "Now then," he murmured against her lips, "about that Jell-O..."

A long while later Erin lay in Max's arms, her head cradled on his shoulder. She felt boneless, her body satiated from the hours of delicious lovemaking they had shared, but her mind would not let her rest.

One of her legs was hooked over Max's, and her hand lay on his chest, her fingers threaded in the crisp mat of hair. She smiled as she felt the slow rise and fall of his rib cage with each deep breath of slumber. Absently she rubbed her foot up and down his leg and shivered as its hairy roughness tickled her sole.

Outside, traffic still rushed by and the garish sign in front of the motel flashed on and off. With every blink the red glow spilled through a crack at the edge of the draperies, lanced up the wall and bounced off the mirrored ceiling in a thin line. Erin watched it, bemused.

Never in her wildest imaginings had she thought she'd spend a night in a tawdry dump that was little more than a brothel. Yet it didn't seem to matter. The hours there with Max had been the most wonderful she had ever known. Sighing, she snuggled against his shoulder, knowing in her heart that she would be happy anywhere as long as she was with him.

Where would they be a week from now? she wondered, gazing into the darkness. More important, would they still be together? Though she didn't want to admit it, Erin knew, deep down inside, that the odds were against it.

The thought brought with it a pain so sharp that she closed her eyes and caught her lower lip between her teeth to keep from crying out. It was unthinkable. Unbearable.

Yet she knew, if it came to that, she would somehow have to bear it. Because if it was a matter of hurting Elise or hurting herself, she was certain what her decision would have to be.

Don't think about it, she told herself. There's no sense in making yourself miserable in advance. Just live each moment as it comes, and enjoy the happiness you have now. Anyway, Max could be right, you know: you could be imagining the whole thing.

Determined to heed her own pep talk, Erin shifted into a more comfortable position against Max's side, closed her eyes and lay perfectly still.

A moment later a tear slipped from beneath her lashes and dripped onto his shoulder, the salty wetness melding their flesh together.

The couple who left the Red Rooster the next morning bore little resemblance to the man and woman who had checked in the day before.

Max wore his western gear with the indolent panache of a longtime cowboy. He looked lean and tough in the tight jeans and shirt, and the cowboy boots emphasized his natural loose-jointed gait. The roll-brimmed Stetson was pulled low and cocked rakishly to one side. Beneath it his eyes were hidden behind reflective sunglasses.

In direct contrast, Erin sat beside him in the battered pickup, stiff as a ramrod. The squaw blouse and full denim skirt he had purchased for her were attractive and comfortable enough, but she felt self-conscious wearing the strange clothes and the long sable wig. In addition, tucked away in the motel room she'd at least had an illusion of safety; out in the open again, she felt exposed and vulnerable.

After a hurried coffee-shop breakfast, they arrived at the car rental counter in the Riviera Hotel at exactly nine o'clock, the same time Ms. Kent was due for work. Two women stood behind the counter, a petite brunette of about thirty and a statuesque young woman in her mid-twenties with streaked blond hair. Both were attractive and impeccably groomed, and both wore that gloss of worldliness that seemed to be a prerequisite for employment at the casinos and plush hotels along the Las Vegas Strip.

After a quick scan of the name tags pinned to their stylish khaki and maroon uniforms, Max spoke directly to the blonde.

"Ms. Kent? My name is Max Delany, and this is Ms. Blaine." He poked the brim of his hat with his forefinger, pushing it to the back of his head. Removing his sunglasses, he gave her his most persuasive smile. "We're trying to locate someone, and we're hoping you can help us."

The woman's face lit with interest when she looked up into Max's handsome face. She spared Erin a glance and dismissed her as unimportant, turning back to Max with a smile. "I'll certainly try. What can I do for you, Mr. Delany?" she asked with an effusiveness that made Erin grit her teeth.

"According to your company's main computer, on Wednesday morning you rented a car to Mrs. Elise Holman. She's twenty-seven, has bright red hair and brown eyes, and she looks a lot like Ms. Blaine. Do you remember her?"

The flirtatious look faded from the blonde's face. This time she made an intent study of Erin's features, a puzzled frown forming between her brows. Erin shifted and tugged at her wig.

"Yes. Yes, of course. With so many people looking for her, how could I forget?"

Max and Erin tensed and exchanged a worried look. "Someone else has been asking questions about Mrs. Holman?" he demanded. "Who? When?"

"Last night. Two men came to my apartment. They said they were policemen and that they'd gotten my name and address from Mr. Lowe, the manager at the main office."

"Did they show you any identification? A badge or anything?"

"Yes. That is . . . one did."

"And were you able to tell them anything?"

"Not much. Only that it was a one-day rental and that she asked which would be the best route to take to Salt Lake City. Also, she bought Nevada and Utah maps."

Max probed, but the woman could remember nothing else about the transaction, so he thanked her for her help and ushered Erin out.

"At least now we know where Elise headed," she said eagerly, hurrying along beside him.

Max's face was like granite as they stepped out into the brilliant Nevada sunshine. Several times Erin was forced to break into a trot just to keep up with his long, angry strides.

"Yeah. And so do those two goons. Only they have a head start on us."

He bundled Erin into the truck and strode around to the other side. When he climbed in behind the wheel his face was grim. He stared straight ahead, then brought his fist down on the steering wheel so hard that Erin jumped. "Dammit! They must have gotten to Lowe just minutes after I left. They probably flashed that badge to get him to give them Ms. Kent's address.'' His mouth twisted in a disgusted grimace. "Which means that Elise was right; at least one of those guys is with the police."

"So? What are we waiting for?" Erin demanded. "Let's go to Salt Lake City."

Max removed his hat and raked a weary hand through his hair. "Sweetheart, don't you understand? If those guys left last night, they're probably already there. They even could have found her by now."

"Maybe. But I don't think so." The barely restrained excitement in Erin's voice drew a sharp look from Max, and she gave him a slow smile, her eyes dancing with secret knowledge. "Because, you see, I think I know where she went, and it wasn't to a hotel, which is where they'll be looking. We have an uncle in Salt Lake, and I'd be willing to bet that Elise headed straight for his house."

The grimness vanished from Max's face. "All right!" he shouted exuberantly. "Now we're getting somewhere." He crammed the Stetson back on his head, pulled the brim low and reached for the ignition key, but his hand halted in midair, halfway there.

"Hey, wait a minute. Instead of driving all that way, why don't we just call?"

Erin frowned. "I'm afraid it will spook Elise. She's determined to protect me by keeping her distance, and if she finds out I'm following her, she might take off again."

"Mmm, you could be right." Pursing his lips, Max drummed his fingers on the steering wheel. "I'll tell you what—why don't I call and speak to your uncle? I'll fill him in on what's going on and ask him not to say anything to Elise. Then we'll drive up there. How's that?"

As Erin nodded her agreement he grinned and reached for the door handle. "Okay. Let's do it."

They went back inside the hotel to use a phone in the lobby. Erin stood beside Max and fidgeted as he talked to her uncle, catching only bits and pieces of the conversation over the hum of activity around them. She expected him to hand her the phone so that she could speak to her uncle also, but to her surprise, after talking for no more than a minute, Max hung up. When he turned to her he wore a worried look, and Erin felt a sudden chill shiver up her spine.

"What is it? What did he say?"

Max took a quick look around, then guided Erin over to a small group of chairs. When they were seated he took both of her hands in his. The concerned look in his eyes made her even colder. "Erin..." Gritting his teeth, he looked away, then sighed and looked back again. "Sweetheart, Elise never arrived at your uncle's. He hasn't heard a word from her."

Chapter Twelve

Erin paled. "Wh-what?"

Her voice was a breathy wisp of sound. She stared at Max, unable to move.

"I didn't tell your uncle what was going on," he continued, tightening his grip on her hands. "I didn't see any point in worrying him. So I simply said that I was Elise's boss and that she was on a business trip and had said she might stop by to visit him on her way. I think he bought it."

"Oh, Max." Erin pulled free of his grip. Bending forward, she propped her elbows on her knees and buried her face in her hands. The cold sensation seeped into her bones, making her shake.

Vaguely she heard Max flag down a passing waiter, but she paid him no mind. She merely sat there, lost in a haze of fear and dread.

The next thing she knew, Max was urging a glass into her hands.

"Here. Drink this."

"What is it?"

"Brandy."

"But I don't like brandy. And it's the middle of the morning, for heaven's sake."

"Just hush, sweetheart, and drink it. It'll make you feel better."

"Max, it isn't necessary. I'm not some weak-kneed little ninny who's going to fall apart on you."

"I know. But humor me anyway." His gaze was tender but unrelenting.

Too shaken to argue further, Erin complied, grimacing with each tentative sip as the fiery liquid burned its way down her throat. Though she hated to admit it, the brandy did drive the chill away. She could feel its warmth spreading through her body like a slow tide of hot molasses, bringing a flush to her skin. By the time she'd consumed half the contents of the glass she was calmer, more in control.

"Feeling better?" Max asked, inspecting the fresh color in her cheeks.

"Yes. I'm fine. Max, what are we going to do now? How are we ever going to find her?"

"I'm not sure. I . . ." He stopped, his expression growing thoughtful. Then all at once he reached over and gave her shoulder a squeeze. "Look, honey, you wait here while I go check on something. I'll be back in a minute." Before she could protest or question him he was striding away through the lobby.

Curious, on edge, Erin fidgeted and sipped her brandy, though more for something to do than for its therapeutic value. She tapped her foot and every few seconds glanced in the direction Max had taken, vacillating between hope and annoyance.

When he returned his face was grim, and Erin was on her feet before he reached her.

"What is it?" she demanded fearfully. "What did you find out?"

Without even slowing his pace, Max took her arm and urged her toward the door. He didn't meet her eyes. "Not now. I'll tell you later."

"Max? Max, please!" Her voice climbed to a shrill pitch in direct proportion to the fear rising within her. She was half turned toward him, alternately trotting and skipping in a sliding sidestep in order to keep up, her eyes wide and beseeching. "*Tell* me, for Pete's sake!"

"In the truck," he growled.

Once there, however, Max still showed no great eagerness to explain. He avoided her eyes, both hands gripping the steering wheel, and as Erin studied his set profile, fear coiled in the pit of her stomach. "What is it, Max?" This time her voice was a shaky whisper. "I have to know."

His jaw moved infinitesimally, and a muscle jumped in his cheek. Erin knew he was gritting his teeth.

After a moment he sighed and turned to her, his face filled with regret and compassion. "I went back to the rental counter. It occurred to me that we should have asked Ms. Kent to check to see if Elise had turned in the car."

"And?"

He looked away again. "She didn't."

Baffled, Erin gazed at him blankly. Then her eyes narrowed. "There's more to it than that, isn't there, Max?" she prodded.

"Erin—"

"Isn't there?"

He slanted her a resentful look out of the corner of his eye and pressed his lips together. Then his face softened, and he turned back to her again and took her hands in his. The gesture made her chest tighten. "Erin, the car Elise was driving was found abandoned in a shopping center parking lot in Grand Junction, Colorado."

Though he had spoken in the gentlest of voices, the words triggered a painful explosion of fear just beneath her breastbone. It seemed to suck every particle of oxygen from the air and to cause her heart to swell until it filled her chest. She couldn't breathe.

She slumped back in the corner of the cab. "When?"

"About an hour ago."

His thumbs swept back and forth over the tops of her hands. "Erin. Darling, I'm afraid that you're going to have to accept the possibility, maybe even the probability, that they found her. That she may even be—"

"No! Don't say it! She's fine!" Erin insisted. "I would know it if she weren't. I'd sense it." Her voice held a shrill ring of desperation that bordered on hysteria. She looked at Max pleadingly, her eyes wide and frantic. Then, as though suddenly weary, she leaned her head back against the door. "I know I would," she murmured listlessly.

"Oh, sweetheart, I hope you're right. But even if you are, we're still stymied. If Elise laid down a false trail, then deliberately abandoned that car to throw someone off the scent, she certainly wouldn't be dumb enough to hang around town long. And Grand Junction is a major crossroads. From there she could have taken off in any direction—north into Wyoming, south to Durango or maybe even New Mexico. Or she could have headed east to Denver. She even could have gone to Utah, though I doubt it. The point is, we haven't a clue as to where to look." He paused, still rubbing her hands. "Of course, that's not all bad," he added in what she knew was an attempt to cheer her up. "It also means those two goons are in the dark, too."

Which way would she have gone? Erin asked herself. She's your twin, your other half. You know her better than anyone. So think. Think! she commanded silently. Her eyes were squeezed shut, her face taut with fierce concentration.

She remained silent for several moments, her mind stretching...reaching out....

And then it came to her.

Slowly at first, like a distant voice calling in the far reaches of her mind. But gradually it grew closer, more distinct, and with it came an image so sharp and clear that she felt as though she were there, as though she could reach out and touch it.

Erin sat up straight, staring at Max, her expression radiating excitement and absolute certainly. "Vail. She went to Vail."

"Erin...honey," Max began patiently. "Look, I know you're desperate to find her, but we can't go tearing around the country with nothing to go on."

"Max, I'm positive. I tell you I can feel it."

"Okay, okay. If you say so." He shook his head, his gaze filled with sadness and love. "But why Vail?"

"Our parents and several aunts and uncles jointly own a cabin there. It's available to any of us anytime we want it. Except, of course, when it's rented out. A local real estate firm manages it, and when no one in the family is using the cabin, it's rented—to skiers in the winter and occasionally to summer tourists."

"I see. And you think that's where Elise headed?"

"Yes. Don't you see? It's perfect. Vail is a busy little village, even in the summertime, with people coming and going constantly. She could get lost in the crowds. The cabin is fairly private. It's also free, and by now Elise is probably running low on money. Plus, if I know my sister, she's been calling David for help and getting that stupid answering machine, the same as I have," Erin added, making a disgusted face. "At the cabin she could hole up and wait for him to come to her."

"It's a possibility, I guess," Max conceded, though he did not sound convinced.

"It's more than that, Max, it's . . . well . . . a certain feeling I get deep inside. It's never wrong. I tell you, Elise is in Vail."

"And you want to go there, right?"

"Yes. Oh, please, Max," she pleaded gripping his arm. "I have to."

He didn't reply for a moment, and Erin held her breath. If he refused, she would go alone, though she didn't want to.

Finally he flashed a lopsided, resigned smile. "Do you want to drive or fly?"

"Fly. But . . . your truck—"

"I'll leave it at the airport and pick it up later, when this madness is over."

Erin's shoulders sagged. Leaning forward, she framed his face between her palms and gazed at him, her eyes misty and adoring. He gave so selflessly—no arguing, no lectures, no attempts to persuade her with logic. He might not agree with her decision or even have that much faith in the telepathic link between her and Elise, but that didn't matter. He loved her and accepted her just as she was. If she felt she must follow her feelings and go to Vail, then he would take her. For him it was that simple.

Erin's throat ached with love for him, and as her thumbs caressed the hollows in his cheeks she smiled tremulously and whispered, "Thank you, my darling."

Breathing fire, David Blaine stormed into the office of Global Imports shortly before they closed.

"Where's Sam Lawford's office?" he demanded of the young woman behind the receptionist's desk.

She blinked and stared, startled speechless by the sudden appearance of the lean, tough-looking, absolutely furious man. "I . . . uh . . . do you have an appointment, sir?"

"Never mind. I'll find him myself." David spun away and started down the hall.

"Sir, wait! You can't just barge in there without an appointment! *Sir!*"

She might as well have been talking to the wind. In less than a minute David located the door that bore Sam Lawford's name.

Wilma Crenshaw started at his brash entry, her hands stilling on the computer keyboard. Her plain face stiffened, and thin gray brows arched imperiously behind steel-rimmed glasses. "May I help you?"

"I want to see Sam Lawford."

His demanding tone sent her brows inching even higher. She gave him a haughty look and made a production of examining the appointment book on her desk. "I'm afraid that is quite impossible. Mr. Lawford is busy at the moment."

"Lady, I don't care if he's in conference with the President of the United States," David said in a low, dangerous voice. Planting his palms on her desk, he leaned over it until his face was mere inches from hers. "I want to see him. Now."

Wilma Crenshaw sucked in an affronted breath and leaned back, her nostrils flaring. "If you would care to make an appointment, I—"

"To hell with that," David growled.

"Just a minute! You can't go in there!"

He charged into the inner office with a sputtering Wilma right on his heels.

At the commotion, the man behind the desk looked up from the papers he was studying, the only change in his expression a slight narrowing of his eyes. David found himself pinned by an icy stare.

"Are you Lawford?"

"Yes." Having delivered the clipped, one-word reply, Sam Lawford waited and watched, not moving so much as a muscle or an eyelash.

Despite the man's stillness and apparent unconcern, David knew he was braced to spring into action. His years with the FBI had taught him to sense danger in men and situations and to meet a threat with whatever it took to subdue it. When David had to, he fought lowdown and dirty, his body as lethal as any weapon devised by man. His well-honed instincts told him he was facing one of his own kind.

"I'm David Blaine, and I want to know what the hell is going on."

"I'm sorry, Mr. Lawford," Wilma inserted. She shot David a furious look, the wattles beneath her chin quivering with outrage. "I tried to stop him, but he just barged right in."

"That's all right, Miss Crenshaw. You may go back to your office."

"But—"

"Leave us, Miss Crenshaw. And hold my calls."

"Very well, if you're sure..." When he nodded she sniffed, poked a hairpin back into the tight bun at her nape and marched out, her thin lips pinched.

"I assume you're referring to this situation your sisters are in," Sam said when the door closed behind the woman.

His voice held not the slightest inflection, and as David met the man's silvery stare he gritted his teeth. Damned icy bastard. "That's right. I returned home this morning after a week of deep-sea fishing off the coast of Mexico and found my answering machine filled with frantic messages from both my sisters. Some babble about a crime and Elise running for her life and Erin chasing after her, along with that other guy, your partner..."

"Max Delany," Sam supplied.

"Right. Now I want to know what the hell is going on around here. So start talking, mister."

"Apparently you know as much as I do."

"Maybe. But suppose you just fill me in on what you know anyway," David insisted silkily.

Taking a seat before the desk, he matched the other man stare for stare, and for a long, tense moment there was absolute silence as each took the other's measure. Then in the distance they heard the faint whine of an eighteen-wheeler climbing the mountain road, and down on the loading dock someone shouted.

Finally Sam nodded. "It seems that, for some unknown reason, Elise came back here late Monday night and saw something that caused her to take off."

"And do you have any idea what it was that spooked her?"

The question held an unmistakable note of suspicion. David knew that it registered on Sam, as he had meant it to, but the man's cold stare never wavered.

"None whatever," he replied, unperturbed.

"I see. Go on."

"Before Elise left town she called Erin and warned her to stay away."

"And of course Erin hotfooted it out here as quickly as she could" came David's exasperated mutter.

Sam raised an ironic brow. "You seem to know your sister quite well. I take it she's the impulsive type."

"Impulsive, reckless and as headstrong as they come. But dammit! Elise should have known that cautioning Erin against anything is like waving a cape at a bull."

"Then it's a good thing that Max went along with her. If anyone can handle a willful female, he can. Women seem to find him irresistible, but if charm doesn't work, he's not above issuing orders and backing them up. Physically, if necessary."

"Huh. I can't see that working with Erin."

"I don't know. He did manage to keep her from being shot in San Francisco."

"Shot?" David jerked forward in his chair. "Are you saying someone took a *shot* at my sister?"

"Several," Sam replied in that toneless voice that made David want to plant his fist right in the man's face. "They flew to the coast to try to intercept Elise, but she had already gotten off the bus. When they walked out of the station two men were waiting for them."

"My little sister very conveniently failed to mention that interesting bit of information in any of her messages," David bit out savagely. He turned the air blue with a string of low, vicious curses and brought his fist down hard on the arm of the chair. "That crazy fool! Even after that, she's still running around out there playing detective. When I get my hands on her I'll ..."

With effort, he regained control of himself and turned his attention back to Sam. "Do you know where they are now?"

"I was hoping you could tell me."

"You mean you haven't heard from them?"

"Not for two days. All I know is they were heading for Las Vegas."

"Mmm. Well, they made it that far, anyway. The last message on my machine was from Erin. She left the number of the motel where they were staying, but when I called this morning they had already checked out."

"Maybe she's called since then." Sam picked up the telephone and placed it on the edge of the desk in front of David. "Why don't you check?"

Without a word, David picked up the receiver and called his home number in Dallas. He had left a fresh tape on the answering machine, but when he punched out the code to play back messages he heard an excited female voice.

"David! I think Elise is in Vail at the cabin. Max and I are going to fly there as soon as we can book a flight. Meet us."

Even as he dropped the receiver back into its cradle, David was moving toward the door. "I know where Erin and your partner are headed," he said tersely over his shoulder.

"If I hurry, I just might be able to catch up with them. Thanks for your help, Lawford."

"Wait a minute. I'm going with you."

With his hand on the doorknob, David turned and looked at Sam, his eyes narrowing on the man's cold face. "Why?"

"Because Max is my friend."

It was midafternoon before Erin and Max were able to get seats on a flight to Denver. They arrived just in time to join the mass exodus of local citizens headed for the mountains for the weekend, and by the time they rented a car and drove the remaining hundred or so miles, it was after eight when they reached Vail.

Erin was nervous and fidgety during the entire trip. Trying to take her mind off the situation and the possibility that they had come on a wild-goose chase, Max kept up a steady stream of conversation, telling her about his family and about growing up in Santa Fe and regaling her with stories of the mischief he and Sam had gotten into as boys. Erin was so distracted that she didn't hear half of it.

"You're going to have to guide me from here," Max said when they saw the first exit sign for Vail.

"Get off the interstate at the main exit." Erin peered out the windshield, her clipped voice and stiff posture revealing her tension.

Following her directions, Max took the off ramp to the south frontage road leading to the west end of town, then turned left. They crossed a bridge, and immediately the narrow gravel lane made a sharp turn back toward the east and began to climb. Set among the stately pines and aspens at widely spaced intervals on either side of the road, summer homes clung to the lower slope of the mountain. Several hundred feet below, the lights of Vail Village sparkled along its base like a scattering of diamonds.

The cabin belonging to Erin's family was an oversize redwood and glass A-frame with a wide deck all around.

There was a two-car garage at road level, but the cabin itself was perched high above it, reached by a long flight of wooden steps.

"Someone's here," Erin said excitedly, craning her neck to look up the mountainside as Max brought the car to a halt in the short driveway.

Light blazed from the triangular wall at the front of the structure and spilled down the slope, illuminating the trees and bracken with a soft golden glow.

Max was impressed by the commanding view the site afforded, but Erin seemed oblivious to it as she scrambled from the car and raced up the steps ahead of him, her footsteps thumping noisily on the wooden planks.

By the time he reached the top she had already knocked on the door. She cast him an anxious glance when he came to stand beside her, but neither spoke. For a minute all they heard was the rustle of leaves stirring in the wind and a staccato tapping on the redwood deck as Erin rapped an impatient tattoo with the toe of her shoe.

Then the door opened, and her face lit up.

"Elise, we've— Oh!" She stopped abruptly and stared, crestfallen, at the unfamiliar woman standing in the doorway. "I...I'm sorry. We...were expecting to find someone else here," she finally managed to stammer."

"Who is it, honey?" a male voice called, and a moment later a large man joined the woman in the doorway. He looked at Erin and Max and frowned. "What's the problem?"

"We're looking for Elise Holman," Max put in. "Is she, by chance, staying here with you?"

"There's no one here by that name," the man replied irritably. "You've got the wrong place."

"No, her family owns this cabin. We thought she was staying here."

"Well, she's not. We leased this place for two weeks, and our time isn't up for another couple of days. You can check with the real estate office in town."

Erin stirred at Max's side and made a despairing little sound. He slipped his arm around her waist and edged her toward the steps. "Our mistake. Sorry to have troubled you."

Excitement had kept Erin from feeling the chill of the mountain air, but as Max guided her down the steps she shivered. He pulled her closer against his side with a murmured "I'm sorry, darling."

She gave him a wan smile and nodded, too despondent to speak.

When they were seated in the car he turned to her, searching her face worriedly. "Well, what do we do now?"

"She's here somewhere, Max," Erin insisted. "I can feel her fear and anxiety. It's so strong that it's blocking out all her thoughts, but I know she's close by."

Max hesitated, and she felt a surge of panic, knowing he doubted her. She couldn't blame him; it must seem to him that she was grasping at straws. But the feelings buffeting her were real, and somehow she had to make him believe in them, too.

Before she could plead her case Max's face took on a decisive firmness. "All right. If you feel that strongly about it, I'll start searching first thing tomorrow morning." He ran his knuckles down her cheek and looked at her lovingly. "Now I suggest we find a place to stay before it gets too late. Tomorrow promises to be a busy day."

Though it was off season, Vail attracted many summer tourists, and they went to three places before finding a vacancy at one of the ski lodges just off Bridge Street, in the heart of the village.

Erin was drooping with fatigue and depression, and when they entered the room she opted for a long, hot bath. Later, after taking a shower, Max emerged from the bathroom expecting to find her curled up in bed, sound asleep. Instead she was standing at the balcony doors, her back to the room.

She was barefoot and wearing a long turquoise nightgown that skimmed her body in a whisper of silk. Her arms were crossed over her midriff, and she was absently massaging her elbows as she gazed out at the lights of Vail.

Watching her, Max rubbed his wet hair with a towel. "Do you want me to order something from room service? You didn't eat much on the plane."

"No thanks. I'm not hungry."

Her pleasant tone didn't fool him; he knew her much too well for that. When he thought about it, it amazed Max that they had met only a little over four days ago. The way he felt, it just as easily could have been four years, because he loved her completely, irrevocably.

They had been four days fraught with intense emotion, the kind that telescopes time and strips away all pretense, exposing with ruthless honesty a person's private self. Erin, he had learned, was a strong, courageous, intelligent and spirited woman. He had seen her angry, loving, terrified, sad, hopeful, despairing. By now he could read her moods as well as his own, and he knew that she had reached a low ebb.

Wearing only a towel knotted about his hips, he crossed the room to stand behind her and cupped the rounded curves of her shoulders, kneading gently. His heart swelled with gladness at the natural way she leaned back against him, and with a smile he rubbed his chin against her crown. The sweet, clean fragrance of her hair drifted to him like subtle perfume. Fine strands caught in the hint of stubble along his jaw, and like slippery silk, the soft curls slid back and forth with each tiny movement.

"I'm sorry, sweetheart," he murmured, curving his arms around her waist and crossing them over her midriff.

Erin sighed and placed her arms atop his. Absently her nails raked his forearms as her fingers sifted through the smattering of hair covering them. "Oh, Max," she said in a forlorn voice. "I was so hoping that we'd find her tonight."

"I know, sweetheart. I know." Her disappointment was a palpable thing, and feeling it, Max gritted his teeth in frustration.

"She's still here somewhere, Max," Erin said quietly. "I know she is."

"I'll start searching first thing in the morning, sweetheart. If she's here, I'll find her. I promise."

It was a promise Max desperately hoped he would be able to keep. He was uneasy relying on something as insubstantial as feelings, especially since he was concerned that they might stem more from desire than fact.

Max wanted to set Erin's heart at ease, but for now there was little he could do. Feeling frustrated and helpless, he held her close and rocked her within his embrace as they gazed down in somber silence at the picturesque mountain resort.

After a moment Max bent his head and nuzzled her neck, then turned her to face him, still holding her within the circle of his arms. His lips met hers in a soft, loving kiss, and when he pulled back he smiled at her tenderly. "You're as taut as a bowstring, and you're dead on your feet. C'mon," he said, nudging her toward the bed. "A good night's sleep is what you need."

Erin didn't argue, and a moment later she was lying in his arms, her head cradled on his shoulder. Max gazed up through the darkness at the ceiling, gritting his teeth. The feel of her, soft and yielding at his side, was sheer torture. He wanted her so much that he ached all over. Every muscle was clenched, his body throbbing and hot with desire.

But she was exhausted, physically and mentally. She needed rest, and he'd promised himself that she would get it, even if it killed him.

Her hand lay curled on his chest, and he felt her breath skim across his shoulder, warm and moist and soft as a feather. One of her legs was hooked intimately over his. The sole of her foot rubbed against his shin, and the soft abrasion sent fire rushing straight to his loins. He swallowed hard and struggled to subdue his raging passion, but when she pressed her parted lips against his neck he could not stifle the low moan that shuddered from him.

"Love me, Max," she whispered. Her tongue trailed a wet pattern over his skin. "I want you to make love to me."

Max squeezed his eyes shut. "Sweetheart," he gasped. "You...you're exhausted. You need rest." The throbbing in his loins intensified. He was so hot and hungry for her that he felt ready to explode.

"I need you more." Erin snuggled closer and moved urgently against him, her soft breasts pressing against his side. Making an inarticulate little sound, she nipped him with sweet savagery. "Please, Max."

It was more than he could take. With a rough, guttural growl, he rolled her to her back and took her mouth in a fierce kiss that sent desire spiraling out of control.

Erin's prolonged moan of pleasure was swallowed up in the kiss as their mouths rocked together. Her hands clutched him tightly, the nails digging into the hard muscles that banded his shoulders and back.

Breathing hard, Max pulled away and rose to his knees. Looming over her, his face rigid with desire in the pale moonlight pouring through the glass doors, he stripped the nightgown from her body and tossed it aside. The wisp of silk fluttered, ghostlike, to the floor, settling in a dark puddle against the ivory carpet.

Stretching out on the bed, his body half covering her, Max cupped her breasts in his broad palms. He kneaded the lush mounds and gently pinched the pink tips. Then he lowered his head, and Erin gave a thin cry, her back arching, as his hot mouth closed over her nipple and drew on her with a slow, rhythmic suction.

Their hands roamed freely, frantically over each other, touching everywhere. There was an urgency about their lovemaking, a silent desperation that drove them both. Sand was pouring through the hourglass; time was running out. They both sensed it, and the uncertainty of their future made them grasp at these precious moments with frenzied need.

"God, I can't get enough of you," Max groaned as his lips trailed over her flesh. He kissed the silky valley between her breasts; then his head slid downward. Heat and moisture filled her navel as he brushed his open mouth back and forth over it. His tongue swirled a wet circle around the tiny cavity, stabbed into it, withdrew and circled again. Erin shivered and moaned, driven nearly mindless by the sweet torment.

"Max. Oh, my love," she murmured ardently. Her restless hands flexed against his shoulders and trailed down his chest, fingers twining through the crisp hairs. Max jerked as her nails flicked the tiny nipples nestled there, then gave a low growl as her exploring hands slid downward. The growl became a groan, and shudders racked him as her warm hand lovingly enfolded his velvet hardness.

Max kissed her nipples and the undersides of her breasts as his fingers threaded through the nest of fiery curls at the apex of her thighs.

"Oh, Max!" Erin gasped at his probing, intimate touch.

He found her warm and wet and welcoming, and the discovery snapped the last tenuous thread of his control. He rose above her, moving into position between her silky thighs, and as their gazes locked, he made them one.

He thrust deep and stilled. Braced on his forearms, he remained motionless for several seconds, his head thrown back, his features clenched in delicious agony. Erin reached up and touched his face, and he turned his head and pressed a hot kiss against her palm.

Then the rhythmic movement began.

For long, ecstatic moments afterward, the moonlit room was filled with sighs and velvet murmurs, the soft, sensual sounds of love.

In the quiet aftermath, Erin slept peacefully, wrapped in Max's arms while, once again, he lay awake in the darkness. He was exhausted, his body sated from their loving, but his mind would not let him rest.

He rubbed his jaw against Erin's hair, his arms tightening around her. God, how he loved her. More than anything in the world. He wasn't quite sure how it had happened, but it had. And love, he was discovering, brought out some very interesting, primitive instincts in a man.

At the moment, he felt an overwhelming need to protect Erin from being hurt, physically and emotionally. But could he?

The mad situation they were caught up in could very well end tragically, especially for Elise. It might have already, though he didn't have the heart to point that out to Erin. He wasn't going to be the one to destroy what little hope she had. He knew, with gut-wrenching certainty, that if anything had happened to her twin, the effect on Erin would be devastating.

Damn! He hated feeling so helpless!

Chapter Thirteen

Erin paced back and forth across the room. She paused by the balcony doors to check her watch and sighed. Max had been gone only twenty minutes, and already it seemed like hours.

Raking a hand through her short curls, she walked the length of the room again, mentally kicking herself for promising him she'd stay put while he checked around. "Why on earth did you let him talk you into it?" she demanded of her reflection when she passed the mirror.

The minute she voiced the impatient question her conscience pricked her. You know why. Because he loves you, and he's afraid for you.

Personally, she doubted that they had been followed this time. But she had seen genuine terror in Max's eyes this morning when he'd pleaded with her to stay out of sight. Lord knew, she hadn't wanted to, but all her arguments failed to reassure him. In the end, loving him as she did, she had given in.

After two more trips across the room Erin came to a halt beside the balcony doors and stared out at the picture-perfect scene below.

The small village, strung out along the base of Vail Mountain, gleamed, pristine and beautiful, in the brilliant sunshine. There was a definite Alpine flavor to Vail. Small plazas, fountains and sculpture abounded at various levels. Lining the narrow winding streets and alleyways were old-world-style half-timbered stucco buildings with rough-hewn beams and bay-windowed fronts that housed quaint shops, sidewalk cafés and Alpine lodges. Everywhere you looked were flowers—hanging baskets, landscaped beds, pots and planters filled with pansies, petunias, poppies and columbines.

From the balcony Erin could see the clock tower at the heart of the village, as well as the very top of the covered bridge over Gore Creek. Beyond, Vail Mountain's massive bulk loomed up against a vibrantly blue sky, its verdant slopes veined with ski runs that stood out as bright green swaths cut through the darker pines and aspens.

The only vehicles allowed within the village proper were the free shuttle buses and bicycles, and with mostly pedestrian traffic there was an air of tranquillity about the mountain town that was very appealing.

But its peace did not touch Erin.

Restless, she whirled away from the glass doors and made another circuit of the room. She stretched out on the bed, telling herself she would rest, but flounced off again a moment later. In desperation, she turned on the television and tried every channel, but nothing distracted her sufficiently and she snapped it off.

"If I don't do something, I'm going to go stark, staring mad," she snarled at the ceiling.

After a moment's consideration, Erin snatched up her purse and headed for the door. She would just pop down to the lobby and get a newspaper. That should keep her occupied for a while.

Erin had already pushed the button to summon the elevator when she remembered that she had not put on the wig. Frowning, she nibbled the end of her index finger and debated whether or not to go back for it, but before she could make up her mind the elevator doors opened. There were three other passengers inside. They looked at her expectantly, and when one young man said, "Well, are you going down or not?" she cast one last doubtful glance toward her room, shrugged and stepped inside.

It would take only a few seconds, she reasoned. The rack of newspapers was just a few feet from the elevator. She would step off, buy one and get right back on.

When the doors slid open Erin was the first one off, but three steps away she stopped as though she had hit a brick wall, every vestige of color draining from her face.

Across the lobby, not twenty feet away, Sam Lawford stood talking to the desk clerk.

For a moment Erin froze to the spot, her mind numb with shock. Then terror welled up inside her, and her heart began to pound so hard that she could barely breathe. She whirled around, but the elevator had already gone. She took a step toward the stairs, then realized she would be trapped if she went back to the room.

Panicked, she looked back over her shoulder. Sam was still at the front desk, but he would soon have the information he was seeking.

Oh, God, she had to get out of there! If he turned his head just a fraction, he would see her!

She looked around frantically. To go out the front she would have to pass right by him. No. No, she couldn't risk it. Keeping her eye on Sam, Erin sidled toward the terrace doors. Trying not to attract attention, she forced herself to move slowly at first, but halfway there panic overtook her and she broke into a run.

Erin snatched open the terrace door so forcefully that it slipped out of her hand and banged back against the wall. She moaned and kept going.

In warm weather the terrace was used as an outdoor restaurant. Erin darted past the startled hostess and cut a zigzagging path through the tables. It occurred to her that there might be steps leading down to the street, but she did not take time to look for them. When she reached the edge of the terrace, she grasped the wrought-iron railing with both hands, vaulted over and landed hip-deep in a bed of columbine. Startled exclamations and murmurs arose from the diners behind her, but Erin hit the ground running. Hardly breaking stride, she tore through the flower bed, leaped into the street and sprinted away.

She ran full tilt, straining for all she was worth. She had to get away. She had to find Max. Oh, God! Where was Max?

At the corner she turned onto Bridge Street, but thick pedestrian traffic forced her to slow down. Nearly sobbing in frustration, Erin bumped and dodged and twisted, weaving in and out among the strolling tourists and bicycle-drawn rickshaws. Oh, please move. Move! she begged silently as she shoved her way through a clutch of people gathered around a sidewalk troubadour.

Every few seconds she darted frantic glances over her shoulder. There was no sign of Sam, but she didn't slacken her pace.

At the clock tower she turned right, raced through a wide pedestrian area for a short way, then veered off between two buildings and up a staired alleyway, taking the steps two at a time. Her lungs were on fire, and the muscles in her legs ached.

At the top, Erin found herself in a small plaza with a fountain at its center. Gasping for breath, she paused long enough to check the alley behind her. Two men were looking into the window of a small shop, and another had stopped to search in his pocket for something. At the bottom a woman and a little girl turned into the alley and started climbing the steps. None seemed in a hurry. More important, none was Sam.

Erin leaned against a building, took half a dozen deep breaths, then plunged across the plaza. The burst of adrenaline that had carried her that far was almost used up, and though she drove herself on, her steps began to lag.

Taking a wandering route around another cluster of buildings, Erin crossed a second plaza and stumbled down a short flight of steps that led to a rushing creek. Along its bank ran a row of shops and sidewalk cafés.

She was no longer running; it was all she could do to put one foot in front of the other. Her heart was pounding painfully, and her quivering legs would barely support her. She also had a painful stitch in her side. Erin glanced behind her, then headed for the nearest café. She had to rest . . . and think.

Even if Sam had given chase, she was fairly certain she had lost him. Just to be safe, though, she decided to go inside and take a seat where she could watch the entrance. Maybe she could get a table near the kitchen, so she could run out the back if she had to. She'd order something to drink and stay just long enough to get her second wind and decide what to do.

Before stepping inside the café, Erin took one last look over her shoulder, then nearly screamed when someone grasped both her arms just above the elbows.

"Why, Ms. Blaine. Where are you going in such a rush?"

Rendered senseless by terror, Erin stared, wild-eyed, at the man a full five seconds before she realized he was not Sam. Her relief was so great that her knees buckled.

"Here now! Easy does it," he exclaimed with a chuckle, tightening his grip as she began to sag. "Why, you're as white as a snowbank." Her chest was still heaving, and perpiration-darkened curls clung to her face and neck. In-pecting her, the man frowned and shook his head. "Don't ou know it's not wise to exert yourself at this altitude until ou've had time to get acclimatized? Two days just isn't ong enough. Here, let's sit down."

Two days? Erin blinked in confusion as the man led her o one of the sidewalk tables.

When they were seated he poured a glass of water from he pitcher on the table and handed it to her. "Here now, Ms. Blaine, you just relax and sip this, and when the wait-ess comes we'll order you a soft drink. You'll feel better in ıo time."

It hit her then that that was the second time he'd used her ıame. Sipping the water, she studied him over the rim of the ;lass. He was tall, in his mid-forties, with a hawkish face hat would be difficult to forget, but Erin was certain she'd ıever met him before in her life. Yet he knew her name.

"By the way, I apologize again about the problem with our family's cabin," the man added. "If I had known in ıdvance that you were coming, I wouldn't have rented it, of :ourse. But I've removed it from the listing, so when the Morrisons leave tomorrow I'll bring you the key and you ·an stay as long as you like."

Erin's heart gave a little leap as, suddenly, it all clicked nto place. Elise had talked to this man! And she had used ıer maiden name! Leaning forward, she grasped his arm. 'You're the agent who handles our cabin?"

"Yes. Yes, of course I am," he said, clearly startled. "We net on Thursday when you came by my office to pick up the .ey. Are you feeling all right?"

"Look, Mr. . . . ?"

"Ledbetter. John Ledbetter."

"Mr. Ledbetter, the person you talked to wasn't me. That vas my twin sister. I came here expecting to find her at the ·abin. I've been worried sick, not knowing where she was."

"Ah, now I understand," he said, looking vastly relieved.

"I take it you know where Elise is staying?"

"Why, yes. I rented her another cabin for a few days until yours is vacant. The next one up the road, actually. I'll take you there, if you'd like."

"Oh, would you? that would be..." She stopped, her expression uncertain. Max. She needed to find him and let him know. About Sam *and* Elise. But how? She hadn't the slightest idea where he was, and she couldn't go back to the hotel. All she could do for Max, she realized with a sick sensation in the pit of her stomach, was pray that he somehow managed to elude his partner.

But she could find her sister.

She gave Mr. Ledbetter a determined smile. "That would be wonderful. Thank you." Standing, she hitched her purse strap onto her shoulder. "I'm ready to go whenever you are."

In his excitement, Max fumbled with the room key, cursing under his breath. When the lock finally clicked, he pushed the door open and quickly stepped inside. "Erin! Sweetheart, I found where Elise is stay—"

He halted, his face registered shock, then fury.

"You!"

"Hello, Max." Sam stood up, his rangy frame unfolding from the chair with that peculiar grace of a big man.

"What the hell have you done with Erin?"

Sam's brows rose a fraction. At the same time another man stepped out of the bathroom. Max swung to face him and found himself staring down the barrel of a gun.

The man smiled, but his eyes were deadly. "Funny. I was about to ask you the same thing, Delany."

It took a second, but when his meaning sank in, relief poured through Max. They hadn't found her. Somehow, Erin had gotten away. A sardonic smile tipped up one corner of his mouth. "Now, if I knew where she was, you don't seriously think I'd tell you, do you?"

"I would if I were you, Max," Sam advised matter-of-factly. "This is David Blaine. Erin and Elise's brother."

Max turned on his partner with a murderous look. "When I want your opinion I'll—" The furious words halted in mid-spate, and his head swung back toward the man with the gun. "You're the brother?"

"That's right."

Max subjected him to an intense, narrow-eyed scrutiny. His brown hair held only a hint of red, but the eyes were the same. Yes, despite his lean, mean, slightly battered look, there was definitely a family resemblance, Max decided. Especially around the mouth. And there was that same stubborn chin. He judged him to be around thirty-six, which would be about right.

David withdrew a wallet from his pocket and flipped it open. "Here's my driver's license. And there's a social security card in there somewhere, if you're still in doubt."

"No, I believe you. but what the hell are you doing here with him?" Max demanded, hooking his thumb toward Sam.

His eyes narrowing, David looked from Max to Sam and back. "You have a problem with that?"

"What's the matter with you, Max?" Sam demanded, and for once his voice was tinged with anger. "I'm here because I'm your friend. I've been worried sick, wondering what happened to you. Why the hell did you stop calling?"

"Because I didn't want those two goons on our tail again, that's why. Hell, Sam, I may be gullible, but I'm not stupid. How long did you think it would take before I realized that every time I called you, they showed up?"

For an unguarded moment Sam looked stunned; then every trace of emotion vanished, and his face took on that set, distant look. "Are you saying you think I sent them after you?"

"Oh, c'mon, Sam!" Max gestured impatiently, his expression disgusted. "What else could I think? I called you from Albuquerque and told you Elise was in trouble and I was flying to San Francisco to intercept a bus, and two guys show up at the terminal and shoot at Erin and me. Then, like a fool, I called and filled you in on everything and told you our plans, and the next morning when we left Bakersfield, lo and behold, the same two appear out of nowhere. Only this time they were just following us. Someone had obviously told them Erin was the wrong sister. You were the only one who knew that, or where to find us."

"I had nothing to do with it," Sam said stonily.

"Did you tell anyone else where Max was or what was going on?" David asked.

"I may have after the first call. Several people did ask where he was," Sam replied after giving it some thought. "That was before I knew how serious the situation was. But after the shooting? No. No, I didn't say a word to anyone."

"Then there is no way anyone else could have known about Erin or that we were in Bakersfield," Max said, his voice rough with bitterness.

"Unless," David offered, "someone tapped Sam's phone."

The comment drew sharp looks from the other two. "Or..." Sam began.

"...someone could have simply listened in." As he completed the thought, Max's gaze sought Sam's, his eyes filled with regret and contrition. "God, Sam, I'm sorry. That possibility never occurred to me."

Sam waved aside the apology. "Don't worry about it. It didn't occur to me, either, and in your place I probably would have reacted the same way."

Helplessly, remorse, regret and a dozen other painful emotions gnawing at him, Max watched the shutters come down, watched his friend retreat still further behind that icy wall. Though Sam dismissed the misunderstanding with that maddening imperturbable stoicism, Max knew his friend was far from unaffected. His own lack of faith was another in a long series of low blows against this man who'd had far more than his share. And the hell of it was there was nothing Max could say or do to change it.

David holstered his gun, faced Max and planted his hands on his hips. "Now that we've got that settled, where the hell is Erin?"

"I don't know." Max raked a hand through his hair. Fear welled up anew as several horrifying possibilities occurred to him, shoving aside, for the moment, his concern over Sam. "Dammit! She wasn't supposed to budge from this room. She knows it's not safe for her to be running around."

David gave a snort of mirthless laughter. "That's never stopped her before. Even scared stiff she'd never be short on bravado," he said with mingled pride and exasperation.

"Or sheer raw courage," Max added. His tone stated plainly that he would stand for no criticism of Erin, not even from a brother.

Faint surprise flickered across David's face. Narrowing his eyes, he fixed Max with a flinty look. It met a blue stare as unyielding as stone. The air vibrated with challenge as the two men appraised each other in silence. On the sidelines, Sam watched the exchange with interest, an atypical smile twitching about his stern mouth.

"So that's the way it is," David finally murmured.

"That's right. Any objections?"

"I'm not sure. Check with me later. After we've found my sisters."

"If you two are through bristling at each other, I suggest we get on with it," Sam commented, and both Max and David had the grace to look sheepish.

David walked to the dresser and picked up the brown wig, fingering the silky strands with a musing smile. "Sam and I went to the cabin last night when we arrived, and there's a family there by the name of Morrison. According to them, no one fitting Erin or Elise's description had been by, just a tall dark man and a woman with long brown hair. The description threw me at first." He tossed the wig back onto the dresser, his expression darkening once again. "Obviously Erin was mistaken about Elise's being here."

"No, she wasn't!" Max's earlier excitement returned in a flash as he remembered what had brought him back to the room. "I don't know where Erin is, but I did discover where Elise is staying."

"All right! What are we waiting for?" David said, striding for the door. "Let's go."

"Now you tell your sister I'll be by tomorrow with the key to your cabin," Mr. Ledbetter called out as he put the car in gear and headed back down the road.

"I will. And thanks for the lift." Erin waved, and when the car disappeared around the curve she climbed the three steps to the porch. Unlike her family's cabin, this one sat just a few feet from the road. It was smaller and more rustic, made of logs, with a covered porch across the front.

Erin knocked on the door. "Elise! Elise, it's Erin." She waited, but there was no sound from inside. With an impatient sigh she looked at the tan Plymouth in the attached carport. Mr. Ledbetter had said it was Elise's; she had to be there. Erin *knew* she was there; she could feel her presence . . . her fear.

From the corner of her eye Erin saw a shadowy movement at the window, and she knocked again, harder this time. "Elise, open up! I know you're in there."

Just as she started to knock again the door opened partway and a hand shot out, grabbed her wrist and jerked her inside. There was a slam behind her as Erin took two stumbling steps into the room; then a tug on her wrist whipped her around, and she was face-to-face with her sister.

Pressed back against the door, Elise stared at her. Her face was pale, and there were dark circles beneath her wide, terror-stricken eyes. Gazing at her, Erin felt a rush of pity and compassion so strong that she had to blink back tears.

"Erin, what are you *doing* here?" Elise demanded.

The sharp edge of hysteria in her voice wrung Erin's heart. Smiling tenderly, she held out her arms and said, "Now is that any way to greet your other half? Especially since I went to so much trouble to find you?"

Elise's face crumpled. With an anguished cry, she flew into Erin's outstretched arms. "Oh, God, Sis. I'm so frightened!" she choked, and then words became impossible as she dissolved into tears.

The pent-up cries tore from deep inside her, terrible racking sounds that reflected the days of terror and uncertainty she had endured alone.

"There, there, sweetheart. Cry it all out. You'll feel better." Battling her own tears, Erin held her twin close, crooning soft, soothing words, rubbing her heaving shoulders, her back, the silken curls so like her own. She rocked her gently, her heart aching with sympathy and love as she strained to absorb her sister's fear.

Gradually, Elise's sobs tapered off, and she quieted. "I . . . I'm sorry," she quavered as she pulled herself from Erin's embrace. "I know that doesn't help. It's just that these past few days have been so horrible." She sniffed and took a deep breath, scrubbing her wet cheeks with her fingertips and the heels of her hands. "I've been so scared they would find me that I haven't been able to eat or sleep. I didn't know what to do except run. And call David. But he isn't at home." Her eyes filled with fresh tears, and her chin began to wobble as she looked beseechingly at Erin. "Oh, God, Sis, what am I going to do?"

"There now, don't get yourself upset again." Erin framed her twin's face between her palms and stared into her eyes. "Everything is going to be all right, Elise. You'll see."

If she had hoped to still her sister's panic, she failed. Suddenly Elise's eyes widened with alarm. "Erin! How did you get here?"

"Mr. Ledbetter brought me."

"No, I mean how did you find me?"

"Well, it wasn't easy, I assure you," Erin said with an attempt at wry humor. "I never realized before what a clever, devious mind you have. I'm impressed, sister mine."

"But I obviously wasn't clever enough. You found me. And if you can, so can others."

"Darling, who are you talking about? What hap—"

Without warning, the door was kicked open. Elise let out a scream, and instinctively both women reached for each other as two men with guns stormed in. They were followed more slowly by a woman. She stopped a few feet inside the door and gave them a superior, malicious smile. "I believe your sister is referring to us, Ms. Blaine."

Erin was so shocked that she barely heard Elise's piteous moan. She stared at the woman, unable to believe her eyes. "Miss Crenshaw?"

"Surprised? I thought you would be." Cocking her gray head to one side, Wilma Crenshaw looked at Elise with something approaching respect. "I must say, my dear, you surprised me. You led Alan and Floyd a merry chase. And that business about going to Salt Lake City fooled them completely. We never would have found you if it hadn't been for your sister."

"You followed us to Vail?" Erin asked, feeling sick at heart.

"No. We followed your brother and Sam to Vail. Actually, that's not quite true. We hired a plane and got here before them. You see, I listened in when he phoned from Sam's office to check his answering machine. When Sam and your brother arrived, we simply waited for them to find you."

"You listened in on..." Erin stopped as understanding dawned. "Then Sam isn't involved in this at all, is he?"

"Straight-arrow Sam? You suspected him?"

The questions came from the burly blond man. Erin glanced at him and nodded, realizing that this had to be Floyd Shulman, the man Max had told her about, the same one who had stared at her when she arrived at Global. God, had that been only five days ago? It seemed like a lifetime.

He threw his head back and laughed. "So that's why you came barreling out of that hotel like a bat out of hell. You nearly ran poor Alan right into the ground just trying to keep up with you." Shooting the other man a taunting look, he grinned slyly. "He's gone a bit soft after ten years of cushy police work."

"Damn you, Floyd—"

"Shut up, you two!" Wilma snapped. "I've had enough of your bickering!"

She turned back to Erin and gave a snort of derision. "Sam Lawford? Hardly. It takes someone daring and clever to handle an ingenious operation like ours. My brother Jerry set the whole thing up," she said with pride. "He sees to it that the diamonds are shipped from Israel, and I take care of things on this end."

"Diamonds?"

"They embed them in marked pieces of pottery," Elise said. Her voice was still shaky, but she had managed to pull herself together. Now she was glaring at Wilma with bitter, defiant anger. "That's how they get through customs undetected. They're hidden, and they don't show up on the X rays. When I went back to Global on Monday night to check the vault, I saw a light in the warehouse and heard voices. No one was supposed to be there, so I went inside to check. That's when I saw them smashing open a shipment."

"We thought it was drugs," Erin said in a dazed voice.

"Don't be absurd!" Wilma snapped. "Do you know what that foul stuff does to people? My brother wouldn't soil his hands with it."

Erin stared at her in amazement, realizing that the woman was offended by the idea. Considering their circumstances, it was almost comical.

"If you feel that way, then why have you been chasing my sister all over the country? Why are you here?" Erin knew it was probably futile to attempt to appeal to the woman's finer instincts, but she had to try.

"This is different," Wilma snapped sullenly. "I can't let you ruin everything Jerry has worked for. Anyway, if you hadn't been so nosy, none of this would have happened," she added with an accusing glare for Elise.

"But why harm us?" Erin persisted. "You can't possibly hope to get away with it. Or hope to continue your smuggling operation. Both Max and Sam know that something is going on, so there's sure to be an investigation."

"All we have to do is pull back and wait it out. Alan will see to it that the investigation goes nowhere, and when it's dropped we'll quietly resume shipments." She smiled at them coldly and folded her hands across her thick middle. "As for you two, you're simply going to have a tragic accident. In your rush to get back to Mr. Delany you're going to lose control of your car and crash down the mountainside."

"Max is here?" Elise asked, her eyes suddenly alight.

The reaction told Erin all she needed to know about her sister's feelings toward Max, and she felt a hollow ache in the region of her heart. She gave Elise's hand a squeeze. "Yes. He came with me to help look for you."

"Why don't we just kill them here and be done with it?" Floyd argued.

"Because, you idiot, it's got to look like an accident," Alan barked, glaring at him. "If the local police suspect murder, the investigation will drag on forever."

"But what if the crash doesn't kill them? What do we do then, smart guy?"

A bitter quarrel broke out between the two men. Wilma tried in vain to silence them, and soon all three were involved in a shouting match.

Watching them, Erin gauged the distance to the door. Their chances of getting away were slim, but she'd be damned if she was going to just let them push her off a mountain without a fight. Maybe if she kept them busy, Elise could get away. Would they shoot? she wondered. She wasn't sure about Alan, but Floyd would. She would have to do something about him.

Under cover of the shouts, Erin poked her sister in the side and muttered under her breath, "When I tell you to run, take off as fast as you can."

"But—"

"Don't argue. Just do it!" she hissed.

David brought the car to a halt the instant they rounded the bend and the cabin came into view.

"Someone's there," he announced tersely, staring at the dark sedan parked behind the compact in the carport. He eased the door open and climbed out, and without a word the others did the same.

They studied the quiet cabin. There was no movement, no sound beyond the distant chirping of a bird, but something was wrong. Max could feel it. His gut was knotting like a twisted rope.

"Keep low and stay close to the trees," David commanded as he pulled out his gun and moved forward. Crouching, the three men raced along the edge of the road, keeping the parked sedan between them and the window at the front of the cabin. To Max, their labored breathing and the crunch of their shoes on the gravel seemed abnormally loud, and he expected at any second to hear a challenge from whoever was in the cabin.

When they reached the drive they stopped behind the car, waited a moment, then, one by one, moved into position, David and Sam flattened against the wall on either side of the door, Max by the window.

"See anything?" David whispered.

Max eased closer to the window, carefully tipping his head out just enough to get a look inside. What he saw almost made his heart stop.

That crazy little fool!

Chapter Fourteen

It all seemed to happen in a flash.

To Erin's relief, Floyd lost the argument. Wilma stalked to the door and held it open, and in response to her sharp commands, the two men began to herd them out.

Elise went first. As she drew even with Wilma she paused to look at her pleadingly, but the woman just stared back, tight-lipped and unyielding.

"C'mon. Get going, you two," Floyd snarled behind Erin.

Erin moved up closer to her sister and drew a deep breath, her muscles tensing. A little hitch of her shoulder sent the purse strap sliding down her arm. When the loop reached her wrist her fingers closed around the double strap, and with her other hand she shoved Elise out the door.

"Run! *Run!*"

As the words left Erin's mouth she threw herself to the side, sending the door crashing back, pinning Wilma to the wall behind it, and in one continuous motion she swung the heavy shoulder bag around with all her might and smashed it into Floyd's face.

The deafening report of his gun reverberated off the walls, but the bullet slammed into an overhead beam as he went staggering backward.

Alan shouted, and from the corner of her eye Erin saw him raise his gun with both hands and take aim. Instinctively, she dived for the floor.

She hit the hard surface rolling, expecting to feel the pain of a bullet ripping through her at any moment, but it didn't happen. All at once the room was full of men and the sound of scuffling. Erin came up against the far wall and scrambled to her feet, her muscles bunching for flight. But to her amazement, Sam had Floyd Shulman in a hammerlock, and Max was pounding the young policeman senseless, sending him staggering back with every furious blow.

Then David was there, standing in the doorway with Elise tucked against his side, a gun in his other hand.

Wilma staggered out from behind the door, and he motioned with the gun for her to stand in the middle of the room. "All right, Max. That's enough," he ordered, as Max's fist smashed into his opponent's jaw again.

Max grabbed Alan by the shirtfront to keep him from falling and glared at David. "This creep was going to shoot Erin," he snarled through clenched teeth, shaking the semiconscious man like a dog shakes a bone.

"Well, he's not going to shoot anyone now. Let him go."

For an instant Max looked as though he was going to argue. Then, with a disgusted growl, he shoved the man away. As Alan crumpled to the floor Max's anxious gaze swept the room.

A look of fierce love and protectiveness blazed from his eyes when he spotted Erin. "Sweetheart. Thank God you're safe," he murmured with heartfelt relief, and started toward her. He had barely taken the first step when Elise flew from her brother's side and flung herself against his chest.

"Oh, Max, darling. I knew you would come," she sobbed as her arms encircled him. "I knew it. I've always known you cared, and when Erin told me you were here, I knew you wouldn't let me down."

She burrowed close, clinging like a limpet, her face pressed against his chest. Stunned, for a moment Max just stood there, not responding, but as she began to weep, he hesitantly raised his arms. They hovered over her back for an instant, then, with obvious reluctance, enfolded her.

Watching, Erin felt her heart break into a million pieces. It was over. Every fragile dream, every tiny shred of hope to which she had so foolishly clung these past few days vanished like smoke in the wind.

Love shouldn't be so painful, she thought with aching sadness as she watched her sister being comforted by the man they both loved. Or so complicated. But it was. Erin's body quivered with hurt that was soul-deep and inescapable.

Somehow, it made it worse knowing he could be hers. A word, a gesture, that was all it would take, and Max would gently but firmly put Elise aside. But like every decision in life, there was a price to be paid, and this one was just too great.

It did not matter that Max would never love Elise; Erin could not deliberately hurt her twin. If she did, she would never know a moment's happiness, no matter how much she cared for Max.

It was all so hopeless and sad.

Max stroked Elise's back as she wept softly against his shirtfront, his hands gentle and soothing, if a bit awkward. Over the top of her head he gave Erin a helpless look. His eyes pleaded with her to let him end it, to let him explain, but she shook her head and silently implored him to say nothing.

With grim acceptance, Max returned to his ministration, his face set and hard as he bent over Elise.

Unable to watch the touching scene any longer, Erin looked away.

By chance, her gaze encountered Sam and halted, her eyes widening. He was staring at Elise, sobbing in Max's arms, and for the first time Erin saw real emotion in that austere face. It was pure pain.

Why, he loves her!

It was a stunning discovery. Despite all that Max had told her, she had been certain that Sam Lawford was incapable of feeling anything. She had been wrong. So very wrong. In that unguarded moment he was gazing at Elise with abject longing and despair, his harsh face twisted in torment. No, there was no mistaking that anguished look; Sam's suffering exactly mirrored her own.

Erin had thought she could not possibly feel any worse, but as she stared at those bleak, silver-gray eyes, her aching heart felt as though it were splitting in two. Dear God, it was all such a mess.

Mercifully, Erin had little time to agonize over the situation. David took charge, and after hearing the entire story, he sent Sam into town to notify the local police and the FBI.

The hours after that passed in a blur. The rest of the day and a good part of the evening were spent going over and over the whole tale from start to finish. They were questioned in great detail by men from both law enforcement agencies, who went over even the most minute detail with relentless thoroughness.

Under questioning, Floyd confessed everything—that he and Wilma had sought jobs with Global for the express purpose of smuggling diamonds. Alan Harper, it turned out, had stumbled onto their operation by accident and cut himself in for a share in return for his silence.

Since he was the only officer involved, a call was placed to the Santa Fe police department, and search warrants were issued. Within only a couple of hours enough hard evidence was discovered in Wilma's apartment to back up their story. Local and federal charges were filed against the three, and the authorities in Israel were informed of Jerry Crenshaw's part in the operation.

By the time the police were finished with them, it was late. The women rejected the suggestion that they stay over and fly home the next morning; Elise, after nearly six days of running scared, was eager to return home, and Erin wanted to avoid the inevitable confrontation with Max. Several times during the afternoon and evening Max had tried to corner her, but she had managed to avoid getting into a discussion. It was not difficult, since Elise never let him out of her sight.

They caught the red-eye to Albuquerque, all except for Sam, who volunteered to fly to Las Vegas and pick up Max's truck. He had once again donned his icy mask of indifference, but Erin knew that he was hurting and that the offer was a self-protective maneuver. She envied him the chance to escape. If there had been a hope of getting away with it, she would have volunteered to go with him.

Erin had forgotten how observant David was. She was sure she'd hidden her feelings well, but, sitting next to him on the plane, she soon discovered otherwise.

They had no sooner left the ground than he said, "Okay, spill it. What's going on?"

"Going on?" Erin looked at him, her eyes widening, in feigned innocence. "Why, nothing."

"Don't give me that. I saw the look that passed between you and Delany. So what's he doing sitting up there with Elise?" he asked, nodding toward the front of the plane.

Erin stared out the window at the black sky and tried to keep her voice steady. "She's in love with him."

"Gee, thanks. Would you believe I'd already figured that out?" he said with brotherly sarcasm. "But then, so are you. And I happen to know that the man is crazy about you. So explain."

Tears threatened. Erin swallowed hard and attempted a nonchalant shrug. "I don't want to hurt her."

"Hell, neither do I," David said impatiently. In a softer voice he added, "But I don't want to see you hurt, either."

"I can take it," Erin insisted, though her wobbling chin belied the claim.

"And you think Elise can't? For Pete's sake, Erin, you've been protecting her ever since you were both toddlers and Tommy hit her over the head with a plastic bat. It's become second nature with you, but that doesn't make it right." When Erin didn't respond, David heaved a sigh. "All right," he continued wearily. "I'll grant you that Elise is sweet and gentle, but believe me, there's a lot of strength beneath that softness."

"David, you don't understand. Elise was in love with Max long before I ever met him."

"So? Do you think that gives her squatter's rights or something? She's a grown woman. If she hadn't already learned that wanting doesn't necessarily make it so, it's time she did."

"I never should have fallen in love with him," Erin maintained stubbornly.

David's stern expression melted into tender concern. He picked up her hand and rubbed his thumb over the soft skin and fragile bones. "Honey, love happens whether you want it to or not. You can't control your feelings."

She slanted him a long look and lifted her chin. "Maybe not. But you can control your actions."

They arrived in Santa Fe in the small hours of the morning. Since Elise's apartment was still in shambles, Max insisted that they all stay at his house.

Erin was horrified, but before she could refuse, Elise had taken him up on the offer, her delight at the prospect obvious.

As the battered Continental began the climb toward Max's home, Erin could not suppress a shudder, recalling the last time she had been on that road and how close she had come to losing her life.

When Max brought the car to a halt in the drive before his home, they all climbed out. Erin waited with the others while he unlocked the door, shivering in the cold mountain air and feeling decidedly peculiar as her eyes skimmed over the sprawling, multilevel structure. Had it been just a little more than five days since she had been there? The house seemed at once strange and familiar.

They trooped inside like weary soldiers. In the entry Elise complimented Max on his home, looking around with avid interest. Erin fidgeted with her purse and pretended not to notice when he attempted to catch her eye.

"There are plenty of bedrooms," he said as he led them up the short flight of steps to the landing. "You can each have your own."

"That isn't necessary. Elise and I will share one," Erin put in quickly, determined to forestall any attempt he might make to get her alone. "We're both still too keyed up and nervous to be alone," she explained in response to Max's sharp look. In truth, she was simply too exhausted and too heartsick to deal with their problems.

By the middle of the week, Max decided that he'd been as patient as he intended to be. He was going to talk to Erin alone even if he had to kidnap her to do it, he told himself as he waited in his car across the street from Elise's apartment complex. They'd been back in Santa Fe for three days, and he had not had an opportunity to say more than a half a dozen words to Erin, much less touch her. Which was what he was longing to do.

They had to get things settled between them, he told himself, shifting restlessly on the seat. They had to make plans for their future. Most of all, they had to tell Elise how they felt about each other. The longer they waited, the more difficult it was going to be. Didn't Erin see that?

Of course she did. She had to have noticed the way Elise looked at him and spoke to him. The day they had spent straightening her apartment, she barely got three feet from his side. And dammit! The only reason he'd volunteered to help was to be near Erin, to maybe steal a moment alone with her.

He had hoped to have her in his home long enough to get everything settled, but Erin had foiled that plan by insisting, almost the moment they awoke that first morning, that they return to Elise's apartment.

Drumming his fingers on the steering wheel, Max watched the driveway of the apartment complex for Elise's car. It had been repaired while they were gone and returned to Elise yesterday. He had suggested that she take the rest of the week off to rest and recuperate and visit with Erin, but she insisted on returning to work today. He had a sinking feeling that her dedication sprang from a wish to be near him.

The little blue car turned out of the driveway, and Max sat up straighter. Okay. It was about time. He watched Elise drive away, and as the car merged with the morning traffic he climbed from the Continental and strode across the street. While Elise was getting things shipshape at the office, he was going to have a talk with her sister.

Erin looked around the room one last time, then snapped the lid shut on her suitcase. She carried it into the living room and set it beside the door. Straightening, she pulled a slip of paper from her pocket and double-checked her flight number and departure time, then glanced at her watch. Four hours until her flight; she had plenty of time.

Nibbling her index finger, she frowned and ticked off the items on her mental checklist. She was packed and ready, she had a plane reservation, she'd called for a taxi to be there in an hour, she'd left Elise a note. Erin cast an anguished look at the telephone sitting on the kitchen bar and bit the inside of her lip. There was only one thing left to do: she had to talk to Max.

Of course, she could write him a letter and mail it from the airport. It would be easier all the way around. Erin thought about it for only a moment before rejecting the cowardly temptation. Max deserved better than that.

Taking a shaky breath, Erin wiped her damp palms on her slacks and walked toward the bar.

Before she reached it the doorbell sounded. The ring was followed immediately by a loud knock. Erin retraced her steps and looked through the peephole. Her heart began to pound.

Bracing herself, she opened the door and forced a weak smile. "Hello, Max."

Without a word, he stepped inside and pulled the door from her nerveless grasp, shutting it with a snap. Then she was in his arms and he was kissing her, all the loving and frustration of the past three days pouring into the hungry embrace.

Erin gave herself up to it without thought of resistance. She melted against him, greedily absorbing his heat and power, her hands running over his shoulders and neck, her fingers twining in his hair. Their tongues danced and stroked in an erotic duel as their yearning bodies strained together. Erin was painfully aware that this was the last time she would ever be in Max's arms, and she clung to him with feverish desperation.

"I've missed you like hell," he said thickly when he ended the kiss. He buried his face in the side of her neck and held her so tightly that she couldn't breathe, but she didn't care. Erin pressed her lips together and squeezed her eyes shut in an agony of despair and love.

"I want you," Max said in a desire-roughened voice. "I want you so much I ache." He raised his head and looked at her, his handsome face flushed and soft with love as his hand curved around her cheek. "But first we have to talk. I promised myself that—"

He stopped, staring over her shoulder at the suitcase by the door. His gaze snapped back to her, and his blue eyes blazed with anger and accusation. "You're leaving."

"Yes," Erin admitted sadly. She stepped away from his arms, her heart crying out at the awful finality of it.

"Just like that? You were going to leave without saying a word?"

"No! No, I was just about to call and ask you to come over so I could—" she bit her lip and looked at him helplessly "—could say goodbye."

"I don't believe this." Max paced away a few steps, raking a hand through his hair, then swung back, glaring. "You planned this all along, didn't you? Here I've been thinking that you were just dreading the inevitable, that you knew we would have to explain to Elise how we felt, but that you were just putting it off. But I was wrong. You never had any intention of telling her the truth, did you?"

Miserably unhappy, Erin shook her head. "Not once I saw how much she cares for you. She's convinced that you came after her because this whole thing made you realize how much she means to you. Since we've been back she's been so bubbly and happy. You're all she talks about. I can't tell her about us, Max. I just can't. Please understand."

"Understand! How the hell do you expect me to understand? Whatever Elise feels, or thinks she feels, you can't prevent her from being hurt, because I don't care for her that way. I never will. And throwing away what we have won't change that."

"Maybe not," Erin said, her eyes glistening with moisture. "But I can't be the one to smash her dreams. She would feel so betrayed that the pain would be twice as bad. I can't do it to her, Max. I can't hurt her that way."

Erin felt torn in two. She adored her sister and wanted to see her happy, and for that reason a part of her almost wished that Max could love Elise. But another part of her wailed in agony at the very thought.

Max's face hardened. "All right, then, I'll tell her."

"If you do, I'll never forgive you, Max," Erin declared. "I swear it." Her taut voice quavered with emotion, but it was not an idle threat. It was there in the determined lift of her chin, the fierce warning blazing from her brown eyes.

Stunned, Max looked at her as though he couldn't believe his ears. "You can't mean that, Erin." His voice rang with desperate anxiety. "Dammit! We love each other!"

Erin wrapped her arms around her middle, as though bracing herself for what she was about to say. "Do we, Max?" she questioned shakily. "We've only known each other a little over a week. Maybe...maybe we just got carried away by all the tension and drama." It wasn't true, and she knew it. Just saying the words made her feel as though she were dying, bit by bit.

"I'm thirty-seven years old, Erin," Max said furiously. "A grown man, not some infatuated teenager. I damn well know what I'm feeling. I love you. And you love me. Don't you?"

Unable to meet the hard demand in his eyes, Erin walked to the window and fixed her gaze on the swaying limbs of the cottonwood tree just outside in the courtyard. "Max...please."

"Don't you?" he insisted.

Erin turned her head and looked at him over her shoulder. Torment darkened her eyes. The temptation to deny her feelings was strong, but she couldn't force the lie out. After a moment of taut silence her shoulders slumped. "Yes, I love you," she said dejectedly, wishing with all her soul that she didn't. "But it makes no difference."

Max flinched as though she had struck him, his face turning pale. The utter bleakness in his eyes tore at Erin's heart, and she returned her gaze to the window, though all she saw through her tears was a watery blur.

"I see," Max said stiffly behind her. "Well, I guess that's that."

Erin sensed him moving toward the door. It opened, and then there was an awful quiet. She struggled to draw air into her tortured lungs.

"Goodbye, my love," Max whispered.

The door closed, and with that soft, final click, Erin's face crumpled. Her eyes squeezed shut against the pain, sending a torrent of tears streaking down her face. They dropped from her chin like rain, and she tasted their salty wetness as they gathered in the corners of her mouth.

Chapter Fifteen

Time heals all wounds. Erin gave a bitter little laugh and leaned back in her chair, swiveling it to stare out the window beside her desk. How many times had she heard that particular homily? She had always believed it, had drawn a certain amount of comfort from it in the past, but now she was beginning to have her doubts.

How much time did it take, for heaven's sake? It had been two months since she had seen Max, and the pain and longing were just as sharp. Erin gave another snort of laughter and raked a hand through her hair. Who was she kidding? If anything, they were worse.

She thought about him constantly. She couldn't eat. She couldn't sleep. She couldn't work.

Grimacing, Erin glanced at the computer monitor. Except for three lines of amber letters, it was blank. They were the same three lines she'd been staring at for the past hour. She had been working on the novel since the beginning of summer, and the French translation was due at the publisher's in three weeks, but she was not much further along than she had been before Elise's fateful phone call. She just couldn't seem to concentrate.

Not that she hadn't tried. In the past two months she had driven herself, spending longer hours at her desk than she ever had, and getting less done.

With a sigh, Erin abandoned the computer, pushing her chair back to stand and walk to the window. Below, several of the tenants were lounging around the apartment pool, and a few others were swimming, despite the slight nip in the October air. She gazed at the supine bodies and envied them their carefree existence, without having the slightest urge to join them. She had tried that diversion a few times, but it had been an exercise in futility.

How was she ever going to forget Max, she wondered dismally, when Elise wrote of little else? Evidently, he was doing nothing to discourage her sister. If anything, from the tone of Elise's letters, they seemed to be drawing closer. Every line of the last one was etched in Erin's brain.

Max took me to dinner last night at Tomascito's. Oh, Erin, it was so wonderful. We talked for hours.

And on the next page there was:

Max dropped by my apartment the other night, even though we didn't have anything planned. Not that he takes me for granted, mind you, but the relationship is progressing nicely, becoming more comfortable.

Then there was:

Guess what Max brought me from his latest trip to Paris? A bottle of Joy perfume! Can you believe it? It costs the earth.

As she'd read the letter Erin had wanted to curl into a little ball and die. Every word had brought pain, as though her heart were being ripped from her body by a sharp-clawed animal. Which, in a way, was true; the animal was the green-eyed monster.

For the first time in her twenty-seven years, she was jealous of her twin. Erin hated the feeling. She almost hated Max for causing it. Almost.

She closed her eyes and caught her lower lip between her teeth to stop its trembling. Dear Lord, she wished she could hate him. Or at least stop caring. But she couldn't. She loved him so, and it hurt unbearably to lose him.

Except you're not losing him to Elise, she reminded herself. You gave him up two months ago, remember? she mused with brutal honesty, striving to subdue the fresh surge of jealous despair. You turned your back and walked away. You can't blame Max for seeking solace with someone else. If they find happiness with each other, you should be glad.

High overhead, a jet was drawing a white line against the vivid blue sky. Erin's gaze absently tracked the tiny silver speck as it inched westward. But, dear Lord, how will I bear it if Max and Elise marry?

The gnawing ache in her heart grew steadily worse over the next two weeks. Erin fought it and the constant urge to weep in the only way she knew how—by driving herself even harder.

She worked at the computer from dawn until late into the night, many times not even stopping to eat. Only when she was so exhausted that she could not focus her eyes would she quit. Then she showered and fell into bed, to toss and turn, tormented by dreams of Max and Elise, their bodies entwined, kissing, loving.

Erin lost weight she could ill afford to lose, and there were dark circles under her eyes, but she finished the novel translation by the deadline. As soon as she shipped it off, she signed a contract to act as an interpreter at an international beauty pageant to be held in Brazil the first week of

November. She was desperately hoping that distance would accomplish what time had not.

It was not until the respite between assignments that Erin realized she had not heard from her sister in almost three weeks. Had it been anyone else, she would not have thought anything of it, but Elise, through good times and bad, had written faithfully once a week since they'd left college.

Though Erin did not crave listening to her sister rhapsodize over Max, she was too concerned to simply dismiss the sudden change in habit.

The telephone call, however, did not ease her mind. Elise laughed and said she'd been too busy to write, but there was a sort of frantic gaiety in her voice that disturbed Erin. Worse, when Elise ended the conversation after only a few minutes, Erin was left with the distinct impression that her sister had not wanted to talk to her at all.

Erin was hurt and worried. Something was wrong. She could feel it. Had Max confessed their brief love affair? The thought gave Erin a moment of panic, but it faded quickly. No, it wasn't anger or hurt she sensed from Elise. It was...agitation.

Erin was tempted to fly to Santa Fe and find out what was going on. Only a heartsick dread of facing Max again, of having him confirm that he was, indeed, in love with her sister, stopped her. She was not emotionally strong enough to face that just yet.

Preparations for her trip to Brazil kept Erin busy, but still she fretted over her twin. She sensed a certain...uneasiness of mind...so strongly that she was not even surprised when Elise arrived on her doorstep.

An instant before the doorbell rang Erin knew she was there, and she jerked open the door without even checking through the peephole.

"Elise!" she cried, snatching her close for an exuberant hug. "What are you doing here? Why didn't you let me know you were coming?"

Laughing, Elise returned the embrace, but before she could answer, Erin bundled her inside. The minute the door closed she grasped her twin's hands and looked at her anxiously. "Now, tell me, what's wrong?"

"Does something have to be wrong? Can't I just visit my sister if I want?" Elise pulled free of Erin's grasp, strolled into the living room and tossed her light cape over the back of a chair. She seemed at ease, her smile serene, yet, watching her, Erin detected a finely drawn tension beneath the calm.

"No, of course not. You know you're always welcome," she said when they were seated on the sofa.

"Thanks, Sis. Actually though, I have to confess, I did come for a reason. I'm hoping I can talk you into going back to Santa Fe with me."

To Erin, Santa Fe meant seeing Max, and her heart gave a little skip at the mere thought. The yearning ache that had been with her for months became a sharp, stabbing pain, and she clenched her teeth to keep from crying out. "I, uh, no. I'm sorry, darling, but I couldn't possibly. I'm very busy right now. I'm leaving on a South American job in ten days, so you see—"

"Erin, you've got to come," Elise said with quiet urgency, laying her hand on Erin's. "If you don't, I'll never forgive myself."

"Wh—what?"

"For coming between you and Max," she added softly.

Erin could not have been more shocked if Elise had tossed a bucket of cold water in her face. She stared. "You . . . you know?" At Elise's nod, she closed her eyes, feeling sick. "Max told you, didn't he?"

"No. He didn't have to." She cocked her brows reprovingly at Erin's puzzled look. "The mental link works both ways, remember? But even without it I would have figured it out. In your letters, whenever we talk on the phone, you avoid even mentioning Max. And he, poor man, can't stop himself from asking about you constantly."

"Oh, Elise, I'm so sorry. I—"

"Don't be. Actually, I'm the one who should be sorry. You see, I've known how things were between you since that day at the cabin. I just didn't want to admit it. I guess I thought that once you left, Max would turn to me. I should have known better. You and I may look alike, but we're very different people."

"But he has, hasn't he? What about the dinner date, and the perfume from Paris?"

"The dinner was business. I neglected to tell you that his attorney and an Australian supplier were there, too. As for the perfume... well... I gave him the money to buy it for me."

"And the night he dropped by your apartment?"

She grimaced sheepishly. "He came to pick up a file I had taken home. He was there all of five minutes."

Elise's soft gaze held remorse and abject apology. "I can't tell you how guilty I've been feeling over this. I knew before you ever came to Santa Fe that Max wasn't for me. But I'm ashamed to say, I was—" she stopped and bit her lower lip "—I was jealous because he fell for you so quickly. That's why I wrote those misleading letters. And I've been feeling absolutely wretched. Lord, Sis, jealousy is so awful. I hate it."

"I know," Erin said with an understanding smile.

"So you see, you have to come back. Max loves you, and you love him."

"But, darling, you love him, too."

"Actually... I don't," she said, smiling wryly at Erin's skeptical look. "Oh, I thought I did. After Tommy died I was lonely. I missed him so much, I guess I was looking for someone to love. Under those conditions it's difficult to distinguish love from infatuation. Max happened to be the first really interesting man I met. Besides being attractive and sexy as all get out, he's a wonderful person, as I'm sure you know, and I suppose I was just sort of bowled over by that. But deep down I've always known that Max and I are not at all suited." Grinning, she reached over and tweaked one of Erin's curls. "You're much more his type."

Relief and joy poured through Erin. For an instant she could not control the glow of happiness that suffused her or the smile that bloomed on her lips. Catching her sister's wry smirk, she sobered instantly, guilt piercing her. "Oh, Elise, are you sure? I couldn't bear to hurt you."

"I'm sure, I'm sure. Now go pack a bag while I call and book us on a flight to Santa Fe."

"Tonight? But . . . but what if Max doesn't want me anymore? I really hurt him when I left. He might not be willing to forgive me."

Shaking her head, Elise looked at her pityingly, as though she were dealing with a not too bright child. When Erin didn't move, she pointed an imperious finger toward the bedroom. "Pack."

Max scribbled furiously, filling the lined yellow pad with his bold scrawl. From outside came the faint sounds of voices and car doors slamming as people began arriving. He had been at his desk for an hour already. The only way to keep his mind occupied, he had discovered, was to immerse himself in work.

When he reached the end of the sheet, he paused. That was when he made the mistake of letting his gaze slide to the desk calendar. Max reached over and flipped the page to the current date, then stared at it as though mesmerized.

Two months, two weeks, and three days since she'd gone. Hell, it seemed like forever.

Making a disgusted sound, he tossed his pencil aside and shot out of his chair. He walked to the window and looked out, rubbing the stiff muscles in his neck. Would it ever stop hurting? Would he ever stop wanting Erin?

It didn't help matters, of course, he admitted wryly, that her mirror image occupied the front office. The sight of that wonderfully familiar face brought such pain that he avoided looking directly at Elise. Having her around was like wearing a hair shirt, but he couldn't get rid of her. She was an excellent secretary. Besides, he couldn't bring himself to sever that last link with Erin.

Hell, Delany, you must be a masochist.

Behind him the door opened, and he looked over his shoulder as Sam entered the office.

"You said you wanted to go over the transport bids first thing," his partner said without preamble.

As Sam strolled in and sat down they heard Elise entering her office. Max returned to his desk and pushed the intercom button. "Good morning, Elise. Would you bring in the file on Robison Trucking, please?"

"Yes, sir. I'll be right in."

With an encouraging smile, Elise handed Erin the file. "Here. You take it in."

"Me? Now?" Erin swallowed hard. Clutching the folder to her, she cast a nervous glance at the door to Max's office, then looked at her twin. "Elise, are you sure about your feelings? I could—"

"I'm sure. Look, don't worry about me. Somewhere out there there's a man for me. I'll find him eventually."

He'll find you, if you'll just let him, Erin thought, remembering the way Sam had looked at her.

"Okay. Here goes." She squared her shoulders, took a deep breath and headed for the door.

When Erin entered the room and saw Sam she was disappointed, but the instant her gaze fastened on Max, the other man was forgotten. As she walked toward him her eyes ran avidly over his beloved face, greedily soaking up every detail. He was thinner, and there were lines around his eyes and mouth that had not been there before, but to Erin he looked wonderful. She wanted to toss the file into the air and fling herself into his arm.

The two men were talking, but as she stopped beside the desk Sam glanced up at her, did a double take and grew utterly still, his silvery eyes widening infinitesimally. Erin knew he had recognized her when his gaze sharpened and flicked to Max, then back to her. She even thought she saw one corner of that hard mouth twitch.

"Just put the file on the desk, Elise," Max said without looking up.

Growing desperate, Erin edged closer. With a hand on the back of his chair, she leaned and placed the folder in front of him, her senses swimming giddily as she breathed in his clean masculine scent and a hint of citrus cologne. She straightened and gazed down at his bent head, itching to run her fingers through his hair, to kiss the little strip of flesh above his collar.

Max shifted in his chair. "That's all, Elise. Thanks."

"Very well. If you're sure there's nothing else I can do for you."

Max's head snapped up before she could get all the words out, his expression thunderstruck. In the next instant it changed to furious.

Erin's smile faltered. She backed up a step, but in a blur of motion he lunged out of the chair, grasped her arm and headed for the door with long, ground-eating strides.

She was aghast. It was not at all the reaction she had expected. "Max, will you stop!" she cried, stumbling along behind him, trying to pry his fingers from around her forearm. "Look, all you had to do was ask me to leave. You don't have to throw me out!"

"Throw you out? Ha! I'm going to throw you on your back. Just as soon as I get you alone."

"Oh!" Her eyes widened in delighted amazement, all the fight going out of her with that one breathy exclamation. As docile as a lamb, she trotted along behind Max, wearing a complacent smile.

Elise gaped, then smothered a giggle as he hauled her through the outer office. Just before he pulled her into the hall Erin glanced back over her shoulder. Sam was watching the spectacle along with Elise, standing in the inner doorway, a shoulder propped against the frame, his arms crossed over his chest. Erin winked and wiggled her fingers at them both.

Oblivious to the attention they were attracting, Max towed her down the hall, through the reception area and out the door. He stuffed her into his car and peeled out of the parking lot as though the place were on fire, sending gravel flying.

In five minutes flat they screeched to a stop before Max's front door. During the short ride not a word passed between them, but the second they stepped into the house he let fly.

He whipped her around and grasped her shoulders. "Now you listen to me. I let you walk away once. I listened to all your arguments and let you have things your way, though it tore my guts out to do it. But you came back of your own free will, and now all bets are off. So if you think you're going to torment me by waltzing in and out of my life when the notion strikes you, you can forget it. This time you're staying."

So that was why he was so furious.

Tenderness flooded Erin as she recognized the fear and vulnerability behind his anger. Making no effort to hide the love shining in her eyes, she met his glare with a smile and said softly, "I know."

"You're mine now, and I'm not—" His head jerked back. "What did you say?"

"I said I know."

"You're here to stay?" he asked cautiously, as though he couldn't quite believe he'd heard her right.

"Well...not literally." His frown returned, and Erin stepped closer and placed her hands on his chest. She slid them up over his shoulders and stroked the hair at his nape. "I'll probably always be a vagabond, so I can't promise to stay in one spot forever." Her fingertips fondled his ears and feathered over the sensitive skin behind them as she gazed at him lovingly. "But my heart will belong to you for as long as you want it."

Joy flared in Max's eyes. "Oh, God, sweetheart, that will be forever," he said with heartfelt relief as he wrapped his arms around her. He looked at her in stunned amazement, like a man who had suddenly been given all he'd ever wanted, his gaze caressing her as it roamed over her radiant face.

Then he focused on her mouth. His eyes became slumberous and heavy-lidded, his lips parted, and as his head began its inexorable descent Erin trembled. His breath was a warm, moist zephyr against her skin as he whispered, "Forever."

Then his mouth took hers in a kiss that was so hotly sweet, so long and loving, that Erin was sure she would shatter with delight. Their lips clung and rocked, hungrily striving to make up for the long, lonely months apart. Love and desire, want and need, all melded together, heating their blood until it rushed through their veins like molten fire.

Max broke off the kiss and lifted her in his arms, his gaze locking with hers. "God, I love you."

Erin cupped her hand around his lean cheek. "I love you, too," she whispered.

Still holding her eyes, he took the stairs to the landing two at a time, then climbed the short flight that led to the private master bedroom wing. He set Erin on her feet beside the bed and kissed her again. When he raised his head his eyes were glittering hotly. "I need you," he said in a raspy voice as his hands went to the buttons of her blouse.

Erin felt weak and trembly, as though her bones were melting. "I know, my darling," she whispered, reaching for his belt buckle. "I know."

They worked feverishly to divest each other of their clothes, but progress was hindered by shaking hands and the need to touch and caress. Finally, between lingering kisses and whispered words of love, buttons, hooks and zippers were dealt with and they were tumbling together onto the wide bed, lips fused, eager hands touching, stroking, learning anew lovers' secrets.

Neither could wait. The long, lonely time apart had built their desire for each other to a fever pitch. Wrapped in each other's arms, they kissed with all the pent-up yearning that had bedeviled them for so long, and as Max rolled her to her back Erin's legs curved about his hips in a movement as natural and as instinctive as breathing.

Their joining was swift and smooth and deeply satisfying, a joyous homecoming. Max thrust deep, then grew still, and for a moment they clung to each other, their bodies taut and quivering as they savored the almost unbearable pleasure.

But soon it was not enough. Needs too long denied clamored for fulfillment, and with a groan, Max began the age-old movements of love.

It was a fierce loving, fueled by hunger and the heartache they had both endured. The driving urgency carried them higher and higher, like a white-hot star shooting across the firmament. And when the end came it was breathtaking.

They tumbled to earth in a cloud of languor, clinging to each other, their bodies slick with perspiration, their breathing labored. A soft smile curved Erin's mouth as she stroked Max's damp back.

"Mmm, I like that," he mumbled drowsily.

Rousing himself, he braced up on his forearms and smiled down at her, his eyes filled with satisfaction. He stroked her temple and caught a darkened curl, watching, fascinated, as it wrapped around his forefinger and clung. His eyes met hers, his look questioning and confused. "No more doubts?"

She shook her head. "No. None."

"I'm almost afraid to ask, but . . . you're not worried about Elise anymore?"

"My sister, it seems, has decided that you are not the love of her life, after all." Erin slid her hands up his arms and over his shoulders, clasping her fingers behind his neck.

"Actually, you have her to thank for my being here. She came to Houston and practically dragged me back to you."

Max grinned and rolled to his back, bringing her with him, tucking her close against his side and cradling her head on his shoulder. "You know, Elise has been a wonderful secretary, but something tells me I'm really going to like having her for a sister-in-law."

Erin jerked up onto her elbow and stared down at him, shocked. "Sister-in-law? You mean...you want to get married?"

"Of course I want to get married. What did you think?"

"B-but, Max," she exclaimed worriedly. "I'm no good at marriage. I-I'm too much of a gypsy at heart, I guess. Settling down in one spot is just not for me. At least, not yet it isn't. And after a while my flitting from place to place would start to irritate you."

Anger flared in Max's eyes. He hooked a hand around the back of her neck and pulled her down for a swift, hard kiss. When it ended his handsome face was set and determined. "You're forgetting a few things," he said gruffly. "Number one, I'm not that stupid ass, André. I happen to love you just the way you are, and I have no intentions of trying to change you. Number two, I'm not exactly a homebody myself." He tugged her earlobe and grinned. "I own an import company, remember? We can travel the world together."

"Really?"

"Sure. The arrangement that Sam and I have works out great for both of us. I enjoy going to new places, meeting new people; he doesn't. After his experience, he's happy to stay at home. So you see, my love, there's nothing to worry about; we're ideally suited."

Dawning delight widened Erin's eyes. "Why...we are, aren't we?" she said in amazement.

With a sigh, she laid her head on his chest and rubbed her cheek against the damp mat of hair like a contented cat, savoring the peace and happiness the discovery brought. She knew that from now on, no matter where in the world she roamed, Max's arms would always be home for her.

"So. Now that we have that settled," he said, lazily stroking her arm, "will you marry me?"

"Mmm. Whenever you say."

"Good. We'll plan it for next week."

"Next week!" Erin raised her head and gave him a sultry look. "What's wrong with tomorrow?"

"Nothing, except I don't think we could get a minister to perform the ceremony here," he drawled wickedly as he rolled her onto her back. "And I don't plan on letting you out of this bed for at least a week."

*   *   *   *   *

FOOLS RUSH IN where angels fear to tread...

If you've concluded that impulsive Erin is no "fool," you might be tempted to discover that her gentle twin is no "angel." Watch Elise's halo tip— and maybe tumble off?—in Ginna Gray's WHERE ANGELS FEAR, coming from Silhouette Special Edition in the summer of 1988.

Available November 1987

Silhouette Desire

Falcon's Flight

Visit with characters introduced in the acclaimed Desire trilogy by Joan Hohl!

Flint Falcon—first introduced in *Nevada Silver*—valued his freedom above all else. But then he met Leslie Fairfield. Would the beautiful redhead's love tame the proud falcon in flight?

Don't miss *Falcon's Flight*—Flint and Leslie's story. And coming soon from Special Edition, *Forever Spring*— Paul Vanzant's story.

D390

ATTRACTIVE, SPACE SAVING BOOK RACK

Display your most prized novels on this handsome and sturdy book rack. The hand-rubbed walnut finish will blend into your library decor with quiet elegance, providing a practical organizer for your favorite hard-or soft-covered books.

Only $9.95

Approximately 16" x 8" when assembled

Assembles in seconds!

To order, rush your name, address and zip code, along with a check or money order for $10.70* ($9.95 plus 75¢ postage and handling) payable to *Silhouette Books*.

Silhouette Books
Book Rack Offer
901 Fuhrmann Blvd.
P.O. Box 1396
Buffalo, NY 14269-1396

Offer not available in Canada.

BKR-2A

*New York and Iowa residents add appropriate sales tax.

Silhouette Special Edition

COMING NEXT MONTH

#421 NO ROOM FOR DOUBT—Tracy Sinclair
No job too small or too difficult, Stacey Marlowe's ad boasted. But then she hadn't considered the demands her first customer would make. Shady Sean Garrison wanted—of all things!—her trust.

#422 INTREPID HEART—Anne Lacey
Trent Davidson would forever be a hero to Vanessa Hamilton. After all, he'd twice saved her life. But how could Trent settle for Vanessa's childlike adoration when he needed her womanly love?

#423 HIGH BID—Carole Halston
Katie Gamble was thrilled when fellow building contractor Louis McIntyre reentered her life. But Louis's gentle deception—and uneasy memories of a night long ago—threatened their bid for a future together.

#424 LOVE LYRICS—Mary Curtis
Ambitious lyricist Ashley Grainger lived and breathed Broadway, while her former fiancé, conservative lawyer Zachary Jordan, was Boston born and bred. Despite their renewed duet of passion, could they possibly find a lasting harmony?

#425 SAFE HARBOR—Sherryl Woods
When sexy neighbor Drew Landry filed a complaint about Tina Harrington's unorthodox household, they battled it out in the boardroom . . . and the bedroom . . . even as they longed for sweet compromise.

#426 LAST CHANCE CAFE—Curtiss Ann Matlock
Rancher Wade Wolcott wanted no part of Ellie McGrew's struggle to build a new life for her daughters. But the lovely, unassuming widow bought the farm next door, waited tables in his diner—and somehow crept into his heart.

AVAILABLE THIS MONTH:

Coming in
November

Silhouette Classics

You asked for them, and now they're here, in a delightful collection. The best books from the past—the ones you loved and the ones you missed—specially selected for you from Silhouette Special Edition and Silhouette Intimate Moments novels.

Every month, join us for two exquisite love stories from your favorite authors, guaranteed to enchant romance readers everywhere.

You'll savor every page of these *Classic* novels, all of them written by such bestselling authors as:

**Kristin James • Nora Roberts • Parris Afton Bonds
Brooke Hastings • Linda Howard • Linda Shaw**

Silhouette Classics
Don't miss the best this time around!

SCLG-1